T0146610

Dreux CLUB BLUES

A NOVEL

SCOTT D. FENNER

DREUX CLUB BLUES
A NOVEL

This is a work of fiction. All of the characters, names, incidents, organizations, and dialogue in this novel are either the products of the author's imagination or are used fictitiously.

iUniverse books may be ordered through booksellers or by contacting:

iUniverse
1663 Liberty Drive
Bloomington, IN 47403
www.iuniverse.com
1-800-Authors (1-800-288-4677)

ISBN: 978-1-5320-3786-3 (sc)
ISBN: 978-1-5320-3788-7 (hc)
ISBN: 978-1-5320-3787-0 (e)

Library of Congress Control Number: 2018900170

Print information available on the last page.

iUniverse rev. date: 02/14/2018

To my friend Earl Primo. Your honesty, compassion, and love of life and family have been inspirations to us all. You fought the good fight till the very end and didn't waver. We will all take strength in your example of courage and determination. Rest in peace, my brother. When I get to heaven, I know you will be easy to find. I will search for the circle of souls laughing the loudest because I know I will find you in the middle of them.

A SHORT NOTE FROM THE AUTHOR

I asked my good friend Professor Madeleine Fulwiler to read my first draft of this book. Since she is an English professor, I figured she could give me insight into any grammatical mistakes. I still remember her kind words of encouragement upon returning the manuscript: "If you were a student in my class, I would have failed ya."

The following is a work of fiction. It is inspired by experiences and memories of my time on the New Orleans Police Department. Any resemblance to real-life events or persons, living or dead, is purely coincidental.

CHAPTER ONE

I loved the Dreux Club. It was the place where I felt most comfortable. The Dreux was on Dreux Avenue, just off Lafaye Street, in the Gentilly Terrace area of New Orleans. Gentilly Terrace was built in the early 1900s by excavating and piling up earth in the area's shallow swamp to create blocks of terraced land where houses could be built. I lived in one of the oldest houses. It was constructed in 1912. Many of the other homes were built in the 1920s. The people of Gentilly were proud of their homes and kept them up. On summer weekends, everyone did yard work and the whole neighborhood smelled like fresh-cut grass.

Among native New Orleanians, the neighborhood you came from said a lot about you. A person could tell your economic standing, the religion you likely practiced, and the high school you went to, among many other educated guesses. My mother's family moved to Gentilly in 1948 when my maternal grandfather bought property there. My dad's family had lived in the area since the early 1900s.

New Orleans's unique culture was not exclusive to the French Quarter. Most New Orleans neighborhoods had small bars and taverns that were frequented by locals, many of whom went there daily to catch up with friends, share news, and gossip.

The building that housed the Dreux Club, like most of the buildings that surrounded it, was built in the early 1930s. On the outside, the place was unremarkable. It was built with wood and brick and covered in cedar clapboards that had been painted white long before. The structure begged for a new coat of paint, but that wasn't going to happen anytime soon. The building stood at street level, unlike the many surrounding homes, which were elevated and had brick around their foundations, as well as ironwork banisters and railings. They were the typical homes built in Gentilly in the 1930s.

The Dreux had no off-street parking. Most of its patrons just walked from their homes nearby. This was not a business that would ever be well known. It was a simple neighborhood club that scraped a living from the locals and friends who patronized it.

The Dreux had a very small addendum at the bottom of the sign above the front door. It read, "Private Social Club." After all, in the late '70s in that area, they couldn't be open to just anyone. They had to pick and choose who they wanted in their establishment, or else any troublemaking asshole could come through the door and cause nothing but problems. The front door was one of those one-way-mirror doors that allowed everyone inside the club to size you up as you stood outside and judge whether you were fit to be buzzed in. I always got buzzed in.

That cold night in January 1979 was no different. Inside, the Dreux Club smelled like cigarette smoke and old spilled beer. The bar was shaped like a square and backed by a wall of shelves filled with glassware and liquor bottles. A counter with storage underneath ran along the length of that wall; the cash register and telephone sat on top of it. A mirror hung behind all the shelving. I guessed it was supposed to give the illusion of more liquor bottles and glassware than was there. I was sure it had worked in the 1930s, but now, with the buildup of more than forty years' worth of dust and mistreatment, it held no true reflection, only twinkling of light here and there.

The old bar had seating along the other three sides in the form of chrome bar stools with padded black plastic seats that were held together mostly by duct tape. The bar's wooden top had been covered long before with sheets of copper. Whoever did the work had done a surprisingly good job. It almost looked too good to be in this place.

Under the bar on the working side sat several chest-type coolers that continuously let off a loud electrical hum. You first noticed the humming when you walked in, but then it gradually faded into white noise. An old sofa stood against the front wall, near the jukebox, but unless you wanted to take the smell of the Dreux Club home with you, you weren't to sit on it.

Above the couch hung a huge oil painting of a ship sailing in heavy seas. Bursts of seawater exploded in all directions as the ship's bow crashed into a wave. The gray skies in the background looked threatening, and according to its flags and sails, the ship was in a tempest. The painting was in an enormous, intricately carved, dark wooden frame. You could tell it was very old. Everything about it screamed that it did not belong in the Dreux Club.

The walls of the club were murky beige in color. It might have been some other color when it was first applied, but much like a newspaper left in the driveway for a week, it had yellowed into an unintended shade. The place also had painted cement floors and a pool table in a separate room in the back that led to the restrooms down the hall.

This is where we always ended up. All types of neighbors and friends showed up here. We could always relax over a couple of drinks and complain and bitch our ways to happiness.

The bartender, Barry Christopher, was a best friend of mine. We had grown up together. He was wiping down the bar and gave me a nod as I entered. Barry was a good sort. You would be hard-pressed to find a gentler, more honest man. He personified the term *regular guy*. Barry wasn't a big talker, but he was a good listener. He was a little heavy, but in no way fat, and a bit shorter than my six-foot height. He had shaved off the beard he'd had since high school a while back. He had blue eyes and dark brown hair that he parted on the side. We hung out together often.

"Hello, David," he said as I sat down. Barry was one of the few people who called me David. Everyone else called me Dave.

"Damn it's cold out there," I said.

"It beats summer heat," he replied.

"Looks like a good night," I offered.

"Yeah, I think it's gonna be a good night," he said.

He wiped the bar in front of me down with "the rag"—a filthy gray scrap of cloth that had probably been smeared over every inch of the building. He might as well have wiped down the bar with a raw chicken thigh.

"The guys been around?" I asked.

"They gonna be around. They don't miss a weekend," he answered. "What can I get for ya?"

"Give me a Bud," I replied, and he headed toward the chest cooler.

There was a decent crowd that night. They were talking, laughing, and having a good time. I saw Gertie standing with Ron and Greg at the other end of the bar, bathed in a bluish light. Gertie waved her hand that wasn't holding a cigarette at me vigorously until I tipped my beer toward them in response.

I had been friends with Gertie Chauvin for years. Gert was a paradox for me. I loved to see her, but at the same time it hurt me to see her. She had superb boobs, a slender waist, and a magnificent rear end. She styled her hair in a classic '70s style. Sometimes at the end of the night, if she had been laughing hard and cutting up, her lipstick looked like it had been applied with a shoe. Her voice was unlike any I had ever heard. I still remember that she smoked Virginia Slims. Everyone wanted to be around Gert. She was never self-conscious, always said what she thought without a filter, and was never mean to anyone. She was the only female member of our group. All that only made it harder for me; I had loved Gertie Chauvin since we were kids. Sometimes things just didn't work out as one wished. We never had a serious relationship. Some reason or another always kept us apart.

Ron and Greg were two devoted members of the Dreux Club crowd. Ron was stocky with curly medium-length brown hair. He had a short goatee that helped define his smile. Ron was always smiling. He was very outgoing, and strangers seemed to take to him immediately. Greg was tall and lanky. He had blond hair that was always combed perfectly. He wore wire-rimmed glasses that made him look smart and distinguished. Greg was clever and laid-back, but I didn't know how he kept his cool, as he was usually at the receiving end of many of the jokes and ribbing from our group. I guessed he really liked the attention. He never complained about his treatment and was always quick with a comeback or a smart-ass remark.

Gert, Ron, and Greg were laughing about something, but I was too far away to get the joke. I just sat at the bar and waited for my other pals to show up. The buzzer sounded. Through the door, I could see Jerry and "the Satisfier" stomping their feet in the cold, their hands shoved into their coat pockets as they waited for Barry to hit the button that unlocked the door.

That night, the three of us sat at the bar—Jerry, the Satisfier, and me. The Satisfier's real name was Steve. He acquired the peculiar nickname a while back, when a lot of us witnessed an argument he had with a woman he was dating at the time. They had made quite a scene.

"Are you satisfied?" he had yelled. "I hope you're satisfied! Cause I'm a satisfier. That's what I do. I satisfy!"

That was all it took. Everyone had started calling him the Satisfier.

The Satisfier was a big man, clean-shaven with short dark brown hair. His hulking stature made him look very intimidating, but he was actually very mellow and easygoing. He had a great sense of humor that I really enjoyed. The Satisfier also had a very mechanical and analytical mind. He seemed to know instinctively how things fit together and what made them work.

Jerry was a large, strong individual too. He had a beer belly and black hair that he wore in a pompadour. He was clean-shaven and usually very well dressed. Jerry had a razor-sharp wit and a propensity for practical jokes. The two of them worked well in our little band of misfits at the Dreux Club.

The Satisfier and I had recently completed the paperwork and testing to join the New Orleans Police Department. You would think a job as a police officer would be exciting and something everybody would want. That was not the case. As we sat in a row at the bar, drinking our beers, the Satisfier complained, "I don't want to be a cop. I'm only doing this because my mom is pushing me to get a real job."

The Satisfier lived in a two-room studio apartment over his mother's garage. She was charging him $150 a month in rent to stay there but wanted him out as soon as possible because he was an adult and her friends were asking nosy questions. He made good money repairing cars for friends and others who heard he was an honest man. I guessed she figured that a job as a police officer would be good for him and that he would do well. After all, he was a big man and extremely strong. So she was pushing the Satisfier to join the department, but Steve wanted none of it.

"I can't let my mom think that I sabotaged this job." Steve exhaled. "I had to come up with another plan so they wouldn't want me. That's why I started screwing around with the psychological section of the test. Remember that test?" he asked me. "Four hundred and some odd questions, all about if you like ice cream. Do you like chocolate ice cream? Later, do you like vanilla ice cream? Do you like ice cream cones? Have you ever thrown ice cream at a motherfucker? What a bunch of crap that was. I guess they was just trying to see if you was telling the truth by asking the same damn question in different ways, over and freakin' over."

Jerry and I nodded in agreement. I could not respond, because my mouth was full of beer.

Steve leaned forward onto the bar and continued, "I figured after I botched the test, they would just let me go, just give me something to show my mom that they did not want me as a cop. No, I wasn't getting off that easy. You know they sent me to Tulane Avenue to talk to a shrink."

"You shittin' me?" Jerry asked.

"No, man. I went today," the Satisfier said. "That doctor took me into his office. He was an old guy with glasses, looked to be about one hundred years old. I figured they'd have one of those couches with the padded head, the kind you can lie back on, you know, like you see on TV, but they didn't. They just had a sofa. I just sat on the sofa and looked at the floor.

"Then the shrink spoke real soft and said, 'Stephen, I'm looking at the results of your test, and it seems you have some issues. Do you know what I'm referring to?' I told him I didn't know what he was talking about."

Steve continued, "He said, 'Stephen, the results of this test are very troubling, very troubling indeed.' I knew I had to come up with something and come up with it quick, or my ass could end up being a cop. Then he asked me, 'Stephen, is there anything you'd like to talk to me about?'"

The Satisfier paused and looked each of us directly in the eyes for a moment. He said, "Guys, I knew that was my in." Steve leaned forward and gave us the "knowing look."

"I laid it on thick. I told him it was too terrible to talk about, and he said, 'Now, Stephen, Stephen … this is a friendly atmosphere. I'm just here to help.' I told him, 'It hurts to talk about it, Doc, even after all this time.' The doc said, 'Stephen, you'll feel better if you talk to somebody about it.'

"I knew this was probably my one and only shot, so I just went ape. I put my hands on my head, put my head between my knees, and I just started talking," Steve continued. "'It was terrible, just horrible Doc,' I said. 'The ritual, the catechism, the secrecy, like the Freemasons, PTA, or the Cub Scouts.' I whimpered a little.

"Then I told him, 'I remember they took three of us out of the bunch … We had to strip to our socks and stand there naked before the assembly. Then we had to sing, to sing a song. I still remember it today, so many years later.' I put my face in my hands, and I moaned real loud. 'Oh why? Why? I got no singin' voice. I don't even know what a Gadda da Vida is.'

"Then I let out this noise like I was choking or trying to catch my breath. Then I told him, 'I just shut my eyes 'cause I knew the master was gonna get on his knees in front of us and play us like a trained seal on the horns, like at Sea World.'

"Next, I broke down sobbing because I knew this was my only chance. I peeked up at him just for a moment, and dammit, that fucking guy couldn't write notes fast enough. I knew then I would be found unqualified. I was never gonna be no policeman."

The Satisfier lit a cigarette, started laughing, and waved up three more beers from Barry. As Barry banged around in the chest cooler, looking for three more Budweisers, I saw Gertie leave Ron and Greg and start walking our way.

"One of you guys going to buy me a beer?" she asked.

I called out to Barry to bring four instead of three.

"So what's up, Gert?" I asked. "You still working at the bakery?"

"Yeah," she said. "It'll be five years in November."

"Well, that's good. You about the only one around here that's had a steady job for that long," I said.

"That's because I know when I got it good," she replied.

Barry reappeared with four beers, as requested.

"I heard you were going to be a cop," Gertie remarked.

"It looks that way," I said.

"You might as well 'cause you've looked like a cop for years with your mustache and short hair," she said.

She was right. I'd had a mustache since my freshmen year of high school and kept my hair short not only to be a nonconformist to the styles of the 1970s but also because of my stint in the US Marine Corps as a reservist. I still had to attend drills, so I kept my hair short. Since we were all in our mid to late twenties, hair styles really did not mean much to us.

"You shouldn't come around here after you're a cop," she said.

"Why is that?" I asked.

"Because cops make people nervous."

"If you're not doing anything wrong, why would you be nervous?" I asked.

"Because you never know if a cop's gonna bite ya," Gertie said.

"Some people say the same thing about you, Gert," Jerry chimed in.

Gertie shot Jerry a dirty look and then said to me, "You forget that we came up together. I remember smokin' True Green cigarettes in that crawl space under your front porch. You weren't cop material back then. You were a bad little kid."

"I wasn't no altar boy, but I never did anything really bad or hurt anybody," I said.

"I know you used to smoke pot in high school," she said. "How did you get around that?"

"I just told them the truth: I've smoked pot, but I haven't smoked it in several years. Plus, I had to take a lie detector test, and I passed that. They aren't interested in the little shit you used to do. They just want to know if you're an asshole or not."

"Well, you musta busted that machine, because you are one of the biggest assholes I know!" Gertie laughed and shoved my shoulder, very proud of herself to have gotten such a good burn on me.

Barry returned to stand in front of the four of us.

"Barry, you gonna let this guy back in here after he's a cop?" she asked.

"Yeah, we're pals. Plus, David pays his tab, so he's gonna stay," Barry replied and wiped down the bar in front of us with the rag. He had begun to walk off when Gert called to him.

"Hey, you missed a spot." Gert pointed to a spot on the bar.

Barry quickly ran over and wiped it down. Then someone else called him to put in an order.

"There wasn't no spot. I do that to him all the time." Gert snickered.

"Why you want to mess with Barry, Gert?" I asked.

"Because he's so easy." She giggled.

"He won't go so easy on you when you piss him off," the Satisfier warned her.

"Barry?" she asked. "You can't piss him off because he just doesn't give a shit. The only things he seems to care about is this joint and that damn cat."

"Who, Fantome?" I asked.

"Yeah, that cat gives me the creeps," Gert said.

"Again, people say the same thing about you, Gert," Jerry said.

"Shut up, Jerry!" she snapped.

Jerry just shrugged and took another pull of his Bud.

"It may be because she's so big and black that if you ain't right on her, you can't see any features. Just those green eyes, watchin' out of a jet-black shadow. What kind of name is Fantome, anyway?" Gert asked.

"It's old French for ghost," I told her.

"Oh, that makes sense now, Barry and the ghost. That's all this place needs. And now we gonna add a cop."

It was getting late and I still had to get home. I only lived about four blocks away, but I either had to bum a ride or walk. Some wiring in my car had short-circuited, causing the headlights and taillights not to work, so I could not drive it at night.

"Hey, Steve, you gonna be around tomorrow?" I asked.

"Yeah," he said. "You want me to work on your car?"

"Yes, please. I need to have those lights working."

"Okay, come around tomorrow about eleven. I'll be out back."

I said my goodbyes, paid my tab, and headed for the door. As I opened the door, the large black mass that was Fantome pushed past me to go inside. I was not startled; I had witnessed it so many times before. She would wait outside until someone was arriving or leaving and then she would dart inside and find a dark place to settle down until closing.

I didn't know if Barry took her home each night or locked her in the club. I never thought about it until years later.

I started for home but heard Jerry call after me, "I'm leaving too. I'll give you a ride."

CHAPTER TWO

The next morning, I went to visit the Satisfier in the lot where he fixed cars for cash. It was behind his house in the Seabrook Place subdivision, at the corner of Saint Roch and Robert E. Lee Boulevard. He worked under a clump of trees, a true shade tree mechanic. The Seabrook Place subdivision was very near mine. Most of the houses were built in the 1940s, and it was hard to tell where Gentilly ended and Seabrook Place began. Back in the 1970s, it was an upper-middle-class neighborhood.

As I approached, I could see a vehicle jacked up and two legs sticking out from underneath it.

I walked up to the pair of legs and asked, "What are you doing?"

"What does it look like I'm doing?" the Satisfier replied.

"Looks like you're nursing off the teat of a '73 Buick."

"Funny guy, funny guy," his muffled voice said from underneath the car. "You brought that crappy little shit wagon of yours?" he asked.

"Yeah, it's daylight, so I can drive it."

"What you think is wrong with it?" he asked.

"I was driving the other day, and I smelled this electrical-type smoke. Then I noticed my lights weren't working anymore."

"Yeah, those MGBs are known for their electrical problems," he said. "Could you hand me that hammer? It's over there on the blanket."

Steve had all of his tools carefully arranged on a blanket nearby. I picked up the hammer and put it in the hand that emerged from under the car.

"Aha, the claw hammer, the tool of the surgeon," I said. "What you gonna do with that? Pound in a screw?"

"Now I know why you have so few friends. You're constantly screwing around," he scolded.

"Yeah, but I got you," I said.

"Who told you I was your friend?" he mumbled.

"Then I would have one less acquaintance if I turned the handle on this floor jack."

"Don't even talk like that," he said. "Besides, I always use jack stands. I set the stands in blocks of cement. That way if any weight did come on them, they wouldn't sink into the dirt."

"Living under constant fear of attack?" I asked.

"No. I just believe in being cautious."

He squirmed out from under the Buick, stood up, reached into his shirt pocket, and pulled out a pack of Marlboros. He shook it at me, and I took one of his cigarettes. I had no problem bumming smokes.

He lit his own cigarette, took a deep puff, exhaled, and then said, "Let's take a look at that cheesy little car. Why do you drive this thing? It's too small. I've built go-carts bigger than this."

"It's cool. It's an MGB, a foreign sports car," I replied.

"Look, pal, late-model British Leyland products lost a lot of horsepower after safety and emissions regulations kicked their asses. If you had an old one, like from the '60s, that's back when they would scoot. If you get into a little accident while driving this, you're going to end up underneath an American car." He looked over my car for a minute and then asked, "What color is this anyway?"

"It's Damask red," I said.

"Damask red? What's a Damask? A bruise? Some kind of skin cancer?" he asked.

I admitted that I did not know.

"It ain't red; it ain't purple; it ain't maroon. What the hell?" he said. Steve then bent over and started digging under the front seat.

He was right, I thought. I'd never seen this color before. Maybe it was some special hated British color, illegal to export unless it had been slapped on something being sent to America, some sort of passive-aggressive nationalism payback because they were still sore from losing the colonies in the Revolutionary War.

"Here's your problem," the Satisfier declared. "This wire bundle is shorted and burned. That's why your lights ain't working."

"Can you fix it?" I asked.

"Sure," he said. "Anything can be fixed for a price."

"Man, you know I ain't got a lot of money," I said.

"I'll work with you on it," he promised. "But you know this foreign stuff is always gonna cost more than domestic. I think I have a connection on a wire bundle for it. But you gonna have to work with me."

"That's what I was afraid of," I said.

"Look, let me fix it and then let's get rid of it. I can put you in that Buick over there."

"Oh, the one you're fixin' now?" I asked.

"No, dumb shit, I'm just changing the oil on it. It runs great," Steve assured me. "I got a good friend of mine who lives uptown. He's fruit, but I think he's looking for a car like yours. I want to give him a good deal 'cause he is a friend, and you know I don't screw over anybody. I will talk to him and we can all come to a fair price. You know, fruits like little sports cars like this."

"Are you insinuating that I'm queer?" I asked. "Just because I drive a certain brand of car?"

He just looked at me and chuckled.

"You know I'm not queer, 'cause if I was, I would not be seen in the light of day in public with the likes of you. Then no self-respecting man would ever want me after that," I said.

"Yeah, you right," he said. "Plus, I always see you trying to catch a glimpse down Gertie's blouse."

"Don't everybody?" I said.

"Yeah, that Gert is something," he agreed. "So, what's it gonna be? You gonna bust open your piggy bank and buy the Buick?"

"Look, let's just get this fixed, get you paid, and then I'll look at my money situation," I said. "May I bum another cigarette?"

"You as bad as my mom," he said.

The Satisfier was as good as his word. His uptown friend was interested in the MGB, and I got a fair price for it. I bought the Buick and still had a few hundred bucks left over. I was now the proud owner of a 1973

Buick Regal. I had gone from driving a skiff to driving a tugboat. It was a lot bigger than the MGB, and I did feel safer in it. And if I ever had any trouble, I could always take it to the Satisfier and get it fixed for an honest price.

All in all, it was a trustworthy car. It was a good thing that I was able to get that Buick when I did. I started the academy very soon after, and I depended on its reliability. In fact, I ended up driving that thing throughout my time at the police academy and my first several years on the job.

My time in the police academy was just like going back to school. Sure, we had physical training, police procedure courses, Louisiana criminal law education, police codes and policies classes, but it was just 8:00 a.m. to 4:00 p.m. It lasted about three and a half months, but after the training, cadets were ready to hit the streets with a seasoned officer as their training instructor.

One of the strangest things about it was putting on my uniform for the first time. I looked into a full-length mirror and saw a young New Orleans cop looking back at me. My first gut reaction, which came from the old part me, was *run!* That feeling soon passed, and I just kept staring at that guy dressed new black leather, with a Smith & Wesson Model 19 on his hip and the shiny chrome badge of a New Orleans police officer hanging on his shirt. Some thirty-eight years later, I still remember the impression it made on me and just as intensely as I did back then. I would wear that uniform for many years to come. I was always proud to wear it, through good times and bad.

I was happy wearing that uniform as well as miserable. I lost friends wearing it and saved lives. I was welcomed as an angel by some and despised as a devil by others. It was torn in accidents and attacks and stained with blood, both of others as well as from me.

Sometimes I wonder if I had known then what I know now, would I have kept it on? Would I have chosen another path? I don't think so. All those experiences forged the person I am today. Confidence, self-reliance, determination, discipline, and honesty are all traits that were hardened into my personality through my experiences on the police department. To be in the police is to be part of a very special family. If you have never been a member of it, you'll never know what it means to be in it. I did not know it at that moment, but my life was forever changed. I would never again be the man who put on that uniform for the first time. That guy was gone.

I met a lot of new people in the police academy, some of whom I'm friends with to this day. Jake Couvillion is one of them. Jake lived about two miles from me back then. I think he drove an old VW Bug, but it had been giving him lots of problems, so he needed a ride from me daily. Jake smoked like an old stove. He used to smoke Camels without filters. I cannot take credit for this description, but many of our academy classmates said he looked like a man-sized baby. He had a round baby face, a baby's lack of hair, a baby's fat body, only he was six foot two. I guess they were right; he looked like a giant chain-smoking baby. Only this baby could probably beat the shit out of you. He had an incredible sense of humor. He was always good for a sarcastic one-liner. I hit it off with him from the first day.

I remember one time when the instructors were showing us a tremendously gory, graphic movie of a traffic accident. We watched movies from a projector, if you know what that is. It was on celluloid film. There were no such things as VHS tapes or DVDs back then. I guess the movies were meant to shock the senses of younger drivers and warn them to use caution or else end up dead. Showing them to us as police recruits was an attempt to steel us for what our police duties would inevitably cause us to encounter. In one accident, a little convertible had smashed into the side of a hill, throwing the driver onto the passenger seat and dislodging a boulder that crashed down onto the driver's seat. The video was focusing on the dead driver and the overall scene when out of the darkness came Jake's unmistakable voice: "I told him not to let the rock drive."

Most days on our way to class, we stopped at Lawrence's Bakery at the corner of Elysian Fields and Fillmore, about six blocks away from my house. That was the best bakery I have ever known. To the present day I mourn its closure. The smell of the place when you walked in was so deliciously overpowering. The staff had been baking all night. Doughnuts, French pastries, petits fours (tiny cakes layered with buttercream and other icings), cheesecakes, rum cakes, and every other sort of baked culinary delight. Lawrence's Bakery was famous for its wedding cakes. Many New Orleans couples used to fuel up on a Lawrence's Bakery wedding cake before consummating their wedding vows. And don't start with the cops-and-doughnuts shit. We gladly paid full price for everything we got from Lawrence's.

After the bakery, we would drive to the old police academy complex on Navarre Street near City Park. There we parked in the lot, always in the same spot under an old cypress tree, and had our breakfast. It was also where Jake would have his obligatory ten last cigarettes before class.

As I mentioned, going to the police academy was like going back to school. I did not like school very much. In my senior year of high school, I made mostly As because it had finally dawned on me how important education was and the fact that it could be enjoyable. Before that enlightenment, I had detested school and was just an average student.

The subject matter at the police academy kept my attention. Unlike my past education, it was easy to understand the relationship between what was taught and how to apply it in real-life situations. It wasn't like learning algebra only to graduate and never use it again. All the skills taught at the academy directly related to law enforcement work and staying safe in an unforgiving environment. I'm not going to bore you with all the skills or types of classes that made up the curriculum. Suffice it to say that once I completed the program, I had the basic skill set necessary to do the job under the watchful eye of a veteran instructor.

I remember my academy days with fondness. There was no pressure. We just went to class and made the best of it. For lunch, we would walk down Navarre Street and get a po'boy at Weavers Sandwich Shop or pile into several vehicles and go to Bud's Broiler on City Park Avenue for a burger with cheddar cheese, chili, and smoke sauce, along with fries and a shake. We were a very diverse group, black and white and four women. The recruits came from all sorts of different backgrounds. Some were from out of town like Tommy Sheridan, but most had been born and raised in New Orleans.

The mayor of New Orleans came to address us one afternoon shortly before our graduation. He stood in front of us and pontificated about how he had broken the back of the police union during their strike earlier that year. He spoke of how great he was, and one could tell from his speech that he viewed the police department as an adversary rather than the guardian of safety and order in the city. No one said anything after his sermon. But as he went on and on, I thought of how foolish it was for him to come before twenty-five people who would be presumably spending the next twenty years protecting the city of New Orleans and basically calling them a bunch of assholes.

Several years later, dressed in police uniform, I stood over his lifeless corpse as he lay in repose in his casket at Gallier Hall on Saint Charles Avenue. My partner, Wong, and I had taken a break from our tactical unit assignment of running off the winos and homeless in that area to give him a last adios. The city managers did not want the people who were coming to pay their respects to the deceased mayor to have to look upon the drug addicted, alcoholic, and downtrodden who frequented that part of the central business district. So tactical platoon two's job was to run them out of the zone.

Aside from the mayor's speech, I don't recall any other classes or instruction that I did not agree with. I did well in the academy and basically had fun learning the art of being a good policeman. The instructors were top-notch, and the personnel were invested in our success. After all, we would be one of them soon.

My academy class was the last class in the old academy complex on Navarre Street. After we graduated, it was demolished to make room for expansion of Delgado Community College. I believe the cypress tree under which Jake and I used to park and eat breakfast is the only thing left standing. The rest of the police complex was bulldozed to accommodate a parking lot.

Several days before we graduated, we were given our district assignments. Jake was assigned to the sixth police district. I was assigned to the seventh district. The seventh district comprised all New Orleans East, from the Industrial Canal to the Saint Tammany Parish line. It was the largest district in the area, but many of the other districts were far more laden with crime. People kidded me, saying that the seventh district was a retirement district. By the time I left the police department twelve years later to join a federal law enforcement agency, the seventh district had become a crime-ridden hellhole.

In the early '70s, the seventh district was the up-and-coming place to live. It had good neighborhoods, expensive homes, and a new mall. It was an area full of promise. Then the city management, in their infinite wisdom, decided to start closing down the inner city's squalor and moving its inhabitants to Section 8 Housing in New Orleans East. It seems when folks pay nearly nothing for their properties, they don't have pride of ownership. Many people just let their properties go. That dropped property values faster than shit through a tinhorn. It happened so fast that long-time property owners could not recover.

A friend of mine owned a house valued at $150,000—a lot of money in the '70s. He was forced to sell it for $32,000. That was all he could get for it. He was not alone. Many people lost a lot of money because of the city's lack of forethought. Or was it their lack of give-a-damn?

Along with plummeting real estate values came the inevitable spike in crime. It went from property-type crimes to violent crimes practically overnight. When I first got to the seventh district, it was unheard of to have a backlog on the night watch. By the time I left the department, it was routine.

The seventh district was not my only assignment on the police department. In the time I spent there, I was assigned to seventh district patrol duties, the district task force, and the Asian unit. Then I left the district to go to the mounted division, SWAT (tactical unit), and finally the detective bureau. I eventually sold my police experience to the federal government, joining a federal law enforcement agency and essentially doubling my pay in the first year. As cops, we never really liked the feds much, for myriad well-deserved reasons. As a fed, I liked them even less.

Me and three other recruits were assigned to the seventh district. Upon our arrival, we were assigned to field training officers. These officers had at least five years on the job and were tasked with honing our skills and turning us from recruits into self-sufficient policemen. We patrolled with these officers for a month each so that by the end of four months, we had ridden with four different instructors who had different sets of experiences to impart. This seemed so logical and worked so well that I was amazed when I went to a federal agency and they had not thought of it. But the New Orleans Police Department did, and I am a much better law enforcement officer because of it.

Each of my field training officers was totally different. One was large and oafish, one was small and skinny. One was older, near retirement, and the other was a medium-build black man. Each had a diverse outlook on what made a good policeman and so much information and experience to teach in two months. There was no way to absorb it all.

The time I spent with these instructors was not completely filled with the instructor-student interactions. We laughed and kidded each other. I think this type of instruction, low pressure from someone you truly believe cares about you, works best.

I remember once I was riding with my black field training officer, Calvin Woodrow, and we received the call of a bomb threat. The policy of the New Orleans Police Department was to never publicize bomb threats or finding any device because that was what bombers wanted. They wanted the notoriety and media attention. The department would never give it to them. We arrived at the location and, with the location personnel there, conducted an exhaustive search for any unknown packages. You couldn't just have the police running around searching for that kind of stuff. They wouldn't know what belonged, what didn't, or what was out of place. Only the people who were there every day could spot that. That was why we had to solicit their help in the search.

We searched the entire building and found nothing. Calvin was still inside talking to the people at the scene when I walked outside to do a search of the exterior of the building. That day was freezing cold, and the wind was howling. I walked around the entire building but did not find anything. I did see a pipe sticking out of the ground with a red ribbon tied to the top of it, blowing in the wind. It was between the building and landscape hedges in front of the business. I looked it over carefully and determined it was just a hollow pipe, so I didn't give it any further thought. Since it was bitterly cold, I went back to the police cruiser, which was parked about twenty feet from the pipe. There I waited for Calvin's return.

As I waited in the car for Calvin's return, I knew he was too conscientious not to go look at the pipe. I picked up the radio microphone, turned the system to the public address mode, and turned the volume all the way up. Then I waited.

I observed Calvin come out of the building. He saw me sitting in the car. Just as I had supposed, he did not disappoint me. I saw him look over at the pipe. He approached it. As he put his hand on it, I immediately brought the mic up to my mouth and made an explosion type noise. The volume was deafening. Calvin leaped about ten feet into the air. He knew he'd been had and whipped around to face me. He laughed and shook his head.

He got in the car and remarked, "You're a very funny guy."

"I couldn't resist," I told him.

"I only wish I had thought of it first," he said.

We had about twelve or so calls for service each shift. It sounds like a lot, but it was less than two an hour. That was when I first got to the district. The workload on the seventh district officers today is probably twice that. We handled all types of calls. Since we were a two-man car, we were assigned any code two calls. A code two is an emergency call, a need for a police presence immediately, such as crimes in progress, life-or-death medical emergencies, injury accidents, suicide attempts, stabbings, shootings—the list goes on and on.

There were also one-man cars. The job of the single-man units was to handle cold calls for service—burglaries, simple traffic accidents, thefts, and crimes where the perpetrators had committed their deeds and had left the scene.

Domestic disturbance calls could be code one or code two, depending on the facts of the incident. If there was ongoing physical violence or the threat thereof or a weapon involved, they would be elevated to a code two.

In my third month of field training, I rode with the large oafish officer. His name was Allen Gregory. He had been on the force about five years and had always been in the seventh district. He was a big man, about two hundred thirty pounds, and had been born and raised in New Orleans. He had a big black mustache and thick black hair he wore in a crew cut. He was one of those guys who loved *being the police*. Not that he abused the position. He just flat out loved the job.

Allen and I got a call of a violent domestic disturbance at a three-story apartment complex near the corner of Wilson and Chef Menteur Highway. We arrived and could hear the hollering from the third-floor apartment as soon as we got out of the vehicle. Another two-man unit that was close by also came to the call to back us up. We climbed the three flights of stairs and were met outside the apartment door by the female complainant. She was in her thirties and looked as though she had been in a tussle. Her blouse was torn, she had blood in the corner of her mouth, and she was so upset that she was shaking.

She told us her boyfriend had been drinking, and they had gotten into a fight. She said he shoved her around, cursed her, and punched her in the mouth. We asked her the usual questions: Is he armed? Does he have any weapons? She told us he did not. As we entered the apartment to confront him, I noticed three young boys sitting in the living room. The oldest one looked about seven.

The boyfriend was tall and solid, shirtless, and very amped up. He was very tense and kept his hands balled into fists. It was obvious from the start that this was not going to be an easy arrest; this fellow was not going to come along peaceably. He seemed to know he was going to be arrested. The punch to his girlfriend's mouth had sealed his fate. He gave us some bullshit story that she attacked him while he was sleeping—a last-ditch effort to prolong the inevitable.

We all stood in the small living room, the perpetrator, the girlfriend, four police officers, and three young boys. We ordered the perpetrator to turn around and put his hands behind his back. From that point on, it was his goal to fight his way through us to the door of the apartment and possible freedom. Our goal was to subdue him, cuff him, and get him down three flights of stairs to a police unit for his trip to central lockup.

Who would have thought that such a tall, skinny fellow could put up such a fight? Since he was sweaty and shirtless, there was not much of him to grab. We all tried to grab his arms as he wildly threw punches. Sometimes having too many cops could be a problem. In those instances, we tended to get in each other's way. In another scuffle of the same type, I had a good hold of a guy only to get my hand whacked by the nightstick of an officer in the back of the pack.

We fought the guy to the floor twice only to have him squeeze out and make another attempt at the door, flailing all the way. To his credit, he did make it out the door but was taken down for the last time at the top of the stairs. Even after he was cuffed, he struggled all the way to the police unit, protesting that he had done nothing wrong and yelling for his girlfriend to help him. I supposed the recollection of the punch in the mouth prevented her from doing so.

Since Allen and I were originally assigned the call, it was our job to do the paperwork. We went back to the apartment to get the woman's personal information and details of the event, but the seven-year-old constantly interrupted us.

"Mama, is Harold going to jail? Mama, Mama, is Harold going to jail?" he kept asking relentlessly.

Finally, Allen lost his patience with the child and declared, "Yes, yes, Harold is going to jail. He punched your mother. Didn't you see him fight us? Yes, he's going to jail!"

So the boy asked his mother, "Then can I have his pork chop in the refrigerator?"

After four months of riding with my field training officers, I was ready to assume all the responsibilities of seventh district patrolman. I spent most of my time in a one-man car at first, handling cold calls. I rode in two-man cars when the need arose. But as the months passed, I patrolled with a partner more and more.

It was during this time that I met Tommy Laws. Tommy was a police officer trained as a paramedic. He worked on the medical rescue unit assigned to the seventh district. We ran into each other on both routine and emergency calls. Tommy was an accomplished cop and, as it turns out, a very good cook. He invited me to his apartment for dinner with him and friends on several occasions. I also attempted to show off my cooking ability by having them over to my place. If he had been in the patrol section, we might have ended up riding as partners.

One night, I was patrolling on the night watch, 11:00 p.m. to 7:00 a.m., in a one-man patrol unit when I got the call of an injury accident with possible fatality on Interstate 10 near the Saint Tammany and Orleans Parish line. When I was dispatched to the call, Tommy Laws and the seventh district medical rescue unit (1807) was also assigned to go. The area where the accident occurred was all low-lying swamp; most all of New Orleans East is swamp. It was a warm night, and a storm was coming. I could feel and smell it in the wind. There were no streetlights or buildings that far out. The only lights were from vehicles on the interstate.

Upon my arrival, all eastbound interstate traffic was at a standstill. I went to the front of the traffic and parked my unit sideways on the interstate, lights flashing. The accident had occurred at a place we called the crabbing bridge. It was a bridge over a small bayou. All seventh district officers knew the location.

The lights of the stopped traffic adequately lit the scene. The I-10 was three lanes wide at this location. In the far left-hand lane stood a white pickup that had struck the cement rail of the bridge. Both the driver's and passenger's side doors were open. The truck had sustained heavy damage. In the center lane, about three hundred feet farther down the road, stood a stopped semitrailer truck. In the right lane and across from the white pickup, there was a vehicle with two tires up on the curb of that far side of the bridge and two still on the road.

I was the first officer to arrive on the scene; 1807 was still en route. The driver of the vehicle that had come to rest angled on the curb of the bridge ran up to me first. He said, "You have to hurry. There is a woman under my car."

I shined my Maglite underneath the vehicle and could see a woman there. I called out to her but got no answer. I didn't know if she was dead or alive. If she was alive, I knew she was in a bad way and in a bad place because I could smell her sizzling on the hot engine.

Just then, Tommy Laws in 1807 arrived. Tommy ran up to me, and I advised him of the woman under the car. I shined my flashlight under the vehicle so he could see her position and contemplate his best approach for medical treatment. He went immediately to the front of the vehicle and crawled on his stomach, pulling himself along with his arms, under the vehicle to reach the woman.

I could hear Tommy talking to the woman, and I heard the woman moan. I knew then that she was still alive. I was standing about three feet from the vehicle when I felt something hit my right boot. I shined my Maglite downward and it illuminated half of a jawbone with the teeth still in it lying on the pavement.

I bent down and yelled to Tommy, "That ain't hers, is it?"

"No. I just found it under here and it was freaking me out," he said.

Tommy's partner on the emergency unit was with him, so I informed Tommy that I was going to the eighteen-wheeler.

As I started walking toward the semitruck, its driver walked over to meet me. He told me he did not see the original incident that left the pickup in the left lane. He said that as he approached at highway speed, he saw a man and a woman in the middle lane. The man was trying to get up. The woman was helping him until she saw his semitruck barreling down on them. She ran from the middle lane into the right lane to get away from the truck only to be struck by a vehicle traveling on the right side of his that ended up on the curb. The vehicle must have hit her at the same time it hit the curb, elevating the passenger's side of the car. This timing probably saved her life. The semi driver said he was unable to go to the left lane because of the pickup truck or to the right lane because of the vehicle that hit the lady. His only option had been to attempt to brake and stay on course, heading straight. The eighteen-wheeler had struck the man in the middle lane at about fifty miles an hour. Looking at the aftermath, I was sure the man was killed upon impact.

When the fatality unit arrived, they measured 117 feet of a solid bloody skid, punctuated by body parts, some recognizable, some not. There were more gruesome details of this fatality accident, but it serves no purpose to delineate them now.

Tommy and his partner extricated the woman from underneath the vehicle. To my surprise, she had been conscious most of the time. She was badly injured, but she would live. She told us later that she had been having an argument with her boyfriend while driving the white truck. Somehow during the argument, she had crept to the left and struck the bridge rail. The initial impact threw the man out of the vehicle because he had not been wearing a seatbelt. She had then exited the vehicle and attempted to help him out of the road. She said she had seen the semitruck coming and had instinctively fled for what she thought was safety. She'd been screwed either way.

Several months later, after she had recovered, she came to the seventh district and took Tommy to lunch as a thank-you. We didn't usually see the victims come back to give thanks to the cops that helped them, but in this case, she did.

The seventh police district was full of colorful characters when I worked there. We had every kind of cop imaginable. There were big tough ones, skinny geeky ones, old ones, young ones, smart ones, dumb ones, eager ones, and lazy ones. They ran the gamut.

They all had their own peculiar personalities too. There was Lieutenant Baby Ruth, the Mole, the Jock, the Flash, Doug Tanner, Chuckles, Christianson, Duffy, Sergeant Joe "the Goat," and so many more.

Once I asked, "Hey, Joe, why do they call you the Goat?"

"Because I got a hard head and a stinkin' ass," was his reply.

At about two thirty in the afternoon one Friday, officers from the first watch were coming into the station to end their shift, and guys from the second platoon were just showing up to begin theirs. Everyone was meeting in the squad bay. That's when Mikey Duffy hobbled in on his crutches. A few months back, Mikey had been chasing an auto burglar when he stepped off a curve and took a nasty spill, fracturing his hip.

As he entered the squad bay, Tanner said, "Mikey, what are you doing?"

"I'm here to pick up my check," he replied. Mikey's wife had been coming in for the last few months to pick up his paycheck, but today he must have felt good enough to attempt to get to the station himself.

Tanner said, "That's a cocksucka beard!"

During Mikey's long recovery, he had grown a beard. Uniformed police officers were not allowed to have beards, but since Mikey's status was injured on duty, he was under no obligation to follow grooming standards.

"No, that's a cocksucka beard, I'm telling ya," Tanner persisted.

Mikey tried to brush him off, but Tanner had found a victim and wasn't letting go.

Tanner called out, "Flash, go get the Jock."

Flash left the room and soon reappeared with the Jock in tow.

The Jock was Jacques Toulouse Gaspard. Gaspard was the second platoon's desk officer. He was a little Creole whose family had been in New Orleans for a million years. One of his ancestors reputedly fought with the famous pirate Jean Lafitte in the Battle of New Orleans in

1814. The Jock was the station's resident expert in trivia, policy, and procedural issues.

Tanner said, "Jock, look at that beard. That's a cocksucka beard, right?"

The Jock walked up to Mikey, stroked his own clean-shaven chin, and inspected the beard from all possible angles and distances. Mikey just stood there on his crutches staring straight ahead, his happy reunion with his fellow officers now in jeopardy.

After what seemed like an eternity, the Jock straightened up and proclaimed, "This is *not* a cocksucka beard."

"How do you know?" Tanner asked. "Where I come from, they call that a cocksucka beard."

"Well then, sir, you come from a zoo. I was born and raised in New Orleans!"

The gallery of officers murmured understanding and agreement with that qualifying statement. Those sorts of facts were learned early on, from schoolyard to schoolyard and playground to playground, like learning to throw a football, skipping a rock, or pulling a wheelie on your bike.

"You see," the Jock began, "a cocksucka beard is cut very close. It adds color and texture to the face. It tickles a man's balls like a feather, not scrubs 'em like a horsehair brush. This beard, as you can see, is long and casually grown. It shows no sign of manicure. This is not a cocksucka beard."

The Jock put his hand on Mikey's shoulder, nodded, and gave him a smile. The beard could stay! Mikey's masculinity was still intact.

CHAPTER THREE

I had been on the job as a cop for about eight months. During this time, I always tried to visit the Dreux whenever my schedule would allow. I had gone to the club a little earlier one evening; I just felt like a beer. I hadn't even rung the bell when the buzzer sounded as the door unlocked. Barry must have seen me coming through the reflective glass.

"You're here early," he said.

"I just figured I'd enjoy a beer before everyone got here."

"You want your usual?" Barry asked.

"Yes, please," I said.

He brought over a longneck bottle of Dixie Beer and placed it in front of me.

"I usually drink Budweiser," I said.

"Well, my friend, I got no cold Budweiser, so you gonna drink Dixie."

Dixie Beer was founded by a guy named Valentine Merz in New Orleans in 1907. The old signs and memorabilia, which are still all around the city today, say *Dixie 45* on many of them. They say it's because Merz had frequented Nick's Bar across the street from the brewery, where owner Nick Castrogiovanni told him that Dixie "had the kick of a Colt 45." They brewed Dixie Beer on Tulane Avenue until Hurricane Katrina flooded the brewery in 2005; it never recovered. Now I hear they are bringing Dixie back to New Orleans with the original recipe, to be brewed again in a new factory located somewhere in Orleans Parish. I started drinking Dixie as my beer of choice after Barry chose it for me that night.

"She likes you," Barry said, nodding to the spot next to me. I looked to my left and saw Fantome on the bar stool beside me. I had neither seen nor heard her jump up. Like her namesake, she had appeared like a ghost. I gently pet her head. She pushed up into my hand as I did so.

"I've always liked her too," I said. "How old is she?"

"She's about a year old now," he said.

"Man, she's big, being just a year old. Why don't you let me take her and give her a good home?"

"She's got a good home here with me," Barry said. "She caught a rat today. You got any rats at your place for her to catch?"

"No," I confessed. "I could not afford her such luxury."

"See, now what kind of owner would you be? She's gotta have stuff to do. She can't just be lying around. She needs excitement," Barry said.

Her green eyes were looking at me as if she agreed.

"Yeah, maybe you're right," I said. "She's got a lot of things around here to keep her entertained."

Fantome turned quickly to look at the front door. Then she jumped off the stool and disappeared into the darkened recesses of the bar. Just then, Jerry and the Satisfier appeared at the door and rang the bell. It was as if she had known they were coming before they were there.

Barry buzzed them in. The pair came in and took their seats at the bar next to me. The Satisfier was wearing an old military type jacket. It was a drab olive in color but was not an army field jacket.

"That's a cool jacket," I remarked.

"It was my dad's," he said.

"What kind of jacket is that?" I asked.

"My dad's jacket."

I took this to mean that he had no idea what kind of jacket it was.

"I found it in a bunch of his stuff after he died."

"What did he die of again?" I asked.

I knew Steve's dad had been dead for a couple of years, so I didn't think the question was all that inappropriate.

"Testicular cancer," he said. "He thought he had gotten a hernia from trying to pick up a transmission. He was so fat. I guess he didn't see that his balls were ate up with cancer. It spread, and that's what killed him."

"He was in the hospital for a long time," the Satisfier recounted.

"They finally told us to take him home 'cause there was nothing else they could do. He died where he wanted to, I suppose," Steve said. "At home, surrounded by the things and people he loved. After two weeks at home, he semiquietly passed. Now every time I hear somebody scream, 'Take me to da hospital, you fuckin' bitch!' I can't help but think about 'im."

"You hated him," Jerry said. "He used to beat your ass bad when you was a kid."

"Don't talk bad about the dead. It's a sin," Steve proclaimed.

"What sin?" Jerry asked.

"Thou shalt not hate the dead. It's like the sixteenth commandment," the Satisfier preached.

Jerry looked at me as if I was supposed to say something, but I wasn't. I just pointed at my empty bottle of Dixie beer and Barry shuffled toward the chest cooler.

About twenty minutes later, Gertie, Ron, and Greg arrived. They made their usual boisterous entrance, hollering at Barry and slapping our backs as they greeted us enthusiastically.

"Why don't you buy a pitcher, Jerry? We can all split it," Ron suggested. Ron was quite capable of buying his own pitcher, but he likely figured the evening would last longer if he got a free one out of Jerry. Jerry nodded his agreement to Barry.

"So what's up, guys?" the Satisfier asked.

"Same old stuff," Ron said, pulling out a stool for Gert.

Greg had left to go to the restroom.

Gertie said, "Ron, tell them about the bug."

"Oh yeah," Ron said and looked around to make sure Greg was gone. "We were over at the Barrel the other night. It was packed. There was a bunch of single women in there. Greg went down to the other end of the bar—I guess to get rid of me and Gert. We watched him for a few minutes as he ogled the ladies.

"Then Gert told the bartender to send him a Budweiser and tell him it was from that girl down there. But don't point out any particular girl. The bartender brought him the beer," Ron continued. "Ya shoulda seen that dummy looking around for the girl who sent the beer. He was lost.

29

He kept standing on the bar rail to get a higher vantage point. He was looking all around. If he'd had a flashlight in his mouth, he could've been a lighthouse. He was trying to make eye contact with all the girls there."

"We were killing ourselves laughing," Gertie said. "Two minutes later, we sent him another one and did the same thing, told him it was from that girl over there. So now he's got two beers. He picks up both beers and starts walking around, getting close to all the women. He's holding the beers up to his chest. He looked like a freaking praying mantis." Gert laughed.

"He'd go up to different girls and just smile at them. They would look at him like he was nuts. He would know then that he had the wrong girl and go up to another," Ron said.

"We were pissing ourselves. This went on for twenty-five minutes." Gert laughed again and everyone joined in.

Greg returned from the restroom while everyone was still laughing.

"What's so funny?" he asked.

"Oh nothing," Ron said, reaching for the pitcher to pour a glass.

"Greg, you want one glass or two?" Gertie asked, and we all laughed again.

Greg looked puzzled and said one glass would do.

I was very close to my friends at the Dreux. After all, we had known each other since we were in elementary school. I was very lucky to have them. But if you stop and think about your friends, how much time do you really spend with them? Do you see them every day? Several hours on the weekend? If you were on the force, you would spend more time with your partner than with anyone else in your life. Finding a partner that you can work with is not always easy. If you were lucky, you would find another officer who you could get along with for eight hours a day. Sometimes that takes time. You would bounce around riding with just about everybody to find the right person. It's hard to find that one personality type that you not only really enjoy working with but also could trust with your life.

B. J. Wong Jr. was my partner throughout most of my police career. Baldomero Jose Wong Jr. (My God … junior? Do you mean there were two of them?).

B. J. grew up in New Orleans like I did. He went to Holy Cross High School, which was down below the bridge in the lower Ninth Ward. His daddy was in charge of helicopter maintenance for a large oil company in New Orleans. Their maintenance facility was located at Lakefront Airport. His daddy, the original Baldomero Jose Wong, had migrated to the United States from Nicaragua when he was very young.

B. J.'s great-great-grandfather was from China. He had come to the United States for a job building the railroad in the "untamed West." As the story goes, he got really pissed off at the working conditions, the pay, and the way he was treated, so he packed a satchel and started walking south. They say he either got really tired of walking or found a hot gal in Nicaragua, because that's where he stopped walking and put down roots. Four generations later, his daddy came to New Orleans, married, and raised B. J. and his sisters.

I do not know what they did to B. J.'s bloodline in Central America—maybe they pelted him with gamma rays like the Hulk—but he was six foot four. He had an oval face, but you couldn't tell he had any Chinese in him. But when he was born in 1958 in New Orleans; if you were 1/32 of any bloodline other than Caucasian, you were classified as that heritage. Thus, B. J. Wong Jr. had a birth certificate that said his heritage was Chinese. B. J. should have been born in Persia, because he rode that birth certificate like a flying fuckin' carpet. When given the choice between Negro, Caucasian, American Indian, US Samoa, or other, B. J. Wong Jr. always checked other. He didn't just ride the minority train for all it was worth; he wore the conductor's hat and waved to folks from the engine house.

I started riding with B. J. when he and his longtime partner, Bucket Head, went their separate ways. They were partners in the second police district of New Orleans but wanted a change of scenery and to work closer to where they lived. They put in transfer requests to go to the seventh police district. B. J. and Bucket rode together when Mikey Duffy and I were partners. Duffy transferred from patrol to the task force, and Bucket transferred to the detective bureau, so B. J. and I started riding together.

Bucket moved up to the detective bureau robbery section. Bucket Head was his last well-known nickname, but he had many others. His real name was Charlie Barlett. Charlie and I had gone to high school together, so I knew him very well. Charlie joined the police department a year or so before I did. From the academy, he went to the second district, where he met B. J. Wong Jr., and the two soon started riding together as partners

Once during a routine investigation of a citizen's complaint, the captain of the second district dragged Wong and the Bucket into his office. The captain said, "I'm not even going to ask you what happened. Because I know you'll lie, and he'll swear to it. I'm wasting my time talking to you blockheads."

Police officers are closer to their partners than they are to their spouses. Let's face it: we spend eight to ten hours a day with our partners, in a patrol car for most of the shift, except when we get out to handle myriad people, situations, and challenges, and our safety is always in jeopardy. Sugar can turn to shit at any time, and we have to depend on each other. That's the way it was between B. J. Wong Jr. and me. And that's the way it was between Wong and the Bucket.

Before he was Bucket Head, Charlie Barlett had many nicknames: Choo Choo Charlie, Gas Can Charlie, and Pool Table Charlie. All were well deserved. He got Choo Choo Charlie early on in his career when he and Wong were working the night watch, which was 11:00 p.m. to 7:00 a.m. They were driving to the Second District station for the shift change when a call of a signal 62A was broadcast over dispatch. A 62A was a burglar alarm call for service. Because they were close to the location of the alarm, they informed dispatch that they would check it out before returning to the station. As they were en route, they had to cross the railroad tracks at Washington Avenue. They had crossed those tracks hundreds of times and had never seen a train, so while approaching the tracks, they didn't see reason for elevated caution. There were no crossing lights or signals of any kind. When they crossed the tracks doing about thirty-five miles per hour, they were broadsided by a train.

Wong said it happened so quickly. The train hit them and pushed the car along the tracks (thank God it was moving extremely slowly). He turned to see if Charlie was okay on the passenger's side, but the door was open and Charlie was gone. Somehow, Charlie Barlett had been able to turn himself into smoke, wisp away from the moving vehicle, and rematerialize on the side of the tracks. Because the train was going slowly, it was able to stop within a few hundred yards. Luckily for Wong, those yards had not been obstructed by any polls or objects that could have torn the car to pieces with Wong still inside.

"How the hell did you get out?" Wong shouted.

"I jumped out. I thought you were going to do the same," Charlie called back.

"No, asshole! I had a train on my door!" Wong yelled.

"Well, I ain't hurt," Charlie said.

"You ain't hurt yet," Wong said.

That incident gave birth to the name Choo Choo Charlie.

Gas Can Charlie was another of his nicknames. Charlie got that one from the time he was driving alone on Wisner Avenue alongside City Park and came upon a vehicle broken down in the right lane. Charlie wasn't on duty; he was in plain clothes and was driving his personal vehicle. He got out to berate the driver, who was filling his gas tank from a one-gallon metal gas can. I don't know why Charlie would give the guy a ration of crap. That stretch of Wisner Avenue had no shoulder to pull off on in an emergency, but he got out and harangued the poor guy, who was silent throughout the incident.

When the last bit of gas had been transferred from the can to his car, without saying a word, the guy crowned Charlie over the head with the gas can. He dropped Charlie like a bad habit. Before Bucket could get back to his feet, the guy had gotten into his vehicle and left the scene. One would think that a sensible individual would collect his thoughts and realize his mistake. Not Charlie Barlett. That chump came back and told us the whole story—his second huge mistake that day.

Charlie, Wong, and I were good friends with the Sheridan brothers, Tommy was the oldest of the three. I went to the police academy with him. He was the first Sheridan I met. He had learned that there were open positions on the New Orleans Police Department and relocated to the city from Minnesota, the North Pole, or some such cold-ass place up north. He completed the academy and once on the job, he liked it so much that he sent for his brothers. That's when Jimmy and Dewey moved down. It was sort of like how Wyatt Earp called his brothers to meet him in Tombstone. The rest was history. Though I had met Tommy first, I was closer to Jimmy. We all remain good friends to this day.

When Jimmy graduated from the academy, he was assigned to the second police district. Charlie Barlett and B. J. Wong were already riding as partners when he arrived. Jimmy soon fell in with Charlie and B. J. and the three became close friends.

Several years later, Charlie Barlett and Jimmy Sheridan were drinking and shooting pool at an establishment on Saint Charles Avenue. This establishment had a clientele of all sorts of eclectic characters. Jimmy and another patron were playing the table, and Charlie was sitting on a bar stool, watching the game of eight ball, when two professional football players approached them to play a game.

I will not mention their names. I would not want to feed in to their overinflated egos or give these testosterone-laden numb nuts even two minutes of infamy. For the sake of this story, let's just call them Tweedledum and Tweedledee.

The match was Tweedledum and Tweedledee against Jimmy Sheridan and another customer in a game of eight ball. Now, I need to advise you that Jimmy Sheridan was a slim 180 pounds. He was in good shape but by no means a muscleman. The guy he was playing pool with was smaller than Jimmy. Tweedledum and Tweedledee were current NFL players, each weighing in at close to three hundred pounds.

At first, the game seemed to be going well. At least that's what Jimmy and Charlie stated later. But in hindsight, they realized these two gridiron goons were just out looking for trouble.

Jimmy and Charlie were well known by the management and staff of this establishment. It wasn't very crowded that night, so the bartender and manager were also watching the game. Tweedledum made a shot and sunk several balls but had failed to call them.

Jimmy announced for all to hear, "Hey, no luck shots."

Tweedledum immediately shot back, "Nobody said no luck shots."

Jimmy said, "Oh yes I did." His teammate agreed.

"Bullshit." Tweedledum snorted.

Jimmy said, "Hey, man, I called it."

Tweedledum put his pool cue on the table and walked over to

Jimmy. He bent down and got right in Jimmy's face and said, "Fuck your mama."

I don't know what Jimmy would've done next, but he didn't have to decide, as Charlie proclaimed from his stool, "If he told me that, I'd have to hit him."

Tweedledum walked over to Charlie, bent down and got in Charlie's face, and said, "Well, fuck your mama."

Charlie punched him square in the mouth. I don't think Tweedledum expected that. I'm sure he'd had many years of experience intimidating people with his size and having things his way because in the land of halfwits, might makes right.

Tweedledum grabbed Charlie and slammed his head into the top of the pool table. That move would get Charlie six stitches later that night. Tweedledum gave Charlie quite a beating, but Charlie kept swinging like a trouper.

During the trading of blows, Tweedledum stopped and declared, "You tore my shirt." It was kind of a dumb-shit thing to say in the middle of combat, but it happened.

Charlie walked up to him and said, "Let me see," and then punched him again in the mouth.

Tweedledee, who was standing next to Jimmy, watching the fight, said to him, "You don't know who you're fucking with."

Jimmy replied, "No, I don't think you know who you're fucking with."

That's when Tweedledee and his more than three hundred pounds of cowardice coldcocked Jimmy, knocking him out.

At the beginning of this episode, the bartender had called the police and apprised them of the situation. They were on their way soon after the first blow was exchanged. By the time the first of the cavalry began to show up, the fisticuffs had rolled out the front door and onto the sidewalk. Sgt. Bobby Cantrell was the first officer out of his vehicle. Cantrell knew Charlie well; they worked in the same district. Charlie and Tweedledum were on the ground. Tweedledum had straddled him and was beating Charlie in the back of his head. Charlie was grabbing at something affixed to his ankle. Sgt. Cantrell recognized immediately what Charlie was positioning himself to do.

The sergeant grabbed Tweedledum by the back of the shirt and yanked him off Charlie. He then jumped on Charlie, bear-hugging him. More officers grabbed Tweedledum as others rushed inside to assist Jimmy and hold Tweedledee. It was clear to anyone looking at him that Jimmy was badly hurt. He spent the next two days in the hospital with a concussion. After the incident was secured, Jimmy would not press charges on Tweedledee if Tweedledum did not press charges on Charlie for throwing the first punch.

Before everyone went their separate ways that night, Sgt. Cantrell spoke to Tweedledum and said, "Son, I believe I saved your life tonight."

"What are you talking about?" Tweedledum asked.

"I know that man very well. He is not known for rational actions and good decisions," the sergeant said.

"I could've killed him," Tweedledum said.

Sgt. Cantrell looked him right in the eye and said, "No, son, I believe it was fixing to be the other way around."

Charlie transferred out of the district and into the detective bureau. It was then that we started losing touch with him. He started hanging with another group of cops. I don't know if they had anything to do with his ultimate downturn, but I'm sure they didn't help. His wife left him, and he started dating women I would call less than pedigree.

I knew the following story well even before hearing it straight from Charlie's mouth. Charlie's version painted him and his brother in a better light, but the facts were the same. One Saturday he was watching the three-year-old daughter of one of his girlfriends while she was at work. He and his little brother had driven his brand-new Camaro IROC Z-28 to the Pontchartrain lakefront to drink beer. Charlie was the oldest of the three Barlett brothers. I knew them, and take it from me, if his mother had had a fourth one, he certainly would've been a total idiot.

I don't know what started the fight between them and six other guys on the lakefront that day, but I'm sure the Barlett brothers shared some responsibility. You would think the two-against-six matchup, especially when the two were weighed down with a three-year-old girl, would evoke some feelings of trepidation or reservation. Not so with the Barlett brothers. Lucid thought and association of actions to consequences— those were two cables not hooked up in their brains. Those instincts just flopped around loose in their heads. So Charlie and his little brother received one hell of an ass whipping.

Somehow during the melee, it dawned on them that they were losing. The two brothers didn't even speak as they scooped up the child and attempted to make a tactical retreat via the Camaro. When they got to the vehicle, Charlie threw the youngster into the backseat. He and his brother entered the vehicle amid punches and kicks from their opponents. Assailants were even cracking them in the head through the open T-top of the Z-28.

One of the combatants leaped onto the hood of the car and started jumping up and down. In Charlie's mind, a beating in a semifair fight was one thing. Attempting to maliciously and willfully damage a man's brand-new Camaro IROC Z-28 was inexcusable. For Charlie, there was only one appropriate action to take in such a situation. He pulled his revolver out from under his seat and shot the guy once in the stomach.

The hostiles must have realized that they were in a confrontation with a true madman. They withdrew a safe distance from the vehicle, and Charlie and his brother made their escape. After they had put some distance between themselves and their adversaries, Charlie stopped the vehicle to make a call to the New Orleans Police Department's command desk. At this point in history, Jimmy Sheridan was now a sergeant in charge of the command desk shift. Sheridan had already received word of a shooting at the lakefront. Charlie got him on the phone, and Jimmy informed him that the police were already at the shooting location. Charlie told him about the fight.

Jimmy said, "Charlie, you gotta go back. I think you shot one of those guys."

"Shot him? I hope I killed that son of a bitch," Charlie replied.

To make a long story short, Charlie went back. The young man he shot did not die. In fact, he turned out to be the son of a policeman from another jurisdiction. The guy decided not to press charges and notified the district attorney's office that he wanted nothing further to do with the case. I guess he either thought that Charlie was in enough trouble with losing his job over the incident or that if he did press charges, he may have to look over his shoulder the rest of his life. Either way, Charlie's connections in the police department and district attorney's office resulted in him facing no criminal charges. In retrospect, considering the events that resulted from the aftermath of that whole affair, as well as the rest of his life, it would've been better if Charlie had taken that bullet.

The incident not only cost Charlie his career but added to the trauma of having lost his wife and kids in a divorce. He struggled from one failed relationship to another. And because he was no longer "on the job," he started losing touch with his lifelong friends.

Charlie was in the dumps. He had lost the only thing he was ever really good at, and that was being a police officer. Folks kept telling him that he needed to get another skill, maybe get computer training or become a cowboy or something. I speak for every cow in America when I say that we were happy and relieved that he chose computer training.

After several uneventful years, Charlie started getting his life back together. He met a nice woman, settled down, and got married. She had a couple of kids from a previous marriage. Charlie seemed to be doing well with his computer repair career. I don't think he was hanging out with any police officers; I think he let that part of his life go.

What happened next occurred because a drunken imbecile struck a guardrail with his vehicle and complacent municipal workers were not instructed by their superiors to remove the bent section so it didn't stick out into the nearest lane of traffic. The workers only completed what they were told to do, which was to spread sand in the area of the wreck.

Municipal workers are not typically known for their initiative and self-motivation. The lummox streets department laborers got back into their truck and drove away—not recognizing or caring about the dangerous situation they were leaving behind—to continue their malingering somewhere else. As luck would have it, Charlie Barlett, hurrying to get to an early-morning computer repair job, was the one who found it next.

I can't tell you if he saw it sticking out. I can only tell you that somehow it and the rest of the guardrail went through his automobile and cut off both of his legs. I have seen several of these types of devastating injuries in my career. As massive and terminal as these type of injuries are, typically a victim doesn't suffer too long. It's a cold consolation. I'm sure Charlie didn't think about that. He was probably thinking, *I can't believe this is happening to me.*

After all the dangerous situations he had faced and come through on the police department, this senseless thing was going to be what killed him?

Was Bucket a knucklehead? Was Bucket prone to bad decision making? Sure. But he was also my longtime friend, an old pal. Charlie Barlett did not deserve to die alone on that wet, foggy morning.

CHAPTER FOUR

Later that same summer, I arrived at the Dreux early in the evening on a Saturday. I pushed the bell but got no reply. I rang the bell a second time. I wondered what was taking Barry so long. I didn't see a lot of cars parked on the street, so I didn't think a crowd was keeping him busy. Then the buzzer sounded and the door unlocked. I stepped inside. The place was dead. Just a couple of the older regular customers. Gertie was the only one at the far side of the bar. Barry was bent close to her, saying something in a quiet voice. He then straightened and gave me a very odd look.

I walked over and sat next to Gertie. I could see she was upset about something.

"Are you okay, Gert?" I asked.

"I flashed Jerry last night," she blurted.

"What, why?" I yelled and then knew by her look that I had reacted too loudly. "You gotta be kidding me," I whispered.

"I know, I know. I can't believe I did it either," she said regretfully. "We were arguing about something. I don't even know what it was. I just wanted to knock him off the stool. In frustration, I just grabbed the bottom of my sweater and lifted it up, along with everything underneath."

"What did he do then?" I asked.

"He looked at me as though I had just slapped him in the face. He didn't say anything. Then he looked around as though he was trying to find another witness, but nobody else saw.

"I feel so embarrassed," she said. "What would the nuns at Saint James say?"

"I don't think the nuns of Saint James even know what flashing someone is," I said. "I know that's true because evidently no one has clued them in as to the street meaning of your school's mascot. Come on, Gert. Saint James, an all-girls high school, with the mascot of the Fighting Beavers? That's gotta be the biggest inside joke of the entire New Orleans Catholic high school system."

"Yeah, I often wondered why they never changed that," she said. "But we have to get back to the problem at hand. What am I going to do? Jerry is always bugging the shit out of me. He's such a smart-ass, always fooling around and practical joking," she complained.

I knew what she was talking about. Jerry's antics were well known among the local purveyors of jackassery. He recently acquired blank bumper stickers and drew lewd caricatures on them, along with large text. One said, "Professional Jock Smith." Another said, "Honk if you're a homo." He then put them on the rear bumper of Greg's van. That poor goofus drove around for a week before finding them. He never put two and two together as to the reason he was having so many people honking and waving at him. That was Jerry's sense of humor. He liked to clown around.

"He's gonna be here with Steve any minute. You know they're here every weekend," Gert said.

"Look," I told her, "first things first. Take a deep breath. Everything is gonna be okay." Then I said, "I think you should go ahead and open your shirt and give me some perspective on just what we're dealing with here."

"Don't you start joking around. Not now!"

"Sorry," I said. "Guess it's too soon."

"If you weren't the only pal I have right now, I'd punch you in the head," she said, raising one of her fists to my face.

"I saw you talking to Barry. Does he know?" I asked.

"Barry knows everything that goes on around here. He's not gonna say anything. You know Barry don't play around. He doesn't mess with people. I was asking him if he overheard anything. I can't let Ron and Greg know. They'll ride me around like a pony!"

"Bareback, I hope?" I said.

"So help me God … I'm gonna smack the crap out of you. Now, are you going to help me like a real friend or keep fooling around like the jackass I know you are?"

"I'm gonna help, 'cause we're big boobies—I mean buddies."

She hauled off and punched me in the arm with all the fury of a Catholic high school girl in trouble. It hurt.

We did not have a chance to make any real tactical plans. I was still rubbing my arm when Jerry and the Satisfier rang the doorbell. Barry shot Gertie a here-we-go look as he hit the buzzer to let them in. I turned on my stool to watch them as they approached. I paid most of my attention to Steve, waiting for any expression of awareness of the recent event, but I could discern no difference in the Satisfier's demeanor.

The Satisfier walked up and sat next to me. Jerry put his large hand on the back of my neck and squeezed as he said, "Hello, Bronze. Hello, Gert. How's it going, Barry?" He sat down and asked us what we were drinking.

His calling me Bronze did not escape me. It was a slang reference meaning a police officer from the 1979 movie *Mad Max* with Mel Gibson. He starred as a cop in a postapocalyptic society. I was surprised that Jerry knew the term.

I was deep in that thought when the Satisfier shoved my shoulder. "Wake up, Goldilocks. Jerry is buying. What are you drinking?"

"Dixie for me," I said.

"You want to split a pitcher with us, Gert?" Jerry asked.

"That sounds nice. Thank you, Jerry," she said.

That night went like all the rest. We laughed, told stories, smoked cigarettes, and joked around with each other, needling Barry and interacting with the rest of the neighborhood regulars. Ron and Greg showed up too. We all stayed late that night. I didn't see anything out of the ordinary. Nothing had happened to lead me to believe that Jerry had told anybody about the flashing.

When they went to the back to play pool, I leaned over and whispered to Gert, "I don't think he told anybody."

"You really don't think so?"

"I've been watching. They're the same numbskulls they always are. Besides, if they knew, you know one would have said something smart-ass by now."

"Yeah, maybe you're right," she said with apprehension. "I'm sorry I hit you so hard."

"I guess I deserved it," I said.

"That wasn't the time to be playing around," she reprimanded.

"Sometimes I can't help myself."

"I know. You're a jerk. I seem to like jerks. I guess that's why we've been friends all these years."

I excused myself and headed for the restroom. I completed my business, washed my hands, and headed back to Gert and my beer.

"Well, Gert, he told them," I warned her.

"Why? Did they say anything to you?" she asked.

"No, they did not say a word to me."

"Then how do you know he told them?"

"Because they are all playing pool with their shirts off," I said.

That night ended like most of my visits to the Dreux, with just Barry and me locking up. Gentilly didn't have much crime back in those times, but you still had to be careful. Many times I would hang around with Barry as he closed up the place. He would hide the night's profits well away from the bar, protecting them in case of burglary that night. The owner would come in the next morning, retrieve the money, and make the bank drop. Barry never left the club with money. We did not see proactive police patrols in our neighborhood very often. I'm sure the third district was doing them, just not around Gentilly Terrace. When we locked up and left, I always looked around. It always happened when you least expected it, so it was best to counter that by expecting it.

My friend Jake Couvillion from the academy hadn't been expecting it. He was assigned to the sixth district. It was much smaller than the seventh, but it was much busier and had more crime. Jake spent many years there. One morning, he was on patrol in a two-man police unit. Often in this area of the city, the police would stop in at different businesses just to check in and make an appearance. It was good to let the business owners know that they were in the area, and it let would-be perpetrators know the same.

The pair decided to make a business check at one of the local bars. Jake was the first to walk in. It was a small place with a wooden bar and chairs running the length of one side of the narrow room. He saw immediately that there were only two people in the bar: the bartender and a woman holding a gun on him. She turned and saw them and immediately started shooting.

Jake also started shooting. His partner later told me that he felt like he was standing next to Machine Gun Mulligan. Bullets were flying everywhere. They were each in the open without cover. They continued to fire at each other until they both ran out of bullets. They were standing about fourteen feet apart. When the smoke cleared, much to everyone's amazement, nobody had been shot. Believe me when I tell you that this is not the typical outcome of these types of events. They arrested the woman without incident and charged her with armed robbery and attempted murder of a police officer.

After this incident, Jake took firearms training much more seriously. He now knew what it was like to shoot at something that was shooting back. Speed and accuracy do not come naturally. Back then on the police department, you only had one day a year to practice firearms training and qualify. When I was with the feds, it was mandatory every three months and encouraged even more often if we could find the time. Unlike the New Orleans Police Department at that time, money for ammunition was plentiful with the feds.

As it turned out, Jake needed that extra training shortly thereafter. It was on a weekend and Jake was off, so he decided to visit one of the sixth district's watering holes. He went in and hung around with his pals for a couple of hours. He had a few beers over that time, but he knew he had to drive home, so he stopped drinking well before he left. After he said his goodbyes, he was walking down the sidewalk toward his vehicle, which he had parked a few blocks away, when he noticed two men on the other side of the street. He knew right away they were up to no good.

How could he tell, you ask? I will give you this one piece of advice: When the hair stands up on the back of your neck and something in you starts telling you that something is wrong, listen to it. It could be something that your subconscious caught but your conscious self did not. *Always listen to that voice.* I know all of you have heard that voice before. Perhaps that time it turned out to be nothing. You were lucky. Do you want to look stupid and turn around? Or do you want to just ignore it and bet your well-being and possibly your life that you're just being overcautious? That voice has saved my life on several occasions. Trust me on this one.

Jake turned out to be right. They were up to no good. As he approached his car, the pair left the sidewalk and started walking in the street toward Jake.

Jake later told me he heard one of them say, "No, no, man, I think he's a cop!"

But the other guy ignored him. Jake was on the driver's side of his vehicle when the guy drew his gun. Jake already figured he was in deep shit, so he had his weapon in his hand. When he saw the perpetrator pull a gun, Jake shot over the top of his car. The perpetrator's bullet hit Jake in the shoulder. Jake's round hit the perpetrator in the stomach. As with most criminal partnerships, when sugar turns to shit, the partnership dissolves and it's every man for himself. The second subject fled.

The perpetrator was down in the street. Jake opened his vehicle, got on his police radio, and kicked in the call. Because the sixth district was small, the cavalry was there within moments. Two EMS units showed up. They loaded Jake into one, and it left immediately. Then they loaded the perpetrator in the other, and they were both en route to Charity Hospital.

Charity Hospital was the premier trauma center of the South. There was an old saying that if you ever got shot, there was no place better to go than Charity Hospital. Charity was the government-subsidized hospital. But that wasn't why they were so good. They were good because they got so many gunshot wounds each year. *Thanks, New Orleans.* Charity was also a teaching hospital.

When I became a detective assigned to homicide, I would often follow victims to Charity. If the victim lived, he or she was not my problem; the investigation would be a district matter. If he or she died, the case was mine. The trauma team worked on all of these individuals with great expertise and enthusiasm. One old homicide detective gave me the inside scoop. "You can tell if he's going to be one of ours by watching the trauma team," he said. "They will be working with passion. Watch and see if they are sticking him with any hoses. If they're just practicing, they're not going to be wasting any supplies. If that's the case, don't go nowhere. He's yours."

Both Jake and the perpetrator survived the shootout. Jake was out injured on duty for about a month. During that time, he showed up at my house to ask a favor. He said his arm and shoulder still hurt and asked if I would be kind enough to clean his gun. I could see why he needed it cleaned. It was covered in blood, and that blood had gotten into every crack and crevice and had started to rust. I had to pull the weapon all the way down to get it clean. It was then that he recounted the entire story of the incident to me. I told him he was very lucky. He agreed.

I guess Jake was never going to let himself be surprised like that again. Surprise in our line of work is usually never a good thing. As a policeman, you need to expect to find the subject when you are searching that burglarized building. Yes, he is going to be around that next corner. You should get to a point where nothing really surprises you.

Once I responded to a call while in a one-man car. Someone had reported a nude woman, possibly a rape victim, on old Gentilly Road. I knew this area. It was dark and remote. Prostitutes often used the place with their Johns.

When I got to the area, I noticed women's clothing lying in the middle of the street. I stopped and picked up a blouse and bra. A little farther down the road, I found underwear, pants, and shoes. I just put them in the back of my vehicle. I drove a little farther, but I did not see anyone, so I turned around, activated my blue lights, and started driving slowly. That's when a naked woman stepped out of the brush alongside the road. She walked up to my car as I exited the vehicle to meet her.

I said, "I believe I picked up your clothes in the roadway back there. They're on the backseat." I opened the rear door of the patrol vehicle to let her in.

She dressed in the back of the police car. She was not very upset, which led me to believe that she was not a rape victim and this was a prostitution date that had gone wrong.

As I drove to a less remote location, she said, "I know this might sound strange, but you don't show any shock or emotion. I admit I didn't know what to expect when I walked up to you, but no reaction at all really surprises me."

I said, "Lady, nothing surprises me anymore."

I did have one unexpected surprise from this job. That was meeting

B. J. Wong Jr. I had no idea that we would eventually become lifelong friends and brothers. We went through a decade together on the New Orleans Police Department and both transferred to a federal law enforcement agency together. I cannot think of anyone with whom I would have rather shared those incredible experiences. Wong was solid as a rock.

Once our rank tried to implicate us with damage to a patrol unit that we did not do. They split us up to interrogate us separately, like we'd never seen that movie before.

Wong said the sergeant came into the office where he was being interviewed and said, "B. J., you best come clean because your partner is telling us everything."

Wong told him, "Really? Is that a fact? I guess either he's lying or you are. I know him, so I'm going to bet it's you."

During ten years of riding with each other day in and day out, we probably discussed just about everything there was to talk about. Silly picayunish stuff. It turned out that when we were kids, we had the same toy rifle, the Monkey Patrol Rifle. The Monkey Patrol rifle was cool. It had a really strong spring built into it that shot a potato-sized green plastic grenade. The pistol grip separated from the rifle itself to become a stand-alone toy pistol. Wong lost his, not in the heat of an imaginary battle but after he shot his sister in the eye with the plastic grenade. She ran inside crying and ratted him out. His dad came out, grabbed the rifle from B. J., and smashed it against a tree. B. J. was crushed. His father had single-handedly decimated the Monkey Patrol. There were no survivors.

Once, while we were driving through City Park, as we went over one of the bridges crossing the many of the parks lagoons, Wong related this story: He said he was about fifteen and had just started driving. He had a pet turtle named Dudley. He'd had Dudley forever. Dudley was now old and blind, and B. J. figured he would free Dudley for the remaining years of his life. He drove over and parked near that very bridge. He got out and went to the top, and after saying goodbye, he dropped Dudley into the lagoon. His heart rejoiced as Dudley started to swim away. He was still waving when a large-mouth bass swallowed his friend in one gulp. After witnessing the horror, he plodded back to his car and began his guilt-ridden drive home.

Wong always tried to best me. The competition between us was never ending. When I look back on it now, it was juvenile, but back then it was simply entertainment.

On one very cold winter's day, we were patrolling the seventh district. The wind was blowing at about twenty miles an hour sustained. He stopped the vehicle alongside one of New Orleans East's many drainage canals. This canal was probably one hundred feet across. It had a big pipe running from one side to the other.

Wong looked at me and said, "Would you walk that pipe for twenty dollars?"

I carefully considered the challenge. If I fell into that water, it would be bone-numbingly cold. If I made it, I would be besting Wong. I loved besting Wong.

"Yeah, I'll do it," I said.

"You can swim, right?"

"Yeah, I can swim," I assured him. "But I get to take off my gun. If I go in the drink, I don't want it getting wet."

"Yes, of course," he agreed.

We got out of the vehicle. I put my gun belt in the trunk and walked over to the pipe. I was thankful that it was a bit wider than it looked from the road. The wind was whipping as I hopped up onto the pipe and started to cross.

Wong hollered after me, "You gotta walk it back too."

I just kept putting one foot in front of the other and concentrating on just the next few steps. I held my arms outstretched for balance. I was relieved when I made it to the other side.

I did not want to delay too long on the opposite bank. I jumped back onto the pipe and started to cross in the opposite direction, using my proven method. I looked up and saw that sap Wong on the pipe, walking toward me.

"What are you doing?" I yelled.

"I'm not gonna let you do it and me not do it," he said.

That was Wong. There was no way he was going to sleep that night with me having bested him. At that point, I had not made it very far on my way back across the pipe, but it was still a pain to turn around and go back so that he could proceed. We both returned over the pipe without incident to the patrol car. As usual when I beat Wong, I did not take his money.

The seventh district had a separate unit called the Asian unit. This group's job was to police the section of New Orleans East that we called Vietnamese Village. New Orleans had a huge population of Vietnamese, as large as those in Houston, Texas, and Garden Grove, California. In 1975, Catholic charities were instrumental in the relocation of a large Vietnamese refugee population to New Orleans. Policing the Vietnamese was very challenging. At that time, we had no native speakers. We relied quite a bit on children, who had a rudimentary understanding of English because of their schooling here. As a people, the Vietnamese are very religious and have an incredible work ethic. Their society did not wholeheartedly trust the police. Back in their country, police corruption was a way of life. That wariness of police made them excellent victims for Vietnamese criminals. They could be taken advantage of and they would not report the crime to the authorities.

Wong and I were the first members of the Asian unit. A lieutenant in the seventh district, Jack Wickfield—himself a Vietnam veteran—had been collecting information on Vietnamese criminals and keeping the intelligence section of the New Orleans Police Department posted of his findings. Jack liked Wong and me, and the three of us worked together for nearly two years in the Asian unit before Wong and I were assigned to the mounted division of special operations.

We were in the Village late one evening when we got a call for a hostage situation at a restaurant on the main drag. We were familiar with all the businesses on the strip. We knew right where to go. At this restaurant, the owners had installed reflective film over the business's large front windows. But they installed it backward, so outside you could easily see in, and inside you just looked at your reflection. It was easy to see the middle-aged Vietnamese man sitting at a table, holding a man and woman at gunpoint.

I told Wong to follow me. I knew the kitchen areas of most restaurants were hot as hell, so they usually left their back doors wide open with screen doors to keep out the bugs. My hunch paid off, and Wong and I entered the kitchen area unseen by anyone but the cooks. We quietly motioned for the cooks to exit out the rear door. The kitchen area had two doorways that led into the main restaurant—one through the kitchen, opening to the counter area, and the other into a long hallway with restrooms on one side and a straight line to the seating area in the other direction. As luck would have it, at the end of this long hallway sat our perpetrator. He was sitting sideways to me, pointing the gun at the couple. If I had to shoot him, this was the perfect setup.

I signaled to Wong to head for the door through the kitchen. As political correctness had not yet taken hold of the country, I had no qualms in shouting, "Freeze motherfucker!" as I drew down on him. Good for him, he turned only his head to look at me. If he had shifted his body or changed trajectory of his weapon at any time, he would've been a dead man.

I then heard all kinds of crashing and banging coming from the kitchen. I walked up to the hostage taker, my gun trained on him, as he put down his weapon and raised his hands. I didn't see Wong until he was almost right next to me. He was covered in moo goo gai pan, fried rice, and assorted vegetables. I guess when I had stepped into the hallway, he had gone through the kitchen like a bull in a china shop.

As we cuffed and searched the guy, I asked Wong, "What the hell was that all about?"

"I wasn't going to let you shoot him and me not get a chance to shoot him," Wong said. As always, he was not to be bested.

Wong and I worked for the seventh district task force, a separate unit made up of officers from the district, for about two years. This unit was proactive and not tied down to answering calls for service. The unit's mission was to make arrests and combat crime anywhere in the district it was needed. This is when I got sideways with Sergeant Emile LeBeau.

LeBeau did not like me. To this day I cannot tell you why; I can only guess. Emile had a personality that did not play well with others. Consequently, others did not play well with Emile. I tell you the following story with this caveat: I swear on my dad's grave that I had nothing, nothing to do with these events. I'm not saying I would have had a problem with them, but even if I had known who was behind it, I wouldn't have assisted in their perpetration. I don't know if the suspects did not trust me or if they just kept their deeds close to the vest, away from everyone but their closest cohorts.

Emile had a leadership style that I would characterize as nonexistent. He was a natural at pissing people off. Maybe it was the way he talked to them, his smug attitude, or his self-righteous demeanor. Suffice it to say he rubbed folks the wrong way. Not a good idea when your subordinates are practical jokers of the highest caliber.

Emile lived in a condo with his girlfriend. Remember there were no such things as cell phones back then. It would even be a while before beepers became popular, so if you wanted to make a call, it had to be on a hardline phone.

Emile came to the station off patrol to call his girlfriend and check in. He called the phone at his condo and got a recording that said his phone number had been changed to an unlisted number. Highly miffed, Emile called the phone company and gave them a piece of his mind. He yelled that he had not changed his phone number and demanded the new number. The operator told him she could not give him the new number, as it was unlisted.

"I am Emile LeBeau!" he screamed.

The operator replied, "If you're Emile LeBeau, then you would know your new number." Then she disconnected the call.

Emile was fuming. He seemed to know that someone in the district, maybe even someone in the same room right now, had figured out a way to change his home number. It would be war on anyone he thought was guilty or had any knowledge of this offense. Innocent noncombatant causalities would be an accepted by-product.

Since he didn't know who the guilty party was, he just made everyone suffer. This did not sit well with anyone, and I was sure it did not sit well with his nemesis. Several weeks later, Emile went home to his condo after his shift only to find that a semitrailer truckload of topsoil had been delivered to his front door. He was beyond angry now. What in God's name was he going to do with a seven-foot pile of mud at a condo?

He tried to find witnesses to the delivery. If he found a company name, perhaps he could track down the person who purchased the mud. His girlfriend and his neighbors had been away at work at the time, so no one saw a thing. He was at a dead end. The only thing he could do was sit atop his pile of mud, seething.

Since he didn't know who was behind these jokes, he did everything in his power to make life miserable for his subordinates. Then someone started doing what I considered beyond the pale. They started clicking him out. That means whenever he got on the radio, someone would key up theirs and override his transmission. The police communications section was not as sophisticated as police communications are today. There was no way to track the culprit.

This was done as an act of true hatred and contempt. But it wasn't just a foolish thing to do; it was dangerous. If Emile was unable to transmit, there was no way of knowing if he was calling for help. Unfortunately, there were personality types among the rank and file who were very hard of heart, and they didn't care if he was calling for assistance. I did not agree with this practice, and I would have been placed in quite a moral dilemma if I had known who was responsible. The right thing to do would've been to turn that person or persons in. But back then, a rat was worse than a killer. Luckily, that cup passed me by. I didn't know who was doing it.

One Friday afternoon, Emile had been clicked out several times that day. He was overheard to say that this was going to stop that day. He called the officers he thought were responsible into the station—Chet, Mat, and me. I knew that B. J. and I were not guilty, and when I talked to Chet and Mat later, they swore it was neither of them. As usual, Emile was going to hurt the wrong people. We were called into the task force office, and Emile gleefully informed us that he was kicking us off the task force. We asked him why. He said he did not have to tell us why. He was the sergeant, and that was just the way it was going to be! He was as giddy as a coed who had just given her first hand job.

He saved the best for last. Since the district had gone to permanent shifts just the previous month, I would be assigned to the night shift for the next three months. B. J. and I would be broken up as partners. I had enough seniority to be on the second watch. But Emile had fixed it so that wouldn't matter, at least not until the next seniority shift vote. The three of us then requested to see the commander of the district, Captain Carol Hutchings.

I knew Captain Hutchings as well as any district officer could without being part of management. She was a female police officer who had risen through the ranks to make sergeant, lieutenant, and then captain. This was extremely difficult to do, particularly for a woman in the early '80s. Carol was a good captain and a fair woman. Emile entered her office with me to gloat. Captain Hutchings saw what he was doing and asked him to leave so that she could speak with me privately.

I asked her what was going on. She told me everything I already knew about Emile being clicked out and that he was sure it was Chet, Mat, or me. He had arrived at this conclusion because the three of us were usually working when it occurred. If Emile had taken off his shoes, he probably could've counted past ten—the number of officers working any one shift. I told Captain Hutchings that I'd had nothing to do with it and that I had no knowledge of the offending parties. I'm a pretty good judge of character, and I could see that she absolutely believed me. But this was my first lesson in management sticking with management. She had to back up Emile regardless of what she personally thought of him. She said I could get off the night watch on the next vote. She told me that if I wanted to transfer out of the district, she would assist me in getting any assignment I wanted. I had no desire to go anywhere else. I thought of the seventh district as my home. I thanked her for her time and walked to the door.

While I was in the office with Captain Hutchings, Emile had informed B. J. of his suspicions about me and how he had sentenced me to the night watch. He cheerfully informed Wong that he was assigning him a brand new take-home car strictly for himself until my replacement could be found.

Wong didn't say anything to Emile. He knew where I was and waited at the captain's door for me to come out. When I opened the door, he pushed past me and walked up to her desk.

"Captain, I heard my partner has been relieved of his task force duties and has been reassigned to the night watch."

"Yes, B. J., that's correct," she said.

"Ma'am, I would like to request to quit the task force and be assigned to the night watch with him."

"B. J., are you sure that's what you want?" she asked.

"Absolutely, ma'am," he said.

She simply said, "Permission granted."

To this day, I believe it was just her way of cheating Emile out of part of his victory.

I had to hurry outside to the parking lot, not out of anger but because I did not want B. J. to see the tears welling my eyes. No one had ever shown me such loyalty before.

B. J. and I started working the night watch. I wish I could say it all went smoothly, but of course it didn't. The watches were made up of personnel with different levels of seniority. The day watch was made up of all the older guys who'd been on the job many years. The second watch was the next group in seniority. The night watch was made up of new officers who had fewer than two years on the job.

All the newbies were put off by Wong and me coming to their watch and being treated differently. We automatically rode together. We chose the district area we would be patrolling. We picked what days we wanted off. All of this did not sit well with the other night watch personnel. They complained to their rank and asked what made us so special.

"It's because they have years of seniority over all of you," was management's answer to their complaints. "Instead of getting pissed off at them, how's about trying to learn from them?"

It didn't help that we were closer to their sergeants and lieutenant than they were. They knew Emile and why we were on the night watch. They were aware that we had gotten a raw deal. It would not have surprised me to learn that Captain Hutchings had greased the skids before our arrival on the watch.

There were no two ways around it; the night watch sucked. We were busy at the beginning of the shift, and then it would slow down until about five thirty in the morning. Then it would pick up again until we got off at seven. That was the way it was then. I'm sure officers of the seventh district today go nonstop all night long.

It was during one of those increases in activity that Wong and I got a complaint of unknown trouble at an apartment complex off Read

Road. This complex always reminded me of a giant birdcage. It was made entirely of wood. The wood had a raw, unfinished look. It was multistory, and the second story had bridges that connected one side of the building to the other. Residents would walk up very wide stairs to get to the second story. At the top of those stairs was a breezeway and a wide balcony that overlooked the parking area.

This was not a code 2 call, so armed with the apartment number, we parked and started walking toward the building. That's when we heard a voice calling from above us in the second-story breezeway.

"Officer … Officer … I had to kill 'im!"

We looked up to see a black man in a white T-shirt. He was short and stocky like a little fireplug. He looked like he had just butchered a pig with his bare hands. His arms and shirt were covered in blood.

Wong drew his weapon and at gunpoint told him, "You stay right there."

I ran up the stairs to confront him. When I got to the top, I told him to put his hands on the rail. Then I frisked him and cuffed him. As soon as I was on him, B. J. holstered his gun and met me in the breezeway. The fireplug kept telling us that he had to kill him and that he would show us where he was.

We walked about five or six apartments past the breezeway to an open door. There I saw a man lying on the floor with a cocked .357 Magnum in his hand. The man was still moving, so I drew my weapon and cautiously moved toward him. The movement was just the death throes of a dying individual, but I did not know if he would involuntarily clench his hand and fire the gun. I bent down and grasped the gun, putting my thumb between the cocked hammer and the chamber to ensure it would not accidently fire.

There was no need to call for an emergency unit. I didn't have any formal medical training, but I didn't believe there was anything they could do for him when the only thing holding his head on was the skin on the back of his neck. The fireplug had practically cut his head off. We requested dispatch to send the rank and to notify homicide.

As we waited for the homicide detectives to arrive, the fireplug, who was still handcuffed, told us his story. It seemed that he and the dead man had been friends. They had been drinking and smoking click'ems. A click'em is a marijuana cigarette that has been soaked in formaldehyde. I had seen these on the street many times before. Smoking them makes a dopehead crazier than a scalded ape. Somehow the dead guy got it into his head that the fireplug had screwed him over. I don't know if it was over money or narcotics, but in his pickled brain, he had been grievously wronged.

They had started physically fighting each other, but I guess that got nowhere fast. The future corpse drew a .357 he had been concealing. This action put a little distance between the two as he ordered the fireplug to sit on the floor against the couch. He recounted all the perceived sins the fireplug had committed against him. He then announced he had no choice but to shoot the fireplug. He pointed the weapon at him and ordered him to turn around. The would-be victim asked why he needed to turn around.

"Because I don't want to look you in the eyes when I shoot you," he answered.

"You might as well shoot me because I'm not going to turn around," the fireplug said.

"You gotta turn around or else I can't shoot you," the gunman said.

That's what click'ems do. They tend to fog your brain so you can't even shoot a guy correctly.

Our would-be victim realized by this time, even through the click'em haze, that he was in deep trouble. The gunman picked up a mop and placed a raincoat he removed from the back of the chair over the handle. He held it out to the fireplug and said, "If you not going to turn around, put this over your head." That was the break the stump had been waiting for. He feigned a reach for the jacket but instead leapt on the gunman. The fireplug wrestled the gun away from him and beat him like his life depended on it.

The little numbskull beat the gunman unconscious. He kept beating him even after that, just for good measure. If he had taken the gun, called the police, and held his friend there until they arrived, he would not have even taken so much as a ride downtown that night. But again, those damn click'ems don't allow you to think straight. He could've run away. He could've gone to another apartment. He could've taken the gun, dragged the guy out of his apartment, and locked the door. But apparently none of those solutions were as appealing as going to the kitchen, getting a large wooden-handled knife, straddling his unconscious friend, and trying to saw off his head. Once the gunman's head was mostly off, the fireplug stuck the knife into the gaping hole so that only the last inch and a half of the wooden handle could be seen.

It was only after he took a break from his butchery that he figured it best to call the police. I guess he was concerned about how the overall scene would look to us, so he retrieved the .357, cocked it, and placed it in the dying man's hand. Again, bad drug-addled planning. There was no reason to cock a revolver in a fight. No one would do that. There was no way you could have a life-and-death physical altercation with a cocked weapon in your hand without it going off. It all was obviously staged, which he confessed to later.

When the homicide detectives arrived, we briefed them on what he had told us. When they interrogated him, he told them the same story. Since the detectives were now driving this train, we gave them our information and left. We were no longer needed.

I don't know what he was charged with. B. J. and I were never summoned to court. That means he probably pled out to second-degree or manslaughter. You might think that you would want to follow it through, that you would want to know. Truth be told, once your part is finished, you move on. You don't even think about it anymore unless you are summoned to testify in court. If a police officer cared about running down all the events he or she was involved with to their final dispensation, that person would drown.

The ending hours of the night watch were when another set of shenanigans came to light. One night, Wong and I spotted a car in an area where a new subdivision was under construction. There were no structures there; only the roadways had been completed. There was no reason for a vehicle to be parked there at this time of the morning. Daylight was just breaking, so we approached without headlights. We got out of our unit and walked over to the car. There were two people in the front seats. I tapped on the glass with my Maglite and told the driver to get out. He complied, keeping his hands at his chest where I could see them. He had on a nice checkered collared shirt. The problem was that was the only thing he had on.

The woman started telling Wong that she had been raped. We separated the pair so we could get individual stories and compare them. If both stories matched in substance and in detail without an opportunity for collusion, that story was probably the truth.

The man told me that they had been out on a date and had stopped there to have sex. He gave me her name and address. He said she still lived with her parents. He protested that he hadn't raped anybody. He said he did not know why she would accuse him of such a crime. Wong spoke to her, and her story didn't make sense. All the details were good up until the time of the rape.

She finally ended her false accusations and told us she had just panicked. Her parents were going to be mad at her for coming home so late. She knew she had better have a good reason, and being raped, in her mind, was a damn good reason. It was a good thing that she came to her senses. She'd been about to destroy the rest of the man's life.

CHAPTER FIVE

I arrived at the Dreux later than usual one night. I was off work, and the weekend crowd was already there. My companions were energized and getting boisterous. They gave me an enthusiastic greeting as Barry opened a bottle of Dixie and gave it to me, smiling.

"You're late," Steve said as I sat down. "We were starting to worry about you."

"Yeah, we figured you might've had a date or something," Gertie said.

I told them that the girl I had been seeing had decided to call it quits.

"That's a shame. Didn't she come from money?" Greg asked.

"I don't know. I guess her family had money," I said.

"Well, there you go. That's the problem," Gertie said. "You see, there's old money, there's new money, and then they got you, no money. Why don't you let me fix you up with one of my friends?" she offered.

"I don't know, Gert. My schedule is all over the place right now," I said.

"How come you're gonna fix him up and not me?" Ron asked.

"Because most of my friends know you, honey," Gert said.

"Is Ron really that bad, Gertie?" I joked.

"No, I love this guy," Gert said, patting Ron's leg. "He's a hoot. Ron is like watching a monkey playing with a hand grenade. It's entertaining, but you better do it from a distance."

We all laughed except Ron, who just smirked.

"Were you working last night?" Jerry asked me.

"Yes, I worked last night," I said.

"What happened at the Burger King over on Chef Highway? There were about ten police cars out there when I passed."

I looked down at my beer for a moment and then said, "Guys, if I wasn't part of it and I didn't handle it, I really don't care about it. Just because I'm on the department doesn't mean I have direct knowledge of all the crimes committed in this city. I'm not even assigned to this district." I had given this explanation to the same crowd more than a half a dozen times since I'd become a policeman. I didn't blame them, though. It was just natural curiosity. "I go to work, I do what I have to do, and then I leave. I come home and take off my uniform, and I don't think about it until I have to go back."

"If you don't have anything to tell us, then why don't I tell y'all about my experience with the police yesterday afternoon?" Ron said. That captured everyone's attention. We were all ears.

"Did ya hear about the NOPSI bus accident yesterday afternoon?" Ron asked me. I told him I had not and begged him to continue.

"I was on the Franklin Avenue NOPSI bus yesterday evening, coming home from work," Ron said. NOPSI is an acronym for New Orleans Public Service Inc. They ran the public transportation and the power grid of New Orleans. Power poles were NOPSI poles. NOPSI had an identification number on each one. A "NOPSI pole" was also slang for an erection.

Ron continued, "My car wouldn't start yesterday morning. It turned out to be the battery."

"It was dry as a bone," the Satisfier acknowledged.

"Steve put distilled water in it and charged it while I was at work. Runs good now. Thank ya very much for doing that."

Steve nodded, accepting the appreciation.

"So I took the bus to and from work. On the way home, as the bus stopped at Gentilly Boulevard and Franklin Avenue, *bam*, we were hit in the rear by a dump truck. The truck was gonna turn on to Gentilly Boulevard, so he wasn't going fast. It was more of a bump. Enough of a bump to let ya know something hit us, but that's about it.

"There were about twenty people on the bus, including myself," Ron said. "The bus driver got out to speak to the truck driver. He then went to use the pay phone across the street. I was wondering how long this was going to take. I was still about eight blocks from the house and I didn't want to walk the rest of the way." As Ron had all our undivided attention, he took a long sip of his beer, then continued.

"The truck was still resting where it struck the rear of the bus. As we waited for the driver to return, assholes started climbing out of the sewers and dropping from the trees. They started coming onto the bus and taking the empty seats. Cars were stopping, and shysters were getting out and getting on the bus. When the bus was full, they started lying around outside! When the poor driver came back, he saw what was going on; he didn't know whether to shit or wind his watch!

"By the time the cops arrived, there were nearly one hundred and twenty-five people injured from the accident. The bus could only seat thirty-five. The cops knew what was going on, but what were they going to do? Kind of destroys your faith in humanity when you witness such dishonesty," Ron said. "I said screw it and got up to walk home. One of the most critically injured grabbed my seat."

We were all expressing our collective disgust on the present state of human integrity when Jerry called to Barry and made a large circle gesture over our beers, indicating his request for another round. It was clear that a final decision on the ultimate fate of mankind required additional alcohol-fueled discussion.

As the guys continued to rant, Gertie leaned over to me and whispered, "Really, I can fix you up with one of my friends."

"Let me think about it, Gert," I said. "I'm just coming out of one relationship. I don't think I need to jump into another one right away."

"When you're ready, I think I might have someone you would really like," Gertie said.

As Gert and I attempted to have our private discussion, Ron, Jerry, and Greg were having their own conversation on mankind's condition. She and I unwittingly became an example of some obscure point Jerry had just made in their debate.

"What are they whispering about?" Ron asked in an accusing tone.

"That's exactly it! That's the perfect example of just what I'm talking about," Jerry said loudly. "Secrecy and exclusionism always come first. Then oppression and tyranny, all leading to some sort of homosexual activity. Procreation grinds to a halt. Sodomy rules the day. Visigoths rule the night. The end of the human experience."

"Quite right, professor," Ron agreed. "But have ya considered that life is tenacious? That evolution is constantly at work? Changing and adapting like Neanderthals dying out and the rise of the Homo sapiens. Because of this fact, somewhere on the subcontinent, or in some shrinking metropolis or deep jungle, sodomy produces offspring," Ron surmised.

"Please go on, Doctor. I am quite intrigued," Jerry joked.

Ron continued. "Like in some species, the act of childbirth now becomes fatal. You don't need me to explain why. Now the infamous butt baby becomes real. The poo man, if you prefer. The next step on the evolutionary scale, Turdtacus is born," Ron announced.

"We're all damned, I tell you. Damned," Greg said.

The six of us closed the club that night. Barry did not even try to chase us out. When we were the only ones left at the bar, he turned off the lighted sign outside. The Satisfier dropped some coins into the jukebox. He played "Safety Dance" by Men without Hats. Since we were inebriated to the point that we had no inhibitions to speak of, we all got up and danced. Even Barry danced with us. He had some incredible moves. I never would have expected that. He was all over the floor. The rag slung over his shoulder hung on for dear life; it didn't drop once. Gertie was probably the second-best dancer. The rest of us looked pathetic. We were acting like imbeciles. It was the most fun I'd had in a long time.

The time I spent at the Dreux was not only fun for me but also therapeutic. When I was off work, I needed an escape. Sometimes Wong would meet me there, but I usually went alone. Wong and I were still stuck on the night shift, so my body was used to being up all night. We really wanted to get off that shift.

On weekends that I had to work, I could not help but think about what I might be missing at the club. I would think to myself that they were having a great time, while Wong and I were cleaning up the backlog leftover from the second watch. I was stuck out here but wanted so badly to be there. God loves the working man, but I'm sure he hates the night shift too.

It had been a typical night shift—busy at first and then slowing down to no calls for service. At a little after six in the morning, the sun was just coming up, so it was pretty good light. We got a call of a burglar alarm at Sears at the Lake Forest Plaza shopping center. It was in our area of responsibility, so B. J. and I were assigned the call. We figured we would just check the exterior of the building and if we did not find anything, we would advise dispatch of a code 4. A code 4 meant situation under control and no additional units needed.

We checked the building and found that the entry doors on the west side had been smashed. The building was large and we did not know if the perpetrators were still inside, so we called for a K-9 unit. The K-9 units arrived on the scene within fifteen minutes. It was Paul Teche and Robert "Bob" Dupre and their dogs, Max and Jurgen. I had met Bob Dupre many years before in my marine reserves unit. His stories about the job was what sparked my interest in becoming a police officer. Our friendship started then, and we are still close friends to this day..

B. J. and I and two other seventh district units had been guarding the perimeter of the Sears to prevent any suspects from escaping. Paul and Bob entered the building and began to search it with their dogs. We stood around outside, waiting for their return. While we were waiting, a black Chevy Nova came flying down Lake Forest Boulevard. It must've been doing at least fifty miles an hour. It was early in the morning and there was no traffic, so I guess the driver didn't realize that there were so many cops nearby.

B. J. said, "Let's get that guy." He started running toward our car.

I asked the other guys if they had this scene, and they said, "Yeah, go."

As I started running to our unit too, Paul's dog, Max, who had been searching unleashed, saw us from just inside the doors. Max didn't know blue shirts were good guys. All he knew was men running, chase and bite 'em.

He took off in pursuit. Wong got to the unit first, and as he opened the driver's side door, he looked back to see me running toward the unit, followed by ninety pounds of canine justice.

B. J. screamed at me, "Get in the car! Get in the car!" I jumped in the unit. Then he yelled, "Close the door!"

I had no idea the dog was behind me. I reached out and closed my door, probably rubbing the end of the dog's nose with the edge of the door as I did so. As the realization of what had just happened sunk in, I couldn't do anything except look at the dog outside my window. He must have heard Paul calling to him, because he forgot about us and began trotting back to his handler.

"That was too close," B. J. said.

"Too close," I agreed. "Way too close."

Bob and his partner, Paul, always worked the night shift. They were both permanently assigned to the K-9 division. I hated the night watch. They both had enough seniority to work whatever watch they wanted, but they both enjoyed working 11:00 p.m. to 7:00 a.m. They each had their own vehicles, but they were always together. When you needed to call a K-9 unit in the middle of the night, you always got two for one. They could patrol anywhere they wanted to in the city, as long as they were available to respond to calls.

We would see them often out in the parking lot of a closed business, letting their dogs get some exercise and stretch their legs. Sometimes we would go talk to them, but we always did so from within the safety of our car. When we pulled up to talk, their dogs always sat by them and stared at us like we were raw steaks.

One night, Paul and Bob had just parked in front of a closed strip of shops off Claiborne Avenue and had gotten out of their vehicles to shoot the breeze. While they were standing around, a black man in his early thirties walked up to them.

He said, "Hey, the girl at the Jiffy needs ya."

"What does she want?" Paul asked him.

"I don't know. She's gotta humbug for ya," he said and walked away, motioning toward the Jiffy Spot convenience store and gas station across the street.

The word *humbug* in the *Webster's* dictionary has one main definition and two subdefinitions: One, a deception, hoax. Two, one who attempts to trick or deceive. Three, nonsense. I believe it would have assisted everyone involved if *Webster's* had listed a fourth subdefinition: armed robbery in progress.

Paul and Bob secured their dogs, locked their police units, and crossed the street. They entered the Jiffy Spot and looked for the attendant, who was normally behind the register area located to the right of the entrance. The attendant was at the register, facing a large man in dark clothing who instantly turned to face them.

Bob could see immediately that he had been pointing a weapon at the woman. He shouted to Paul, "He's got a gun!"

Bob said this was when everything went to hell. The guy turned and started shooting. They likewise shot back. Bob said it happened very quickly but that it seemed like an eternity. He said time absolutely stopped. Everything was in slow motion. He could feel when the first bullet hit him in the right forearm. Then a second tore through his right thigh, nicking his femoral artery.

He said, "The guy was on PCP or something. Paul and I were shooting, and we could see that we were hitting him, but he was not going down. He finally dropped about the same time I did. The difference between us then was that I was shot and he was dead."

Paul knew right off that Bob was in trouble. He said there was blood everywhere. He kicked in a signal 108, officer needs assistance, life in danger. This signal brings everyone anywhere near the location to assist.

Bob told Paul, "Tell 'em where we at!"

Paul yelled to the dispatcher, "We're at Jiffy Spot."

Bob yelled at Paul, "God damn it, there's about fifty Jiffy Spots!"

Paul looked directly at Bob and said, "Don't you holler at me!" He then clarified, "The Jiffy Spot on Claiborne Avenue."

Paul attempted to get Bob up. But there was so much blood on the ground that he slipped and ended up head-butting Bob in the mouth. Bob said he thought to himself, *Great, now I got a fat lip.* Paul dragged Bob out to the street, where they collapsed in the middle of the road. Bob said he heard the first police car slide around the corner. The driver stomped on the gas, and the car made a throaty accelerating noise.

Bob said, "Shit, they gonna run us over!" He was still bleeding profusely. He told Paul, "Bro, I don't think I'm gonna make it."

"I will beat the fuck outta you if you die on me!" Paul threatened.

There are very few times that I can remember waiting for an emergency unit when a police officer was badly hurt. We always just threw them into one of our vehicles and went. This time was nothing different. They threw Bob into the backseat, piled in, and sped off.

Immediately, an officer known as "the Saint," tried to find Bob's wound, which was hard to locate after Paul and Bob had rolled around in all that blood. Both of their uniforms were covered in it.

That's when Paul said, "He's shot in the leg."

After finding the wound, the Saint jumped on top of Bob and put his knee into Bob's crotch. He applied all his weight to his knee, attempting to pinch off the artery in Bob's groin and slow down the bleeding. This was pretty hard to do considering the vehicle he was in was going a million miles an hour toward the hospital.

They arrived at Charity Hospital within minutes.

They rushed him to a trauma room. Bob said the doctors searched all over him.

"What are you doing?" he asked.

"We're trying to find your injury," a doctor answered.

"Why don't you hose me off and look for the holes," Bob said. He told me the doctors were not amused.

Bob said to me, "They kept asking me every two minutes or so my name and date of birth. After about the tenth time, I told them, 'I keep telling you and you keep asking me.'" He said, "I found out later that if your condition is that close to death and you forget your name and date of birth, that's when they ship you off to the parts room. It stops being a rescue and goes into harvest mode."

He said they were working on him when Father Peter Rogers came into the room. Father Rogers was the chaplain of the New Orleans Police Department. He was also the head priest of the Shrine of Saint Jude on Rampart Street in the French Quarter. Saint Jude is the Catholic patron saint of lost causes and hopeless cases. It probably would have done Bob no good to know this fact at that time.

Father Rogers came as close as he could while the doctors were working on Bob. Bob saw him and immediately recognized him. All New Orleans cops knew Father Rogers.

Bob was in a bad way. He asked Father Rogers, "Am I gonna die?"

"You're going to be just fine," Father Rogers assured him.

"But you're here to give me the last rites," Bob said anxiously.

"No, son, it's the sacrament of the sick," Father Rogers said softly.

"But I'm not sick, Father. I'm shot!" Bob said.

I guess Father Rogers figured Bob was either delirious or a smart-ass. Either way, it was too early in the morning for this foolishness. He proceeded to give Bob the Catholic last rites. Bob said in receiving the sacrament, Father Rogers dumped oil in his eyes. Bob said he thought to himself, *Oh man, now I'm shot and blind. If this is all the shit that happens to you, I'm never gonna get shot no more!*

About forty-five minutes before the shooting happened, Bob and Paul had been at Crystal Burger. Bob told me, "The girl at Crystal Burger liked us. She gave us free meals. I had eight Crystal Burgers, an order of fries, and a malt. Do you know what happens after you get shot twice and your body dumps about a gallon of adrenaline into you and then doctors pump you full of all kind of medications and you recently ate eight Crystal Burgers, fries, and a malt? You gotta shit!

"They were wheeling me to surgery. I was fully conscious, still giving my name and date of birth when it hit me. I started telling the trauma crew, 'Wait, wait.' They asked what was wrong. I had just received the last rites and I didn't want to say the word *shit*. I was totally clean of sin and I didn't want to mess it up now. I told them, 'I have to poo-poo.'"

He said, "Yeah, it sounds stupid now, but it wasn't stupid to me then. I had all kinds of hoses and cables coming out of me. They brought me a bedpan. They wanted me to crap in this pan in front of everybody while we were still on the move to surgery.

"I told them, 'I can't do this in front of everybody.' One of the doctors said, 'It's okay. We see this with people all the time.' I said, 'Not from me you don't.' The doctor told me, 'You better hurry up; we don't have a lot of time.'

"I crapped in the pan. It was terrible. If they would have known what I was about to do, I think they would have blown off the bedpan and brought me a number five washtub. I then told them I had to wipe. One of them told me, 'We'll wipe you.' I felt about a foot tall."

Bob was a big guy, well over 220 pounds and all muscle. When they got him into surgery, they had a hard time moving him from the gurney to the table.

"They tried to lift me but there was no way. I had to pull my own ass onto that cutting table," Bob said. "I tried to tell a black trauma crew member that I needed to poo-poo again, but he said, 'Too late fo dat. You be gone.' He was right. Seconds later, whatever they gave me dropped me like a ton of bricks."

Bob would spend the next seven and a half hours in surgery at Charity Hospital as doctors repaired all the damage the gunshot wounds had done to his leg and arm. When he woke up, he said that's when it really hurt. He figured the adrenaline had kept the pain away until now. The doctors informed him that if the Saint had not slowed the bleeding by placing his knee in Bob's groin, he certainly would have died. He would have bled out in the police unit while on the way to the hospital. It had been touch and go from the time he was shot until he arrived at the hospital.

After several months, Bob made a full recovery and was back on the street with Paul and his dog. To this day, Bob has a special love and respect for the Saint that saved his life. Many years later when the Saint passed away, Bob and I sat near each other at his funeral. That day was hard for me, but I'm sure it was excruciatingly painful for Bob.

CHAPTER SIX

B. J. Wong had a private pilot's license. He had gone through flight school at Lakefront Airport in New Orleans. He got tied up with two other police officers, and the three went in together and bought an airplane. It was a Cessna 172. It helped that B. J.'s father worked at Lakefront Airport in the aviation section of a large oil company. They serviced mostly helicopters, but Wong's father was an aircraft mechanic. His partners saw this as a valuable asset; aviation maintenance was extremely expensive.

Because Lakefront Airport was in the seventh district, we could always ride by and check on his aircraft. On one occasion, we stopped there in the afternoon. He went inside the hangar where he kept his plane as I waited in the police unit. I had a small radio with an earphone, and I was just rolling the dial, trying to get a decent station. As I did so, I hit the frequency for Lakefront Airport's ATIS.

ATIS, which stands for automated terminal information system, is a continuous broadcast of an airport's current weather, which is updated at least hourly. This eliminates the controller requirement to read local weather data to each landing or departing aircraft. As the forecast changes hourly, it is given a different phonetic identifier. This way, the controller knows a pilot has listened to the most current broadcast. When a pilot would call the air traffic controller, he or she would say something like, "Lakefront Control, November 737 Victor Charlie request permission to taxi to redline with information Zulu."

I knew this stuff because I sat around listening to B. J. talk with his pilot friends on many occasions. Since I was not a pilot, I was considered, in the words of David Gilmour, "an earthbound misfit." When I came upon the radio transmission that afternoon, it gave me inspiration for mischief.

That hour's phonetic identifier for the ATIS broadcast was whiskey. I checked my watch, and it was about fifteen minutes past the hour. I figured I had another forty-five minutes to be safe. I waited for B. J. to return. I knew I had to play this just right or the fish could slip off the hook. Then I saw my mark approaching the car. I had put the radio back in my bag so as not to arouse his suspicion.

When he got back in the car, I asked him, "Did you have fun with your little airplane cronies?"

Of course, I did not expect an answer. It was just a lead-in to throw him off. Then I threw the hook in the water.

"Did you get information whiskey when you were in there?" I asked.

"What?" he asked.

"You know, information whiskey, where they tell you about the airport and the weather," I said, bringing in my stooge.

"It's not called information whiskey, dumbass," Wong asserted.

I could feel my fish nibbling at the bait. Now all I had to do was set the hook. Then I said with deliberate certainty, which I knew would infuriate him, "It's been information whiskey every time I ever heard it."

That was all it took. That fish nearly pulled the pole out of my hands!

"Okay, I tell you what. I'll bet you our next paycheck it's not information whiskey right now," Wong proposed.

You can't tell me I didn't know him inside and out.

"I don't know, man. That's a lot of money." I feigned hesitation. I couldn't move too fast or he might come off the line. I let him harangue me for a few more minutes. I looked at my watch to make sure I was still safe.

"I thought you were so sure," Wong said smugly.

"Okay," I said. "I'll bet you, if just to have you leave me alone."

He started the vehicle and drove quickly to his airplane, chuckling to himself the whole way, proud of the fact that he was surely about to best me. We got out of the car, and he self-righteously pranced to the plane. He removed the keys from his pocket and unlocked the door.

Then he turned on the magnetos and the radio and dialed it to the frequency of the ATIS. The automatic voice came on in the middle of the broadcast, so I got to savor the moment just a little longer. At the end of the broadcast my friend the auto voice said, "Advise control, you have information whiskey."

Holy crap! His legs buckled. He turned to me, and I swear all the color had drained from his face. He did not know what to say. That knucklehead had figured his chances of losing the bet were one in twenty-five. I could see the wheels turning in his mind. He knew I had been in the car the whole time. There was no way I could've heard the ATIS broadcast. How the hell had this happened? What was he going to tell his wife? How was he going to get through two weeks until his next paycheck? I just turned, walked back to the car, and got in, leaving him standing there. B. J. turned off the radio, killed the power switches, and locked the aircraft.

It must've taken him an hour to walk the thirty feet back to our vehicle. His head was bent, his shoulders sagged, and his knuckles were practically dragging on the ground. He looked like a guy who had just discovered his dog had eaten the winning lottery ticket. He got in the vehicle a totally broken man. I was enjoying this too much to let him off now. He started the car, and we went back on patrol.

He requested that I not take his whole paycheck. He proposed that he would pay me the sum over the next four paychecks. That way maybe his wife wouldn't notice. His wife and I are the best of friends today, but back then she hated me. If she found out that he lost his paycheck in a bet, there would be hell to pay. The fact that he lost it to me would cause Armageddon.

I let him stew in his own juices for the next hour. Then I finally came clean and told him how I had done it. I told him I was not going to take his money. As I explained it all to him, I could see the weight come off his shoulders. He was so happy that he wasn't going to have to pay me the money, he totally forgot that I had bested him.

"Do you know how many extra details I was gonna have to work to come up with that kind of money?" he asked.

"Plenty," I said.

When I was on the job, cops worked details. There was no way around it. A detail is a security job done in addition to your forty hours a week for the city. Back then the police department did not control details. They were controlled by individual policemen who had brokered deals with local businesses for police protection for a certain price. I had been working the Plaza Shopping Center detail for many years. Then Sergeant Emile LeBeau took over running the Plaza police detail. When he kicked me off the task force, I asked him if he was going to kick me off the detail at the Plaza too. He said no and that the two had nothing to do with each other. I knew that was bullshit; my days at the Plaza were numbered.

Working the detail at the Plaza was never just sitting around. There was always some lawlessness to police, everything from shoplifters, auto thefts, parking lot robberies, fights, disturbance of the peace, domestic disturbances. It was just like a small city. I remember B. J. and I once had a shoplifter handcuffed and were walking him back to the bubble office. The bubble office was a space the shopping center gave to the police to complete reports and arrest paperwork. It was used as a central staging place. It was called the bubble office because it had a huge Plexiglas bubble window that protruded from the wall and looked out on the ice-skating rink.

On our way to the bubble office, the handcuffed suspect made a break for it. I have never seen a guy run so fast in handcuffs. It has been my experience that these people just have an overwhelming desire to run. That desire is stronger than any good sense they might possess. Think about it for a minute. Where are you going to go? You're handcuffed for heaven's sake. You can't drive away. You can't escape on a bike. There's very little you can do, even if you get away. But those rational thoughts don't enter their minds. The only thing they're thinking is run!

This guy ran. We were running as fast as we could, but he was starting to pull away. B. J. threw his Motorola brick radio at the suspect. It struck the guy perfectly in the back, and he went down. It looked like something out of a cop show on TV. It was a one-in-a-million shot. We rounded up our now exhausted arrestee and, with a firm grip on both of his arms, walked him to the bubble office.

Another Plaza Shopping Center detail adventure was the arrest of a shoplifting juvenile. He was a fat little fellow of about thirteen. We had him handcuffed and sitting in the bubble office while we prepared his arrest paperwork and completed the report to book him into the juvenile division. He refused to admit that he had been stealing. He was adamant that he was only saving his money. I was writing the report, so B. J. had nothing to do. He decided to have some fun with the little fellow. He started talking about how bad juvenile hall was.

He said, "Sometimes they feed you; sometimes they just forget. If they can't find a bed for you, they just make you stand in one place till somebody gets released. It's a tough place. Kids are crying for their mamas; other kids are just shaking like cold wet dogs."

Of course, none of these things were true. The kid didn't say anything. I figured he knew better, or he figured B. J. was full of it.

It was the end of our shift, so instead of calling the district to transport him, we would take him up to juvenile in our car. We called the dispatcher and advised her that we were leaving the Plaza with one male juvenile and our current mileage en route to the juvenile division.

The little guy didn't say anything the entire ride. We arrived at police headquarters, the location of juvenile. When we entered the juvenile office through the unlocked glass front doors, we walked into a foyer area. In front of us was a large, thick pane of glass with speaking holes so we could talk to the officer working the desk. At the bottom of the glass, there was a space of about eight inches from the glass to the counter and a tray that ran the length of the glass. This was so paperwork and property could be passed to either side.

Detective Chris Patton was there to meet us. B. J. and I both knew Patton. B. J. had served in the second district with him, and I had met him some years ago through B. J. and Bucket. Chris unlocked the door and let us into the main office.

"What you got here?" he asked.

"A thoroughly dangerous man," B. J. said.

"Is that so?" Chris said, eyeing the little perpetrator.

"You gotta watch this one," I said, winking at Patton as I removed the handcuffs.

"I know how to take care of these guys," he said.

The little arrestee never said anything. I handed the paperwork to

Chris as he sat back at his desk. It was a Saturday afternoon. Chris was the only detective manning the juvenile office. We said our goodbyes, and Chris buzzed us out. I could hear him telling the kid to empty his pockets and put his possessions on the desk. B. J. and I walked back to our patrol unit and headed back to the seventh district.

We were about eight blocks away when I heard Patton yelling on the radio, "10-28 chasing a black male juvenile in front of police headquarters. White shirt and blue jeans, short hair." You could hear that he was running.

A 10-28 is a code to clear the radio for a chase or a fight and to request the assistance of other officers. B. J. and I looked at each other in disbelief. We immediately turned around and met Patton at the corner of Tulane and Broad Street, about a block from police headquarters. He was out of breath.

B. J. and I searched the area and kept expanding our search range as time went on. We covered about a half-mile radius of the juvenile division and found neither hide nor hair of the agile little escapee. We returned to meet Chris.

We found him inside the juvenile division on the phone. He buzzed us into the main office.

"What the hell happened?" B. J. asked.

He said, "Everything was going fine. The kid never said a word. He emptied his pockets and put his stuff on the desk. Then he just stood there. He didn't show any signs that he would give me any trouble, so I looked down and started to log him in. That's when he bolted.

"I didn't know where he was going because the front door was locked," Chris said. "I swear to God, he turned himself into playdough and squeezed through that little opening at the bottom of the glass counter. If I hadn't seen it with my own eyes, I would have never believed it. He was a chubby kid! How the hell could he do that? His bones must be made of rubber.

"It happened in seconds," Chris continued. "He squeezed through and was on the other side of the glass. I couldn't buzz myself out. I had to get my key and unlock the door. This gave him a good head start. When I got outside the building, he was gone."

We all stood there, looking at that little opening. Nowadays they would have cameras in an area like that. We would have had a video that I'm sure would have gone viral today. But back then there were no cameras. Only three cops standing there in amazement, questioning the laws of physics.

"You two best go back to the seventh district and take your witchcraft and sorcery with you," Chris said.

The seventh district wasn't just suburban sprawl. It had huge tracts of land, mostly swamp. On the east side of the district, that was about all there was. This also had to be patrolled. We found stolen vehicles burned out there, murder victims, stranded motorists, and vehicle accidents on Interstate 10, which crossed through that area. In anticipation of development of homes and businesses, the state had built interchanges off the interstate that went nowhere. They had no exit names. That's why we called them the no-name turnarounds.

Once, Wong and I were patrolling the area of the third no-name turnaround. On the eastbound side, we found a pickup truck. The truck was loaded down with beehives that were covered by a tarp. There were bees swarming all around it but no driver. We pulled up behind the vehicle and ran the license plate. It came back no record.

In typical Wong form, B. J. asked, "Would you go slap one of those hives for twenty dollars?"

I wasn't allergic to bees, but I wasn't stupid either. "No way. They could kill you if enough of them stung you. If you're so brave, why don't you do it?" I dared him.

"How much is it worth?" he asked.

"I'm not gonna pay you anything," I said.

"Then there's no incentive for me to do it," he replied. "No doubt it's dangerous, but it's gotta be worth something."

We haggled back and forth about how much money it was worth in relation to the danger. That's when another truck drove up. An old skinny guy got out and gave us a friendly wave. He was only wearing a T-shirt and jeans. He walked into the swarm of bees, checked the tightness of the straps holding down the hives, and casually got into the truck. He started the vehicle and drove away.

We sat there looking at each other, thinking, *Man we're a couple of dumb shits.*

I liked working patrol in the seventh district. I never knew what I was going to be dispatched to next. One call might be a burglary and the next could be anything.

As I mentioned, much of the seventh district was made up of swamp. That made it a preferred dumping ground for New Orleans murder victims. B. J. and I worked a found body call, again at one of the no-name turnarounds.

This body was badly decomposed. It was what we called a monster. Monsters were bodies that resembled something you would see in a horror movie—no lips, no eyes, and a skeletal face with most of the flesh still on it. Their appearance was quite disturbing to the uninitiated. But once you'd handled many of them, you became callused and it didn't bother you anymore. Homicide detectives met us out there, along with crime lab, who photographed the body and the scene. When homicide detectives were dispatched, the coroner's office investigator is also notified.

It's not like you see on TV. A homicide investigator or responding officer is not allowed to touch the body. You can't dig in his pockets for identification or roll him over to find that little nugget of evidence that will lead to solving the case by the end of the show. The only person who can empty the pockets or roll the body over is the coroner's investigator.

The coroner's investigator usually drove a van and was accompanied by a pair of trustees. These trustees were not hardened criminals; they came from the house of detention. They were serving sixty to ninety days, mostly on municipal charges like public drunkenness, petty theft, and DUI, not crimes against persons. They ran the entire range of personality types. This time, the coroner's van arrived with its usual crew of three.

There wasn't much for the coroner's investigator to do on this scene. The crime lab had finished taking their photos, and it was time to place the corpse in a body bag. That was the job of the trustees. B. J. and I just stood around, watching. The trustees donned latex gloves and prepared to move the body. They unzipped the body bag, and one trustee grabbed the legs while another grabbed the arms. When they lifted the body, its head fell off.

That was all it took for the trustee who was holding the arms. The monster head bounced off his foot. He was evidently shocked, because he dropped the arms, turned, and ran. We all just stood there watching. He wasn't going anyplace. We were truly in the middle of nowhere. But he ran as fast as he could toward Interstate 10.

B. J. and I got into our unit and proceeded after him. We were in no hurry. He wasn't trying to escape. He was just horrified. When we caught up to him, he had slowed from a full-out run to a walk. He was on the shoulder of the interstate. We just drove up behind him and honked the horn. He stopped and walked over to the car. We motioned for him to get in the back. He complied and apologized for taking off. We told him that we understood and no one had any ill feelings toward his reaction. We drove him back to the scene.

When we arrived, the body and the head had already been placed in the bag, and the bag had been loaded onto the stretcher and put in the rear of the van. The coroner's investigator did not give the trustee any ire. We all understood. He was the only one out there who acted like a normal human being. What did that say about the rest of us?

I despised the seventh district night watch. But you know what could make it worse? When your regular partner was absent. Then you would usually be relegated to a one-man car. Such was my fate one night when I pulled into the station at about three in the morning. By then we had caught up on the backlog of calls left to us by the second platoon. I parked my vehicle in the lot and was walking toward the side door of the station when I noticed a subject pacing at the side of the building. This was not an area frequented by civilians. In fact, the door had signage that stated authorized personnel only.

I told him to come toward me, and he complied. He looked to be in his late twenties. He had medium brown hair and was clean-shaven. His T-shirt was untucked, and he looked disheveled. He was acting anxious and was obviously upset. I placed the clipboard I was carrying on the hood of a nearby police unit just in case this encounter turned violent.

He walked to within three feet of me and just stood there. I knew right off that this was not a normal off-the-street complainant. I requested to see his ID, and he slowly complied. I performed a cautionary frisk for weapons, and finding none, I took down his name and information. I asked him why he was here. He did not answer. I asked him if he needed assistance with some matter. Again, he did not speak. He just kept looking not quite at me but almost through me.

We stood in silence, looking at each other for what seemed an eternity. I could see he was not drunk, and I didn't smell any alcohol. In my opinion, he was not impaired at all. His eyes were clear but sad and empty. Then he started to pace again. I called to him again, in a sterner voice this time. He came back to his original position. I asked him if he was hurt or if there was anything I could do to help him. I was again met with an uncomfortable stare and silence.

I then told him that if he did not have any business at the police station, he could not hang around here. I felt as though something was wrong. Was someone after him? Was he unable to speak? Was he in danger? I could not help but wonder why he was acting this way.

After my I told him he could not loiter around the station any longer, he continued to stand there for a long, uncomfortable minute. Then without a word, he started across the parking lot toward the sidewalk and away from the building. When he reached the sidewalk, he turned around one more time to look at me. I watched his melancholy walk until he was out of sight. I found out the next day that he had gone directly home and hanged himself.

CHAPTER SEVEN

As the years passed, lots of things changed for me but not the Dreux Club or my friends there. People close to me told me from time to time that my attitude was changing, that I was becoming cynical and was distrustful of everyone but my closest friends. No one at the club ever expressed those feelings to me. I don't know if it's because they never noticed it or perhaps it happened so incrementally that no one gave it any thought. Was it the job changing me? Or was I just becoming more aware of how the world really was? One thing was a constant: I always looked forward to going to the club and being with my friends.

One of my best friends was Anthony Amato. Tony and I had been friends since sophomore year of high school. In our senior year, a group of us were considering joining the Marine Corps. There were five of us altogether. We figured the marines would make or break us. It was radical thinking back then. Young men of my age were not running to join the armed forces. In retrospect, I had always hung around nonconformists. Tony lived in the New Orleans suburb of Metairie and did not have the luxury of being part of every conversation that we held on this subject. He missed some of the most serious planning stages of this expedition.

So it came as a surprise when, in April, he made a big announcement.

"Guys, I went Saturday and joined the marines," Tony said with pride. "I signed on the dotted line and took the oath."

We were all shocked and quite impressed. He had jumped the gun to be first. He received enthusiastic and patriotic pats on the back.

"Did you sign with the eighty-five-day program?" someone asked over the congratulatory banter.

"Eighty-five-day program? What's that?" Tony asked.

"The program where you go eighty-five days to boot camp and then return to start college. It's that reserve program we talked about."

"Reserve program?" he asked.

"Yeah, we talked about signing up with reserves first," I reminded him. "That way, if you liked it, you could always switch to active duty. If you go active duty and don't like it, there's no way you can switch to reserves."

The expression on his face said it all. It was apparent to everyone that perhaps he should have taken at least one of us into his confidence and explained his plan. We could have explained the parts of the proposal that he had clearly missed. Tony had signed up for active duty, four years, and there was no going back. B. J. Wong was also pals with Tony Amato. He howled with laughter when I told him about this years later.

The home I was living in was huge. I had the entire downstairs. After he returned from active duty in the Marine Corps, I gave Tony the room in the back. He would come and go and stay there on weekends. It was also a place to crash and study when he was finishing college. He and his then-girlfriend, who would eventually become his wife, would stay there together. He often went to the club with me, and he knew the characters there well, most of them since we were in high school.

Once I was sleeping and Tony came to the house late one night. He had his own key, so this was not unusual, but his knocking on my bedroom door in the middle of the night was. He called to me and asked if he could come in. I said sure. I could then see that he was very upset.

Tony was in his last year of college, working toward a business degree. He was doing very well, but he wasn't happy. He had heard me telling cop stories for hours on end. He had thought it over very carefully and decided that he wanted to be a police officer too.

Like any good son, he was proud to tell the news to his mom and dad. He told them he liked the life I was living. It was exciting and there was no dull routine. It was outside and always on the move, and he would always be experiencing something different and challenging. He knew that if I could do it, he could do it too. They did not take it well. They gave him all the reasons why he should not become a policeman.

Then his mother voiced her biggest fear, her major opposition to his career change.

"Do you want to end up an asshole like him?" she said.

I always thought Miss Amato liked me. I don't know what surprised me more, that she would say that or that Tony was dumb enough to tell me she had said it. Either way, it didn't make any difference. I just let it go. Who knew, maybe she was right.

I told Tony, "Do what you feel is right. Don't worry what other people think. Other people aren't going to live your life. You will. If you always do things in life for the sake of other people, you're never going to be happy. Who knows, you might not turn out to be an asshole like me."

The next day I went to the club much earlier than usual. I had bought Fantome some cat treats. I was only going to be able to see her if I got there before everybody else. When customers started to arrive, she disappeared.

Barry was unlocking the door when I pulled up. I followed him inside as he turned on the lights and started getting ready for the evening.

Fantome jumped up on the bar to greet me. As I sat down, I opened the bag of treats and placed several on the bar. She immediately ate them. I petted her head and her long muscular back.

"I really like this cat," I told Barry.

"Yeah, she likes you too," he said.

"My offer to take her still stands."

"No thanks. I need her more than she needs me right now."

I thought this was a peculiar statement. As Barry set a Dixie longneck in front of me, I asked him if everything was all right. He stopped cleaning up and started petting Fantome.

"My brother died about a week ago," he said.

"Philip is dead?" I asked. "Why didn't you call me?"

"We called very few people, David," he told me. "You know how private Mom is. She is absolutely devastated. We had a very small service at the funeral home this morning, and he was buried directly after. It was only family. That's what his wife wanted too. No ... I didn't tell anyone about it. Besides, people come here to forget their problems, not share in mine."

I knew Barry's brother was about six years older than he was. He had been married with two little kids and lived in a town north of New Orleans called Covington. Since he was older than us, we never really hung around Philip coming up.

"What happened, Barry?" I asked.

"He got pancreatic cancer. It was late stage and very aggressive. It killed him about two months after they found it."

He didn't look at me when he talked. It was like he was talking to Fantome and I could overhear him.

"My mother was there at the hospital when he died," he said. "I had just left about an hour before. I can't ask my mom about the last moments of his life. She bursts out crying simply looking at me. She could never answer my questions. You've seen a lot of death, right?" he asked.

"Yeah, I guess I have," I said.

"Have you ever been there just when somebody died?"

"Yes, several times."

"What's it like?"

"Shit, Barry, they're all different. Remember most of the people I deal with are dying from some sort of trauma, not in a clinical setting."

He turned his gaze from Fantome to me. "Do you believe in God?" he asked.

"Yes, I do," I said. "I was raised Roman Catholic, but I kinda have my own religion now. I sort of take the best from a lot of religions and that makes up my philosophy on God. I don't believe in destiny or fate. I don't believe that anything is preordained. I hear people say, 'When it's your time to go, it's your time to go.' I think that's a dumb cop-out.

"Your death is not scheduled in a big book. All risk should be mitigated," I explained. "I believe that God created all of this and then said, 'You can make it as good or as bad as you want. It's all up to you. It's your free will. Keep your feet and hands inside the ride at all times until it comes to a complete stop. I'll see you at the end. Good luck.'

"It's all happenstance," I continued. "If you think about it, happenstance explains why terrible things happen to good people. I personally do not believe that you need any one religion or anyone, for that matter, to be a go-between to reach God," I further testified. "I have a personal relationship with him. I talk, and I know he listens. I don't need anyone else. I believe any religion that thinks they have cornered the market on God is wrong from the get-go.

"I once knew a holy roller who told me, 'The only way to God is to be saved. To request and have Jesus Christ come into your life. If not, you're destined for hell.' I was dumbstruck. I said to him, 'Really? So you're telling me that the holy man who just wears a loincloth, begs his daily meal, and spends the rest of his time praying to God is going to hell? He prays a lot more than you do. He has no material desires. He's ten times holier than you, and he's going to hell?' The guy said, 'Yes, he's going to hell because he doesn't know Jesus Christ.' I yelled, 'They were never introduced!' He said, 'Doesn't matter.' I couldn't believe the arrogance. That's when I concluded that most organized religions are bullshit."

"Do you think he can help me?" Barry asked.

"I'm sure that he can," I said.

"I've been very sad and depressed," Barry admitted. "I don't know where to turn. How do you ask him for help?"

"It's simple," I said. "You just ask him."

"I thought you just said everything was happenstance."

"I did, but he's God. He created the rules. He can bend or change them whenever he wants."

"I can't visualize him," Barry said. "The visual part is important to me. I have no idea what he looks like."

"He looks like whatever you want him to look like," I told him.

"I don't think he looks like the pictures you see above people's front doors," Barry said in a hushed voice. Maybe he was thinking he would piss God off if he were to overhear.

"Long brown hair, long brown beard, European looking," he added.

"No, probably not," I agreed. "But if that's the way you want him to look, I'm sure he'd be okay with it. Or maybe an old man with graying hair and medium gray-and-brown beard. 'Cause I'm sure he doesn't want to be confused with Santa Claus," I joked.

Barry half smiled and continued to pet Fantome.

"All you gotta do is ask him to help you. Then you gotta be smart about it. Because a lot of times when he helps, you don't recognize it," I cautioned him. "I have prayed for a lot of things that I thought I really wanted in my life. Then I wondered why God did not grant them for me. It turned out that he was doing what was best for me all along. If the things I had asked for had been granted, they would have totally screwed up my life. You only see that later, when everything falls into place and you're looking back.

"Death is an inevitable part of life, Barry. We should concentrate on living, not trying to figure out why someone may have suffered an untimely death or spending time contemplating our own ends," I said. "When the angel of death comes for us, we can shake his hand gladly 'cause we know we have lived the kind of lives that have guaranteed us a place in heaven. Remember death is not the end. It's only the beginning of a greater infinite existence.

"Forgive me, brother, if I am getting too deep here," I apologized.

"No, we have been listening to every word you said," he whispered. He was still petting Fantome, who was looking up at him, and tears started to run down his face. It was obvious to me that he was alone. That's why he told me he needed Fantome now more than ever.

"I need God to help me," Barry declared. "I can't keep feeling like this. I need him to help me and Fantome."

He was still crying and leaning on the bar. I put my hand on his and squeezed.

"It's going to be okay, bud. *You're going to be okay*," I assured him.

He looked at me and asked, "Would you help me pray?"

I said, "Barry, we just did."

Barry had a tough time over the next couple of months. He was quieter than usual, and I always tried to be sure that he knew I was there for him. I spent a lot of time with him and his mom over the Christmas holiday. Into the New Year, he seemed to be getting better.

The New Year always brought something else to New Orleans: Mardi Gras. The annual event demanded participation by all police personnel. Fat Tuesday, as it is called, is the day before the Catholic Ash Wednesday and the beginning of the Lenten season. This event brings hundreds of thousands of tourists to the city each year. These tourists, as well as locals, start the celebration in earnest about two weeks before actual day of Mardi Gras. Everyone drinks heavily and has the time of their lives. The only people in the crowd not having a good time are the cops.

I hated Mardi Gras. I haven't liked parades since I was a kid. I am old enough to remember when Mardi Gras parades used to roll down the narrow streets of the French Quarter. The crowds were so large you literally could not move. The drums from the marching bands would reverberate off the old buildings, and you could feel the percussion in your chest. You risked getting your fingers stepped on when you reached into the crowd to retrieve doubloons thrown from the floats. Local kids back then didn't give a crap about catching beads. Beads were useless, but doubloons had the parade krewe's names and the year as well as the theme of the parade embossed on them. They were collectibles.

As police officers during Mardi Gras, it was our job to make sure the party did not get out of hand. We usually turned a blind eye to things that would normally get your ass thrown in jail. If we stopped to enforce all the laws that were being violated by fifty thousand drunken idiots at any given time, there would not be enough jail space or money in the system to prosecute them. We only got involved if people crossed the line into endangering themselves or others.

Mardi Gras also brought in many types of undesirables—pickpockets, prostitutes, scam artists, thieves, armed robbers, and all sorts of reprobates—eager to victimize the inebriated revelers. We were constantly on the lookout for them as we observed the nonstop festivities.

Every policeman who has ever worked the French Quarter on Mardi Gras day can tell you about the number of times drunken people come up to us and tell us how great our Mardi Gras costumes are. They are very proud of themselves, thinking they were the first to come up with that line. I used to just smile in agreement, not mentioning that I had heard that joke hundreds of times. They're not trying to be aggravating; they're just being friendly.

If you've never attended a Mardi Gras parade, I will try to explain one for you. They are made up of marching bands, large floats pulled by tractors, and dance troops performing choreographed routines and accompanied by blasting trucks carrying audio equipment. That is the framework of almost every Mardi Gras parade.

The krewe (the organization to whom the parade belonged) has different themes each year for their parade. This year's theme might be something like Simpletons under the Seven Seas. Then each of the floats is decorated and titled to fit that general theme. The Mardi Gras krewe's members man the floats. They are masked and costumed in relation to their float's theme. When I was a kid, Mardi Gras krewes would just throw doubloons and strings of beads. Nowadays they throw doubloons, beads, horns, spears, cups, coconuts, stuffed animals, panties, virgins, and the severed heads of the unclaimed and homeless.

Mardi Gras assignments usually started two weeks before Mardi Gras day. Each of the districts and each of the divisions in the detective bureau were assigned certain blocks along the parade routes. That was our responsibility until after the parade passed. Then management would decide if they required additional manpower in the French Quarter.

Before a parade, the police had to maintain the flow of traffic on the parade route, crossing traffic from side streets, setting up barricades to stop vehicle traffic, and performing general crowd control. It was always a madhouse. Crowds would move toward the parade route, and vehicles would attempt to get past at the last minute.

I remember once I was assigned to parade duty in the 3600 block of Saint Charles Avenue. We had set up vehicle barricades at the corner of Peniston and Prytania to stop traffic from approaching and attempting to cross the parade route on Saint Charles Avenue. I was alone in the middle of the block on Peniston, and I observed an unmarked police vehicle approach the barricade. A detective got out and moved the barricade, allowing the police unit to pass. The detective then replaced the barricade and got back into the vehicle, which then slowly approached me.

Upon reaching me, the driver rolled down his window and called me over to the car. I knew the officers in the car as detectives assigned to the internal affairs division. He told me there was a woman trying to move the barricade and come through. They told me to tell her it was too late to cross the parade route. Then they left and did the exact thing they told me it was too late to do, which was cross the parade route. Then they disappeared.

I looked down toward the barricade just in time to see a vehicle make the corner and stop in front of the barricade. A woman got out of the car and started to move the barricade. I quickly started walking toward her. She had moved the barricade, gotten back into her vehicle, and started driving toward me, just as the detectives had done moments before. She didn't get far before I was in front of the vehicle, motioning for her to stop.

I said, "Ma'am, you cannot move police barricades and go through them. They are there for a reason."

"I have to cross over," she said.

"It is too late to cross now," I told her. "You need to back your car up to the barricade."

"But I have to cross, officer. Is there anything you can do?"

I told her that I was sorry, but it was too late to cross here. Perhaps if she drove farther toward the end of the route she would have more luck in crossing. I was standing at the driver's side window of her vehicle. I had a clear view of the entire inside of the front of the car. She picked up her purse from the passenger seat and placed it in her lap. She then reached into it and removed a wad of bills.

"Now, Officer, you're telling me there's no way I can cross over?" she said, offering me the wad of bills.

"No, ma'am. Like I said before, it's too late to cross. Now start backing up. I'll move the barricade and stop traffic on Prytania so you can pull out safely." I did not say anything about the wad of bills.

I walked next to her car as she backed to the corner. I removed the barricade, stopped traffic, and put her on her way. I replaced the barricade and started walking back to the parade route. I thought, *How do you like that shit?* Who were they to tell me it was too late to cross anyone over? It was well within my discretion if it was safe to accomplish. They had no parade assignments or parade responsibilities. Why would they give a shit about who or when anybody crossed the route? How would those two douchebag detectives know that a woman was on her way to move the barricade? Even if they were clairvoyant, what would it matter to them if she could safely cross?

They knew she was coming because she was working with them in a sting attempt to bribe me. Those assholes didn't have enough real fucking work to do? I was sure they would go on throughout the evening, trying to find a cop dumb enough to take the bait. In retrospect, I should have yanked her out of the car, handcuffed her, arrested her, and then called my supervisor to meet me on the scene. I could then have waited to see those two morons return and explain to my rank how they were just trying to fuck me over. I wished my mind had worked that fast. It would not have amounted to anything, but everyone on duty that night would have known about their chicken-shit antics within an hour. I may have been an asshole back then, but at least I was an honest asshole.

Working Mardi Gras as a police officer, I saw just about everything. Many things I just had to shake my head at. Sex acts in the street and people doing things they would have never done anywhere else. I once saw a skinny guy entirely painted red like a fireplug. The only thing he had on was a washcloth that read, "Lift in case of fire." As you might imagine, it got lifted a lot more than I cared to observe.

Sometimes I was in awe of people's creativity when it came to their Mardi Gras costumes. I remember a great one to this day. It was an eight-foot-tall monster carrying a cage and lumbering down the street. Inside the cage was a small man calling out to everyone to please help him. It was one of the freakiest things I had ever seen. The monster's arms and torso were made of papier mâché and theatrical-grade latex. From the waist down, the monster was the actual man in the cage's body. He was bent over where his head and arms were affixed to the dummy in the cage. He could stretch his arms out of the cage to beg you and plead for assistance. The guy's body was separated into the man in a cage and the monster. When the monster walked, it was the guy in the cage doing the walking. When you saw the entire ensemble, it was difficult to tell what was real and what was not. He was incredible and disturbing. That was the best costume I saw in all my years of Mardi Gras.

Mardi Gras was supposed to be a happy time for all the participants. I wish I could say that was a fact, but that's not true. Every time there are large crowds of people, there will be incidents. I have been involved in more than my fair share.

One Mardi Gras, the seventh district was assigned a section of parade route between Jackson Avenue and Saint Mary Street on Saint Charles Avenue. I don't remember what parade it was. Saint Charles Avenue was more of a venue for family participation in the parades.

Most of the adult entertainment associated with the parade culture went on near the French Quarter and Canal Street.

The Rex parade had passed and was being followed by the krewes of Elks and Crescent City. Large crowds lined both sides of the street. The weather had been kind to the crowds. It was not cold like some Mardi Gras days of the past. It was a good crowd made up mostly of families. Kids were running all around, attempting to catch the doubloons, cups, and beads thrown from the floats. I was about a block away from the corner of Saint Charles Avenue and Saint Mary Street when we got a call for assistance for a kid who had been run over by a float.

It didn't take me long to get to the scene. One policeman was there already, and he had called for emergency medical assistance. The boy was about seven or eight years old. His dad was kneeling beside him in the street, and his mother was watching from a few feet away. We pushed the crowd back to make room for the emergency medical crew to work when they arrived. The kid had no obvious signs of trauma, which was amazing considering what had just happened. The boy was conscious and moving around a bit. The thing I remember most about this incident was that he was trying to pick something up off the pavement that was not there. He kept grasping at something. He was still trying to get it when EMS arrived.

He had been on his stomach the whole time. EMS tried to assess his situation and saw the same thing I had. His eyes were open, and he was conscious and awake. He did not seem to be in any pain. He looked from the street in front of him upward. In the next second, he was gone. They immediately started CPR. That was when the parents fell apart. The EMS personnel did not wait for a spine board or gurney. They grabbed him and literally ran to the waiting emergency unit. They got the kid in and, with the parents, were off to Charity Hospital. The parade started rolling again, and within ten minutes, you would have never known anything had happened.

They had come to enjoy a beautiful Mardi Gras day as a family, and now their lives would never be the same. It was an accident. These kinds of things happened. You couldn't say lack of supervision or try to assess any blame. It didn't take but a second for a kid to get away from his or her parents. Kids were wrapped up in the moment and just didn't understand the dangers associated with moving floats. Hell, most adults didn't either. My heart went out to those parents, who would probably be reminded of that tragic event every year when Mardi Gras rolled around. It was one of those senseless, stupid things that start out good but end so badly. Happenstance. It all comes back to happenstance.

Shortly after that Mardi Gras season, Wong and I were riding on patrol in the seventh district. We got a call of a shooting on Chef Menteur highway near Wilson Street. It was at a little restaurant on the highway. I don't remember the real name of the restaurant, but on the side of the building in huge lettering was painted, "Stop and eat before we both starve." The building had a black shingled roof and was very small. It was a wooden structure and painted white. Because of the heavy traffic on the highway, smoke, exhaust, and dust had turned it gray. When you walked in, it had about five tables and a long bar where you could sit and eat. It was not a good neighborhood. If you somehow ended up in there, you might have regretted stopping and opted instead to starve. The décor inside was done in a "saved from junk pile" motif.

Our shooting victim was sitting at the bar. If there were any witnesses to the event, they had long since fled. The only staff there were one waitress and the short-order cook. I took a seat next to the victim. He said he'd had an argument with an unknown subject during breakfast, the last of which he was still consuming. I saw a spent brass on the floor and picked it up. He had been shot with a .45-caliber pistol. But as he was looking straight ahead and eating, I could see no wound. I asked him where he was shot. He turned to me and pointed to the hole in his forehead.

The bullet had hit this guy about an inch and a half above his eyes, right in the middle of his forehead. On closer inspection, the projectile had not entered his skull. Instead it ripped a path under the skin around the left side of his head and out the back. I looked around for his guardian angel and hoped I was not sitting on him.

I could not get much information on the perpetrator. Just race and gender. The shooting victim seemed uninterested in pursuing the matter further. I asked the waitress and the cook what they had seen. They told me that they had been very busy doing waitressing and cooking stuff and had seen absolutely nothing.

We had an emergency unit coming. I did not call them off, but I radioed for them to slow down. No use in their getting into an accident when this was not a life-and-death situation. I told the victim that the EMS guys would look at him. I cautioned him if they suggested he go to the hospital, he should probably do so. He told me he would just have to wait and see. He wiped ketchup off his chin with his napkin. He told us he was not interested in pursuing the matter further. Without his cooperation, there was little more we could do.

CHAPTER EIGHT

It was pouring down rain that evening when I got to the club. My pals were there already. Fantome was curled up on the couch asleep. There were just few people around, so she felt comfortable. She was smart enough not to want to go out in that weather. I walked up to the table, said my hellos, and sat next to the Satisfier.

"How's the shop going?" I asked.

"I am doing better than I expected," Steve said. "The location is a gold mine. I am having to schedule repair jobs, and that is something I never did before. I may have to take on some help just to meet the demand," he said proudly. "How are you making out?"

I told him things were going well and that the police department was treating me well; they just didn't pay worth a shit.

"Well, that's the downside of that line of work," he said.

I admitted I'd known that when I got into it.

Greg walked up behind me and set a pitcher of beer on the table and a glass in front of me. "Nice to see you finally made it," he said. "We figured with this weather you might just stay home."

"No, I would not miss this zoo," I said. "Jerry not coming again?"

"He's got a date," Greg said.

"I think it's getting serious. He was talking to me about getting married," Gert said in an astonished tone.

"They have been going out for a while," the Satisfier said.

Jerry had been seeing this gal for several months. He had still been coming to the club every now and again, but it wasn't like the old days. I was happy for Jerry. It also made me sad to face the reality that this group of friends would not be around forever. There were all kinds of reasons folks moved on from one social situation to another.

"I have never met her," Ron said.

We all looked at each other and confirmed that the rest of us had not met her either.

"Why do you think that is?" Gert asked.

"I don't know," I said. "I don't bring everyone I date here either."

"I know what you mean. I don't bring my girlfriend around here either," Greg said.

"That's because your girlfriend's instructions say to deflate her after use," Ron said.

Everyone else laughed at Greg, who just turned red and poured himself another beer. But I asked myself, *Why don't I bring anyone here?* Was it because I did not want to share my friends with anyone else? I was certainly not ashamed of this place or them. I guessed I just selfishly thought of the Dreux as my getaway place. I did not have to put on any airs here. I could just be myself and talk the way I wanted to. I felt totally comfortable with these people. I had known them for years. I trusted them all and had been through so many experiences with each of them. I knew this group was not going to last forever, but I was sure going to enjoy being here with these people for as long as I possibly could.

"I saw on the news about that big police chase on Interstate 10," Greg said as he poured his beer. "Did you see that?" he asked me.

"Yes, I saw that too. That was a big deal, went all the way into Jefferson Parish," I said.

"How many of them run from y'all?" he asked, handing me the beer he'd just poured.

"I don't know the numbers. Just one of those chases is too many," I said.

High-speed car chases were not exciting. They sucked. They are certainly not like you see on police dramas or in movies. They greatly increase the chances of police officers getting hurt or killed. Several officers on the New Orleans Police Department had been killed in auto accidents over the years.

Have you ever had a police unit pass you at a high rate of speed without his emergency equipment? You ask yourself, *Where is he going?*

Why isn't he using his lights and siren? He's just speeding, that hypocrite! In many cases, you are wrong. Most departments require officers to use lights and a siren when exceeding the posted speed limit in an emergency. That looks good on paper. I'm sure it is policy to protect the city from liability. But it does not always work in practical application. It depends on the situation, but sometimes using lights and a siren will cause you more trouble than not.

If I had a quarter for every time I turned on my lights and siren to respond to a call, only to have the vehicle in front of me slam on the brakes, regardless of what lane he or she is in, nearly causing me to rear end them, I would have been able to retire long ago. Many drivers do not know what to do when an emergency unit approaches from the rear. If you think they all pull over to the right lane, you're nuts. Maybe you do, but next time look at what the other drivers are doing. Sometimes not letting them know we're there until we are safely past them is the best option.

There is one thing worse than being in a high-speed chase, and that's being in a high-speed chase as a passenger. You are constantly smashing that imaginary brake on your floorboard. I had my own theory on how to execute a high-speed police chase. It may sound callous to you, but it seemed to work well for me. It's simple, really. Just keep the pressure applied.

People think they are great drivers. They might be very good drivers, but regular driving and driving at high speeds are two very different things. A vehicle's characteristics change greatly at high speeds. Turning, breaking, momentum, traction, and steering principles all fundamentally change at high speeds. I am not saying that I was a racecar driver, but just knowing these facts put me well ahead of the game. All I did was keep the pressure on the suspect. Don't get close enough to be sucked into a rear-end collision. Just stay engaged at a distance that allows you to react and then let nature take its course. There's an old saying among police, "God gets out of the car at eighty-five miles an hour."

There were no pit maneuvers authorized or even well known back then. There were no policies in place that required us to call a chase off when the risk became unacceptable either. Remember this was nearly forty years ago. Don't get me wrong, I appreciate those policies today, but back then, if you voluntarily ended a chase, I'm sure you would not have gotten back to the station without listening to the constant transmission of clucking chickens over the radio. Your name and reputation would be forever tainted. I know you would never understand this, but back then, it was better to be killed than forever labeled a coward or a rat.

One of my chases was on Old Gentilly Road, near the Green Bridge, as a one-man car late one night. The Green Bridge crossed over the Intracoastal Waterway and separated Orleans Parish from Saint Bernard Parish. Old Gentilly Road saw more traffic between the Green Bridge east to Michoud Boulevard. NASA's Michoud Assembly Facility was located at Michoud and Old Gentilly. They manufactured solid rocket boosters for the space program. That small stretch of old Gentilly was used quite a bit by their employees.

Over the radio, control dispatched that Saint Bernard Parish deputies were chasing a vehicle into Orleans Parish over the Green Bridge. From my vantage point on Old Gentilly Road, I was close enough to see the lights crossing the bridge. I figured they would go straight and hit Chef Highway. Old Gentilly Road from the Green Bridge west at that time was in poor condition. It was sparsely populated with industrial complexes. The rest was just swamp area where people dumped trash and the occasional murder victim.

I saw them cross the bridge, but they did not proceed straight to Chef Highway. Instead, they did in fact make a U-turn toward Old Gentilly Road. I saw their lights turn on to the road westbound about half a mile in front of me. I turned my vehicle around and got ready to join the chase. The Saint Bernard Parish vehicle was about a quarter of a mile behind the suspect. When the suspect flew past me, I jumped into lead position in the pursuit.

I resorted to my previously mentioned modus operandi and just kept the pressure on him. I chased him for about two miles until he came to a side street that led to Chef Highway. I kept on him as he made the turn on to Chef. At his rate of speed, he oversteered the turn. As he tried to correct, he overcompensated and smashed into a NOPSI pole. He wasn't hurt that bad and there was no girlfriend, kids, or dog in the car with him. He was just an idiot who thought he could outrun the police.

B. J. and I were involved in another high-speed chase late one night on I-10 near the no-name turnarounds. There were very few cars on the road. The suspect's vehicle and our vehicle were both in the left lane. He was doing an extremely high rate of speed, and we were going even faster in our attempt to catch him. We had our blue lights and siren on. He flew past the only other vehicle on the road, which was a semitrailer truck in the right lane. As we approached, the semitrailer truck inexplicably changed to the left lane—our lane. There was no use in hitting the horn. If the dumbass hadn't heard the siren, he certainly wouldn't hear our horn.

My imaginary brake on the passenger's side was malfunctioning. If I applied any more pressure, I would put my boot through the floorboard. I could see the wheels of the semitrailer truck about six inches from my window and getting closer. Just when I thought he was going to force us off the road, he quickly changed over to the right lane again. We decided to hell with stopping the suspect; we now wanted to stop this truck!

We were the only vehicles on the road. I surmised that the driver had tried to close the back door on our pursuit to assist the perpetrator in his escape. He had to see the suspect fly by him at more than ninety-five miles an hour. Would he have really changed lanes without looking in his mirrors to be sure it was safe? Would you? If he had, he would surely have seen our blue lights and heard our siren. I had no evidence, but I was sure he had done this on purpose. He simply miscalculated our speed. We were on him before he knew it, and he had to abort his plan at the last minute so he didn't get into an accident himself. Why would he do that? That was hard to say. He might have just been one of those people who disliked the police.

He was lucky I was one of the good guys. The thought of drowning him there in the swamp crossed my mind. I was so mad I couldn't even talk. The only thing I did ask was what he was carrying. I had no proof that he had done what I suspected. We just chewed him out and ended up letting him go. On the way back to civilization, I was almost sick with the thought that B. J. and I had almost been driven off the road at nearly one hundred miles an hour by a truck carrying bread bound for Alabama.

Many vehicle chases lead to accidents. That is why you as a driver must drive defensively. Sure, you got the green light, but how about taking a fraction of a second to make sure there's nothing flying up to smash you as you go through it. It doesn't take a police chase to get you into an accident. Sometimes it's not even your fault.

B. J. and I were patrolling when at about nine thirty at night we were assigned a signal 21, which is a miscellaneous complaint. The dispatcher advised us that the caller said there was an elderly man walking on Old Gentilly Road who seemed lost or confused. We proceeded to that location. While heading east on Old Gentilly Road, about a mile from Michoud the street makes a long bend. It was there that we observed a lone man's shoe in the middle of the road. B. J. and I looked at each other, both knowing that it was bad juju.

As we came out of the bend, I saw a vehicle stopped in the middle of the road. The car's lights were on, and the driver's door was open. A well-dressed woman stood next to the door. I figured she probably worked at NASA's assembly facility. We pulled up behind the vehicle and turned on our blue lights. The woman ran up to us as we exited our unit.

"Get him off my car, get him off my car," she begged us.

We walked up to the vehicle, and her problem was apparent. She had hit the old man so hard that he had flipped in the air and landed on the roof of her car. His face was embedded in the windshield at about eye level on the driver's side. Since the vehicle's door was open, the interior light illuminated a ghastly scene. The man's face had not completely penetrated the windshield. But it was close. Blood dripped from the impact area onto the dashboard. It must have been extremely distressing to see that appear in front of her as she was driving.

He wasn't breathing. I checked for a pulse and could not find one. I was not a doctor, but I was confident that he was dead.

"Get him off my car," the woman kept saying. She was stuck in a loop.

I tried to explain that we could not move the man. He was dead, and the traffic-fatality investigators had to come out and process the accident. She was so distraught I didn't think anything I said was sinking in. I placed her in the back of my vehicle and told her to wait there and that the guys from traffic would need to talk to her. I told her that this wasn't her fault. It was dark, and no one would've expected a person to be walking in the road there. There were no streetlights of any kind. She was not in trouble. After all that, she only had one request.

"Officer, could you please get him off my car?"

I tell you to drive defensively to help you avoid an accident. But even if you're not hurt in an accident, it's not over yet. You can bet you'll probably get sued. Everybody wants to sue everybody else today. People figure they can make a quick buck off a lawsuit. I'm not saying that if you are justifiably injured or have suffered an egregious wrong you should not attempt to receive damages. But anyone in the know will tell you that of all the lawsuits filed today, a clear majority of them are frivolous.

Back then, the City of New Orleans was just getting wise to frivolous lawsuits. They started fighting back. It was the best thing they ever did. Before that, they would just offer these people a few thousand dollars to go away. Of course, they would take the quick settlement and be back the next time they had to deal with the police to make another false complaint and get some ambulance chaser to represent them in another lawsuit. This scam spread like wildfire among the unscrupulous entrepreneurs of the city.

As a police officer, I was named in many suits, all of them bullshit. Filing a lawsuit also helped the criminal charges many of the people we arrested were facing. Not only did this rot the entire system, but I'm sure it added extra difficulties for people who had legitimate cases. You had to use all your tools to protect yourself. Any time we were dispatched to a call only to have no complainant meet us or answer the door, I employed a little trick. On the right hand of the door frame, as far up as I could reach, I drew a circle with a little seven in the middle of it. Totally inconspicuous. That way, when someone made a complaint that we never arrived to assist them, I had something to back up my side of the story.

"I want to make a complaint. My boyfriend beat me up, stopped up my toilet, and shot my dog. I called the police, but no one came. Now I'm dizzy all the time, and I got blurred vision. I can't use my toilet, and my dog is gonna be walkin' funny for the rest of his life. I want to make a complaint. It's all the fault of the police who never showed up. I'm going to sue!"

But I could always convince an investigator or judge that I had indeed been there and could prove it with my mark. It would be much simpler nowadays, and I suggest that cops not only do the same thing but, since everyone has a cell phone, also take a picture of it. I'm sure your photo is somehow time-stamped on your phone—further proof that you were there. We did not have cell phones back then. I wish we had.

I will give you an example of what I'm talking about. I was riding with my lieutenant, Baby Ruth. He had spent time in other districts, but now he was a lieutenant in the seventh district with me. Ruth liked me—I believe for my sense of humor. He was the one who told me about the trick of putting the little mark on the far-right top of the door frame. He told me about the time he answered a domestic disturbance call some years prior. A husband and wife had gotten into an argument that turned physical, though I don't recall which of the combatants called the police to begin with. He was dispatched to the location and met a backup unit. Together they proceeded to the scene.

Upon meeting with the complainants, it was obvious that they had been beating the crap out of each other. This was a long time ago when there was no policy or rule that demanded someone go to jail in this sort of instance. We just had to use our best judgment and do what we thought was right after getting the facts and both stories. Neither of them wanted to press charges on the other, and they promised the lieutenant that their altercation had been rectified. They no longer needed the police. Baby Ruth told them that it had better be over because if the police had to come back, somebody was going to jail. He said he left both of them standing at the door, assuring him that everything was okay and waving as he and the other unit drove off.

Not an hour later, they got a call from the same location. He and the other unit returned to the residence, which was now dark. He said they pounded on the front door and went around the back and did the same, but there was no answer. They attempted to shine their flashlights into the windows, but the curtains inside obscured any view. He figured they had just worn themselves out and, being drunk, had probably gone to sleep. He took out his pen and put the little seven in the circle at the far right of the door frame. He said he did it just to prove that they had gone back to the location if they ever needed to prove it in the future. As it turns out, it was a good idea to take out that little insurance policy.

The combatants had turned out all the lights in the house. Maybe they had intended to go to sleep. One of them must've made a last remark and the other just could not let go. I surmise that he was not formally schooled in conflict resolution and therefore did not realize that bludgeoning the other party with a pipe would probably not resolve their differences. After killing his wife, I guess he thought the only sure way to prevent himself from losing his temper to this magnitude again was to put a bullet through his head.

The little mark helped provide Baby Ruth with tangible evidence that he and his partner had indeed returned to the scene. Just one more tidbit for the homicide detectives to put in their report.

I would like to tell you that the times we were dispatched to a call only to have no one there to meet us were few and far between. But that was just not so. It happened all the time. Sure, they had us on the radio, advising dispatch that we had arrived, but it always helped to have a little physical evidence on our side too. We didn't need to use a trick when doing traffic enforcement. We had dispatch tapes of radio transmissions, license plates, subjects we ran, and copies of the tickets we wrote.

As a police officer working the platoons in a district, traffic enforcement was not a top priority. If there was a backlog, we were busy answering calls for service. There was really no time to make vehicle stops and write tickets. Many people thought that we had some sort of quota of traffic citations that we had to write. That was not true. In fact, in the seventh district, management never encouraged or discouraged writing tickets. They just figured if you wrote one, you probably had a good reason. Traffic division might have set some sort of goals for hours worked in ratio to tickets written, but I can't state that as fact. If your job was enforcing traffic laws, I'm sure they wanted some proof that you were living up to the expected standards.

I didn't like to write tickets. They were a pain. If the person contested the ticket, you were subpoenaed to court. This was inconvenient if you, like me, worked the night watch. I used to keep all my subpoenas thumbtacked to a bulletin board near the back door of my home. I put them in chronological order and checked them daily to see if and when I needed to be in court again. There could be twenty or more up there at any given time.

I used to write tickets only on violations that were egregious enough to warrant it. In cases other than those, I would let the driver decide whether he or she got a ticket.

But first came the stop. You may think it sounds simple, but it's more complicated than that. When you stop a vehicle, you don't know who is in it. You think to yourself, *That guy just ran the red light. I'm going to stop him.* He's thinking to himself, *I didn't bury that bitch deep enough. They must've found her. I ain't going to be taken alive!* See the problem?

There's several tactical things you should do on every stop. I will not delineate them here. No use in giving bad guys the advantage of knowing. Some of them have learned to read. But I will say—you must assess the safety of your stop as soon as possible. Is there a threat here? How is this person acting? Do you see or perceive anything wrong? How many people are in the car? Is the vehicle still running? Are people fidgeting around? There are many other questions that I will not go into here for the same reason I stated above.

The good news is that most criminal assholes are assholes all the time. They don't just morph into criminals suddenly. They don't disrespect the law and authority only on some occasions. The criminal's moral compass is broken. Most don't make exceptions. "I'm a murdering, raping, burglarizing, wife-beating, dope-dealing, lawless sack of shit. But dammit, I draw the line at driving without a valid license."

They look like assholes, act like assholes, drive like assholes, and drive broken-down asshole cars, and their friends are all assholes. Their houses look like houses that assholes would live in. In short, they're easy to spot. Sort of like a turd in a punch bowl. If you don't know what I'm talking about, consider yourself lucky because you must live in a place that hasn't been infested with assholes.

Once I established the relative safety of the stop, I asked for a driver's license and proof of insurance. This quickly identified the person with whom I was dealing. I also knew if I had two potential violations right off the bat. The driver had to have a valid license and, in Louisiana, be currently insured. If those two pieces of information were up to date, I would then let them decide where this was going to go.

I would simply ask, "Do you know why I stopped you?"

Most of them would answer no. This question gave them the benefit of the doubt. Folks sometimes didn't realize they were speeding. Some people didn't realize that they rolled right through a Stop sign. They never really thought about it. The sign said Stop. That meant to cease all forward motion. Some folks just didn't see it that way. They came to a Stop sign, rolled slowly, looked both ways, and, if it was clear of traffic, proceeded. That was not a stop. That was a yield. We had special signs for that.

Then I would tell them that they were speeding or that they rolled through that Stop sign. They would answer several ways: "I didn't realize I was going that fast," "I didn't realize I was still rolling back there," or "I thought the speed limit was thirty-five through here." These were all good answers for me. These were honest people who just made mistakes. We're all human. We all make mistakes. I wasn't the kind of hard-ass who didn't give people breaks.

The other scenario went like this.

"Do you realize you are speeding?" I would ask.

"No, I wasn't."

"Do you realize you rolled through that stop?"

"No, I didn't."

"Do you realize you went through that red light back there?"

"You are wrong, Officer. I stopped for that red light."

Sometimes I just wrote the citation. Other times I would explain, "Sir [or ma'am], I do this for a living. I have been trained to observe these things. I see thousands a year. So you think I stopped everything I was doing and, of all the cars on the road, picked you to bum rap on a traffic charge that you're totally innocent of?" Most times my explanation didn't do any good. It just made me feel better.

Once I stopped a guy who was speeding in a Porsche on Interstate 10 Service Road. I walked up to his vehicle, and he looked very uncomfortable. That raised my suspicions almost immediately.

I asked him, "Do you know you were speeding back there?"

"Yes, Officer," he said. "I have to go to the bathroom like right now! I only live a couple of blocks from here. I really gotta go, Officer!"

What could I do? I told him to go ahead but to slow down. "If you get into an accident, you'll end up messing up this Porsche inside and out."

I knew this was a common ruse used by some people to get out of the citation. But sometimes you had to look at the whole situation—body language, facial expression, tone of voice, and several other tells. Then sometimes you just had to take a chance and be a regular guy. If he got out of the ticket this time and it was his habit to drive like that, we'd be seeing him again.

I enjoyed police work; I found it fun. But I worked to live not lived to work. I enjoyed my time off. I had gone to Dorignac's Supermarket in Metairie to stock up. Yeah, it was out of the way for me, but I could find things there that I couldn't find anywhere else. I was pushing a cart around and checking my shopping list when someone snuck up behind me and put something sharp in my back. I heard a deep cartoonish voice say, "Don't turn around or I'll let you have it."

I did turn around, and it was Gertie Chauvin.

"Had you going, didn't I?" She giggled.

"Yeah, that was the voice of a real tough guy," I said. "What are you doing out here?"

"Same as you. I'm getting groceries. I like coming here. It's worth the drive. You off Saturday?" she asked.

"I am," I confirmed.

"I don't get many Saturdays off from the bakery. I'm thinking about having some friends over. The guys said they're gonna come. Barry's even gonna be there. But he's got to leave when it's time to open the club. Why don't you come? You can help me cook," she said.

"So there's the hook."

"It's not a hook, dummy. Don't you want to help me?"

"Anything for you, Gertie," I assured her.

"Tell Tony to come too. He's better looking than you anyway." She had managed to invite him and burn me all at the same time.

"Thanks for the compliment, Gert. What do you want me to cook?"

"Why don't you do your ribs?"

"Yeah, I'm gonna do the main entrée, the hardest one. Why don't we just have this thing at my house?" I offered.

"'Cause, you blockhead, it's my party."

I met Gertie at her place at about noon on Saturday. She lived on

Eastern Street, about four blocks from the club. She rented a place with two other women. It was an attractive house with a large backyard. Several trees shaded the rear porch area. That was where she had set up tables and chairs for her party. The weather was beautiful.

I had started my ribs earlier that day, so they were nearly done. I helped her ice down beer and sodas and put together some chips and dip. She and I spiced up some barbecue beans to go with the ribs. She had a few loaves of french bread that we made garlic bread with. Everything was coming together very well.

"Thanks for your help. I really appreciate it," she told me.

"It's no problem," I said. "Heck, if I drink too much, I can always walk home from here."

Her guests started to arrive, and within an hour, everyone was having a good time.

"How did you do these ribs?" the Satisfier asked me. "These are some of the best ribs I've ever had."

"And you can look at him and tell he's had a lot of ribs," Greg said.

With a mouthful of meat, Steve nodded his agreement.

"Really, how did ya do them?" Ron pressed.

"They are very easy. You just have to use the right stuff," I said.

"Are you gonna keep it a secret, or you gonna tell us how to do it?" Greg said, shaking a bone at me.

"You can do them entirely in an oven, but they're best if you also use a smoker," I said. Then I proceeded to explain how it was done.

First I removed the membrane on the back of the rack of ribs. Next came the rub. There were plenty of different rubs on the market, but I made my own. They all had about the same ingredients. I told them to just look around and find one that they really liked. Next, I put the rub on by hand and used plenty of it; no room for stinginess here. Then I set the racks of ribs in my smoker for around three hours at about 225 degrees. I used apple wood for the smoke. After three hours, I pulled them off, placed them in a large pan, and dumped about a half a bottle of apple juice over them. Then I sealed the pan with aluminum foil to keep in the moisture and put it back in the smoker at about same heat for another hour or two. I told them they could play with the times to get just the right amount of doneness. Once they were done, I drained them and let them rest for fifteen minutes for dry ribs, or I drained and painted them with my favorite barbecue sauce and let them rest for wet ribs.

"You don't boil them first?" Greg asked.

I told him that I did not subscribe to that method. Boiling them would remove a lot of flavor and nutrients.

"You don't boil a steak before you cook it, do you?" I asked him. "Stick to the way I do it, and you won't be disappointed. Ribs are a tough cut of meat. Cooking them low and slow breaks down the connective tissue."

"Well, you done something right, because these are really good," Barry said.

"What kind of charcoal did you use?" Tony asked.

"Kingsford, with some apple wood chunks," I said proudly.

"Sure, that's good, if you like old-time barbecue flavor or traditional taste," the Satisfier said.

"Oh really? What type of charcoal do you use?" I asked.

"Not me. My dad was the outdoor cook."

"Okay, so what type of charcoal did your dad use?"

"Not charcoal so much. He would use old clothes and carpet remnants mostly. Maybe some broken boards or sticks and one of the toys you or your sister left in an inconvenient place, no matter how much you loved it. It's been so long ago now. My dad could really get that burnt, GI Joe or Barbie smoke taste infused into every steak or hot dog," the Satisfier reminisced.

"Man, that's real backyard cooking," Greg said.

"No, that's cooking the backyard," I whispered under my breath.

The problem was that none of us knew whether or not he was joking.

Gertie drafted Tony Amato to help her clean up inside. The rest of us took care of the backyard. That's the good thing about a barbecue: when you're finished, just about everything goes into the trash can. Now it was time to just relax, have a cigarette, and enjoy each other's company.

"Hey, tell us one of ya stories," Ron requested.

That motion was seconded by the rest of the gaggle.

"What kind of story do you want?" I asked them.

"Tell us a Wong story," Tony said.

"Yeah, those are always good," Gertie said.

"Where is Wong anyway? If you're off, he should be off," Barry asked.

"He wanted to be here, but he couldn't get away. His wife had already made plans for this weekend before I ran into Gertie," I said.

"Well, tell us a Wong story anyway, but they're always better when we can watch Wong's face when you tell one," Tony said, snickering.

I knew exactly what he was talking about. Whenever I told a Wong story, Wong would just look at the ground and shake his head. Whenever I got to a good part, he would start making faces.

"Okay, how's about this one?" I said. Then I proceeded to tell them about the time me and Wong got called to pick up and transport a mental patient to the third floor of Charity Hospital.

We went to this guy's location. We talked to his family and got some history on him. He was a long-time mental patient who was now off his medication and giving his family fits. The third floor was Charity's psychiatric ward. This guy was loud and talking about the usual crazy stuff. I could see why his family wanted him taken to the hospital.

On the way to the Charity, he didn't give us any trouble. Just talking stupid stuff. It was best not to attempt to hold a conversation with people in this condition. You weren't going to get anything out of it. We parked near the emergency ramp, which was where all police parked, and escorted him inside. That's when he started getting a little belligerent. He wasn't fighting us exactly, but he was pulling away and just being obstinate.

When you went into the emergency room at Charity Hospital, you walked into a very large room. Along the walls were small cubicles belonging to the nurses whose job it is to triage walk-ins. The police got preferential treatment. We always went to the front the line. Because Charity Hospital treated everyone regardless of their ability to pay, the emergency room was always full.

We took our mental case and sat him on a chair in a cubicle of a triage nurse. These cubicles had no doors, just a desk and two chairs facing it. This cubicle was in front of the chairs of the walking wounded. There had to be at least thirty people waiting to be seen by a doctor. They were holding ice bags to their heads or other extremities. Each was suffering different levels of pain as they waited for medical attention. This was when our friend started getting loud and physical.

He started to give the triage nurse a hard time. He played runaround with her questions and once even stood up from the chair. Wong grabbed him and forced him back to a seated position. The emergency room audience now had a show to watch. The police always drew attention. This was a captive audience, and they were loving it.

Our mentally disturbed friend attempted to stand up again, and Wong pushed him back down into the chair. Wong was getting tired of his foolishness, so now he stood right next to the guy in case he tried it again. The guy might have been crazy, but he was crazy like a fox. He saw all the people looking and knew they could see and hear everything.

That's when he yelled, "Hey!" This got everyone's attention. "Hey … You didn't have to fart in my face!" he screamed.

The crowd of sick and wounded roared with laughter. The man had delivered a knockout blow to Wong without even having to touch him. Wong was absolutely taken aback. He had not broken wind. He was totally innocent—the victim of a madman's wrath.

Everyone at the barbecue was laughing.

"I would have loved to see Wong's face on that one," Ron said.

"Finally, somebody other than me being the butt of a joke. I can't wait to bug him about it the next time he shows up at the club," Greg said with anticipation.

CHAPTER NINE

About a month after Gertie's successful party, the entire group was back at the Dreux Club on a Friday night, anticipating our weekends.

"I'm thinking about opening my own repair shop," the Satisfier announced. He explained that he was getting a great deal of business and the lot behind his house was no longer adequate. He needed a place he could work rain or shine. Then he wouldn't have to lug his tools in and out of his garage either. A business front would also afford him a more professional image. Everyone encouraged and told him they thought it was a good idea.

I asked if he had a location in mind. He told us that was the problem.

"I need to find someplace that is close by. Most of my customers live around here. That's why they use me, because it's convenient," Steve said.

"There has got to be somewhere around here ya can set up shop," Ron said.

"The other thing is I don't have a lot of money to get things started. I'm gonna use some of the money I got when my dad died. I certainly don't want to have to borrow any. If my business went to hell, I would just be back in the lot. I don't want to be paying some bank for something I no longer have," Steve said.

We all agreed to keep our eyes open for an empty building that might meet the Satisfier's requirements. Gentilly had a lot of businesses that were spread throughout the residential area. Finding business space should not be too hard to do. I thought this was a good plan. Steve had a steady clientele. He also bought and repaired vehicles and sold them for a profit, much like he had done for me with the Buick Regal.

The club was busy that night. Tony Amato had even come into town and met us. Barry continued to buzz people in. Some people would stay all night, and some would just have a drink or two and leave. We didn't look at the door every time someone rang the bell. It was hard enough for our group to hold a conversation without being interrupted. So we didn't see the woman when she first came in.

She walked up to our table and singled out Greg.

"You told me you liked to hang around this dump, you little prick," she said to him.

Greg didn't look up. It was obvious that he knew who she was, but we did not. His lack of reaction seemed to make her even angrier.

"You said you were going to call me. You never called. I called the phone number you gave me before you left my apartment, and it was a wrong number. They said they never heard of you," she said. "I guess you forgot you told me you come here. You never thought I'd come and find you, did you?"

Greg clearly didn't know what to do, but looking up and meeting her angry gaze evidently was not an option. He just looked down at the table and seemed to be wishing he could disappear. We were all floored. We sat there looking at her in astonishment. I found myself looking at her hands. They were balled into little fists. I didn't know if she was going to pull a gun and shoot Greg then and there. I didn't say anything, but I formulated a plan in case she did something crazy.

"I'm going to tell all my friends what a no-good bastard you are. I'm sorry I ever brought you back to my apartment. You're a lowlife little worm and even worse in bed. You're a jerk, and all your friends are jerks," she said before storming out.

We all looked at each other. Nobody could say anything. There was a long uncomfortable pause.

"Well, she seems cute," Tony said.

"What the hell, Greg? You better tell us what that was all about," Gertie demanded.

Everyone was looking at Greg like he had just flushed a puppy down a toilet.

"Wait, I'm not the bad guy here. You guys just don't understand," Greg protested. "She ain't the victim. I am. She's crazy. You guys have to hear me out."

"Well, you best start explaining," Gertie said.

"Can this wait till I get another pitcher of beer?" Jerry asked. "Because I'm sure this is gonna be good."

Tony and I had already waved to Barry to bring us two more Dixies.

A few minutes later, everyone was back in the circle. The Satisfier took a cigarette and threw the pack on the table, offering anyone else a smoke. I took one because Steve's cigarettes always tasted better because they were bummed.

"Look, guys, I wasn't going to say anything because it's embarrassing," Greg said.

"You don't think we were embarrassed? I wanted to crawl under the freaking table," Gertie said.

"I'm sorry, y'all. I certainly didn't see this coming," Greg apologized.

"Quit screwing around and tell us the story," Tony demanded.

"Yeah, you little prick," the Satisfier mocked her voice.

"I was over at the Barrel," Greg began. "It was getting late, and that's when I met her. I walked over and started a conversation. She said her name was Wendy, and she works at a shop in the French Quarter. We seemed to hit it off right away. We both liked *Star Wars*. She said she grew up over on Music Street, and she went to Saint James High School. You saw her. She's a cute girl. Everything looked like it was going good. I told her I went to Saint James too, for grammar school, seeing how the high school was all girls. She was drinking enough for both of us. The place was starting to empty out around 1:00 a.m., and she asked if I wanted to follow her to her apartment for one more beer. I said sure. She lives over by UNO."

"She lives at the university?" Tony asked.

"No, she lives in a big house near University New Orleans that has been made into apartments. But it ain't got nothing to do with the university," Greg said and then continued with his story. "We got to her house and went inside. We were drinking beer. We were both getting drunk, so one thing led to another and we ended up in her bed.

"I couldn't believe how good things were going. You know me. Bad luck kinda follows me around," Greg admitted. "We were having sex, and I was doing all my best moves. She was really into it. I was too. This is where it kind of gets embarrassing. I was on top, and I told her, 'Roll over onto your stomach, sweetheart.' But she didn't roll over onto her stomach. She said, 'I'm not your sweetheart,' and punched me in the mouth."

We all laughed.

"Holy shit!" Tony exclaimed.

"I could see why you didn't want to tell us," Gertie said.

"What happened next, Greg?" I wanted him to continue.

Greg went on, "What was I supposed to do then? She hit me as hard as she could. I was bleeding from the mouth. I was in a state of shock. I couldn't believe what had just happened. I was still, you know, sort of plugged in. She didn't say anything else. She just looked at me with those same angry eyes you just saw. I apologized for calling her sweetheart and she seemed to accept that. But there was no accepting it for me. All interest in riding this pony was gone. She acted like nothing happened, and she just wanted to continue. There was no continuing for me. I was still bleeding. So I kinda faked an ending."

"What do you mean you kinda faked an ending?" Gertie asked.

I think Gertie knew exactly what he meant. I just think she wanted to keep Greg on the hot seat a little longer.

"You know, I kinda faked that I had finished," Greg tried to explain. "You know, I did the noises and some rhythmic shaking. It must've been convincing because I think she bought it."

"What did you do then?" Tony asked.

"I told her I needed to go to the bathroom. I looked at my mouth in the mirror. I think it had stopped bleeding. When I came out, she was getting dressed. I got dressed too. I told her I needed to get going because I had work the next day. I wanted to get out of there as fast as I could. At the door, she wanted my phone number. I said okay. I wrote down some bullshit number because I hoped never to see her again. I wasn't thinking straight. I just wanted to go. This girl was crazy. Do you understand now where I was coming from?"

Everyone told Greg they understood.

"I would've done the same thing," Steve said.

When Greg excused himself to go to the restroom, we all looked at each other. I don't know who started laughing first, but it was contagious.

"That was priceless," Gertie said.

"That could only happen to Greg." Tony laughed.

"What are you guys laughing about?" Barry asked from behind the bar.

"Greg," I told him.

"Why, is he drunk?" Barry asked.

"No," the Satisfier said. "But watch it, he could be faking."

It was a good thing Greg was taking a leak, because that meant he couldn't hear us. Even if he had better-than-average hearing, I didn't think he could've picked it up our remarks from that far away. Hearing is a precious thing. Just ask someone without it or someone who has lost it. After spending thirty-four years in municipal and federal law enforcement, I've lost quite a bit of mine. Firearms, jet aircraft, helicopters, and high-performance boat engines have taken their toll on me.

Sometimes you don't know who can hear you and who can't. When you arrive on the scene of a bad accident, a shooting, or a stabbing and someone is hurt severely, you must be careful about what you say. I have heard of near-death experiences when the victims come back and can tell everything that was said in the room when they were allegedly dead. I always tried to keep that in mind. It is also important to give a person confidence that everything is going to be all right. I hope they don't hold it against me in the next life, but I have told a lot of people that they were going to be okay when I knew damn well that wasn't true.

I responded to a call of a motorcyclist who had smashed into the back of a parked moving truck in the fog on Lake Forest Boulevard early one morning. He'd been riding a chopper, so the first thing to hit the back of the truck was the front wheel. This drove one of the front forks into his skull between the top of his nose and his mouth. He was breathing through this gaping hole in his head, labored as his breathing was.

I got on the radio while standing above him and told dispatch this was going to be a fatality and to start rolling in the investigators from traffic. The seventh district emergency medical unit 1807 arrived on the scene to assist me. He still had life in him, so they scooped him up and took him to Methodist Hospital, which was two short blocks away. The guys from traffic arrived and started doing their measurements and photography. This accident was not mine, so I was free to go.

I found out about a week later that the guy did not die. They saved his life at the hospital. He was going to require lots of surgeries to reconstruct his face, but he wasn't dead. I couldn't believe it when I heard the news. What had he been thinking and feeling when he heard me calling for the fatality unit? I hoped he was unconscious at the time. I never made that mistake again.

If a person can hear and he or she speaks the same language as you, he or she should understand you. That's a good presumption to go by. You can use that as a rule. But I would add this one disclaimer: That may or may not be true with mental patients. You can talk to some mental patients all day and your words will bounce off them like bugs off your windshield.

I do not know what your world is like or what you do for a living, but have you ever really stopped and imagined just how many mentally disturbed people are just outside your door? Those of you whose job it is to take care of these folks or render treatment know exactly what I mean. May God bless you for your efforts.

Wong and I once got a call of a signal 21, miscellaneous complaint, in an apartment complex just off Interstate 10 Service Road. We arrived at the location and started searching for the apartment number. The exterior lighting of these apartments was practically useless. We had to use our flashlights. We did not have a lot of information to go on. The dispatcher only told us that the male complainant had called and asked for the police.

We found the apartment number and knocked on the door. We heard someone moving around inside, but no one answered. B. J. gave the door several loud cracks with the butt of his Maglite. The door flew open, and standing before us was a fat naked man wearing only a self-fashioned tinfoil hat. He immediately proclaimed his problem.

"There's a guy on the other side of I-10 who has a ray gun, and he's shooting at me. It follows me around from room to room and stops up my nose."

It was a good thing that I had tactically positioned myself away from the door so that the man could not see me. Have you ever tried to laugh hysterically and remain silent at the same time? It's difficult. B. J. was dumbfounded. There was no training course to my knowledge that teaches the correct action to be taken in a situation such as this. We had to come up with something quick. I had doubts that nude portly men in aluminum headgear were the patient type.

He was alone. We could see no one else in the apartment beyond him. Since he hadn't exhibited any threatening behavior, there was little we could do. There was no law against being crazy as a shithouse rat.

"Yes, sir, I believe I know exactly the man you're talking about," I said matter-of-factly. "We'll go over there and tell him to turn it off. If he cranks it back up again, we'll take him to jail," I promised.

That was all it took. He was no longer amped up. He thanked us for our assistance. He asked us if we wanted to come in for a cup of coffee. We regretfully declined.

That wasn't the only encounter we had with a mentally ill person. I don't know if Johnathan was mentally disturbed. Johnathan and I were not friends. Johnathan and I were not going to be friends. In fact, I don't think Johnathan had any friends. We had not been introduced, but that was what I was thinking when I was dispatched to him sitting on the concrete rail of the Interstate 10 High-Rise Bridge in New Orleans.

I turned on my blue lights and parked my police unit to block as many of the three lanes of westbound traffic as I could. About 120,000 vehicles used the bridge over the Industrial Canal on an average day, per transportation department figures. But they were going to be at a complete stop for as long as this was going to take. I'm sure more than a few of them would have happily assisted Johnathan with a shove if it meant getting to work on time.

The bridge was not as high as the Mississippi River Bridge, but you could see it from almost anywhere in the city. Johnathan was not going to do himself any good by jumping off.

It was about a quarter after six in the morning when I first saw him. I informed the dispatcher that we had a possible jumper. Everyone working the seventh district heard me on the radio. Members of the urban squad also using channel three heard the same.

"You can't sit around up here. You're going to give people the wrong idea," I remarked to Johnathan. It quickly became clear that humor was not going to persuade him. He just looked at me sadly.

"I don't know what's bothering you or what you're thinking, but this is not the fix for any problem," I said. "Why don't you come with me and I can get you some help. I know people who are really interested in helping guys like you. I have seen them do it before. They can help you too."

I was about eight feet away, too far to make a grab for him. He was in his twenties and very thin. He was already sitting on the rail with his legs over the side. If I made a play for him and didn't do it just right, he could end up pulling me over with him.

As I was thinking over my next move, he stood up. I thought maybe he was going to jump or come on my side of the rail. He did neither. He removed a wallet from his back pocket and placed it on the rail next to him. He also removed a small pocketknife from his front right pocket and placed it next to the wallet. Then he sat back down.

I kept trying to get him to start talking. If I could establish some sort of rapport, maybe I could get him to open up. If that wasn't possible, maybe I would just keep interrupting the formulation of his plan to jump. We were located at the apex of the bridge, directly over the Industrial Canal.

The Industrial Canal is a maritime thoroughfare linking the Mississippi River to the Intracoastal Waterway and the Gulf of Mexico. It is deep enough to accommodate most commercial traffic. I somehow didn't believe that Johnathan was thinking of the importance of this specific waterway or how it cut off miles of travel for smaller commercial vessels that could fit through its lock system. No, Johnathan probably just thought it was of sufficient height to end his life.

I remember looking at his feet. He was not wearing any shoes. Had Johnathan walked all this way unshod, or had he kicked off his shoes so they might precede him into the chilly water below? He wore only a T-shirt and blue jeans with a leather belt. I was still trying to get him to talk to me when he broke his melancholy silence and stood up.

He looked at me and said the only two words of our encounter: "See ya." He then calmly stepped off the rail.

I got to the rail just in time to see Johnathan hit the water. I could hear the splash from the top of the bridge over the engine noise of the idling traffic. As I recounted earlier, members of the urban squad shared our radio channel. A unit from the urban squad and one from the third district responded to the west side shoreline of the Industrial Canal.

Officer John Frost was manning one of the urban squad units. John Frost was a character who was known to most police officers in New Orleans at that time. He wasn't known as a tough guy or a funny guy. Everyone knew John because he was such a nice guy. John would do anything for anybody, and that was why he was so well known.

After watching Johnathan hit the water with a splash, I jumped into my car and sped down to the shoreline. By the time I arrived, John Frost had dropped his gun belt and removed his uniform down to his underwear. He then jumped into the water. Frost was as large and strong as he was kind. He grabbed Johnathan and brought him back to the shore. Johnathan was in a daze, but he was breathing. As Frost got dressed again, my fellow officers handcuffed and threw Johnathan in the back of my car. We might be standing in the third district, but Johnathan had jumped from the seventh district, so he was my problem.

I transported Johnathan to Charity Hospital's emergency room. After a cursory check-in at triage, a Charity Hospital police officer handcuffed Johnathan to a gurney and returned the cuffs he had been wearing to me. The emergency room was rather busy even though it was relatively early in the morning. Since Johnathan had done this to himself, he was going to have to wait. While they were going over him to be sure that he had no life-threatening injuries, I took note of several interesting things. He must have hit the water feet first. The force of the water rushing up his pants legs had blown the seat of his jeans completely out. His belt buckle had been ripped completely away, but the belt was still through the pant loops.

Johnathan was still not saying much. It was only then that I finally got his name. He seemed to be just as unhappy now as he had been sitting on the bridge. He told me this had been his third suicide attempt. It has been my experience that these poor people who attempt to end their lives multiple times inevitably succeed. I told Johnathan the same thing I told him on the bridge.

"Killing yourself won't fix any problem you might have. Sufficient help and time will fix most every problem."

He just looked at the wall. I had a feeling he'd heard all of this before.

I took the information I needed to complete my report. I gave Johnathan back his wallet. The pocketknife was a cheap one, so I discarded it later. He wouldn't need it in here anyway. I patted his cuffed hand on the gurney rail. I wished him good luck and told him goodbye. Johnathan kept looking at the wall and did not respond.

I never followed up on Johnathan. I know his last name, but I will not use it here. I guess I just like the way this story ends, with Johnathan alive.

I never considered myself a cowboy, but I did herd several little imaginary men out of a woman's house once. When I rang the bell, she answered the door in a huff. She explained that these little men had shown up and were eating her out of house and home. She told me she lived alone on a fixed income and she could not afford to have these tiny houseguests any longer. She led me to the kitchen, where she presented me to the little intruders. This woman was obviously hallucinating and suffering some sort of dementia. I, being the sane one between us, could see no evidence of anyone else in the house. She announced to the little men that she had been serious when she said she was going to call the police, and here I was.

Now, I fancied myself rather skilled at playing along with mental patients. After all, I had experience with ray guns and tinfoil hats. Now I had to command obedience from several petite perpetrators. I informed the little bastards that they had outstayed their welcome. Now by the power vested in me by the City of New Orleans, I told them I was there to oversee their immediate eviction. I walked to the back door, opened it, and demanded that they leave.

As they allegedly did, the woman called after them, "I told you this was going to happen. I told you I was serious."

About eight months later when I was dispatched to another such call, I arrived with confidence. A frail old lady in her late eighties met me at the door. She was obviously upset. She was shaking and afraid. She told me there was a man in the other room who would appear and just stare at her. She said he was there now and asked me to please make him leave.

She walked me from the front door into a side room. This was an older residence. The room might have once been used as a dining room. It was now sparsely furnished, and the whole house had a musty old wood smell. She pointed to the man in the corner, who of course I could not see.

"There he is," she said with assurance.

"Okay, pal, this lady wants you to leave, so you gotta go," I said, employing my previously successful ruse.

It was obvious by her reaction that what had worked in the past was useless here. She quickly got behind me. While using me as a shield, she began to cry.

"He's not going to leave, Officer," she whispered a warning to me.

I figured maybe I best come clean and tell her the truth. I said, "Ma'am, I don't see anybody."

That's when she squeezed my arm. "You can't see him?" she asked.

"No, ma'am, I cannot," I promised her.

"He's right there. He's wearing a dark blue suit with a skinny tie. He has one of those Irish tweed caps, but it doesn't match his suit," she said. "Please tell me you can see him, son," she begged. "Now he's smiling at us," she said while peeking from behind me.

She began to cry harder. The problem was that this woman did not seem crazy to me. But that could not be true because she was seeing someone who I could not. I must admit it scared the shit out of me. Maybe I was the problem. Maybe I was being purposefully left out of this manifestation.

We retreated to the kitchen area of her residence. I told her that I did not see anyone. I asked if she wanted to come with me. I could take her up to Charity if she thought it would be safer there. Within a short time, she had settled down a little and stopped crying.

She told me this was her house and she did not want to go anywhere. She said, "He never tries to hurt me, but his presence is frightening. He just stands there, looking. Sometimes smiling. He is not there all the time, just every now and again, and only in that room."

I did not let on, but during that conversation, I was a bit frightened too. She seemed to be quite coherent in every other aspect. That made it even more unsettling. If she would just show me she was crazy, I would have certainly felt better.

She walked me to the door. I asked again if she would reconsider coming with me. She thanked me but refused. I told her if she ever needed the police again to please call. If I was working and heard the call come over the radio, I would be sure to show up myself.

"You're a good boy. But I don't think anyone can help me. I guess I'll have to get used to him or find out what he wants," she said tearfully, putting on a brave smile. We said our goodbyes and never met again.

I never really knew until I got into this line of work just how big of a problem the treatment of mental illness is. Remember this was in the 1980s. At least we had Charity Hospital then. Now the voices of the advocates crying out for help for these people are drowned out by the relentless barking of the dogs of crime and the loud droning of mismanaged priorities and feckless leadership.

CHAPTER TEN

"Ya gonna burn 'em," Ron pleaded.

"You want to cook 'em?" the Satisfier asked.

"No, I want to eat 'em, but I don't want 'em burned," Ron said, walking away.

Steve paid Ron no more concern and put the barbecue top back on the Weber grill. He announced to the crowd that the hamburgers should be ready shortly. That was good because I was starting to get hungry. I was on my second beer, and I knew I was far behind most everyone else.

It was nice of the Satisfier to hold a celebration of the grand opening of his automotive shop. He had located a place on Prentice Avenue off Saint Roch. It looked like a good location, and it was very close to the lot where he used to do his work. It would also be easy for his customers to find. Jerry and Ron had helped Steve move in. They moved his tools and the rest of his automotive repair equipment. Steve didn't have everything he wanted, but it was a good start.

Gertie Chauvin was there with some guy we'd never met. It was kind of strange because we were used to having her all to ourselves. The guy stayed near her because he didn't know anyone else. Barry, Wong, Jerry, and Greg were sitting around one of the tables Steve had set up. They had polished off the chips and dip and were eagerly awaiting the burgers. Tony was working and wasn't able to attend.

I pulled up a chair and sat down.

"You didn't tell them about our transfer?" Wong asked me.

"I did not have the opportunity yet," I said. "Besides, it only happened yesterday."

"You are leaving the seventh district?" Barry asked.

"Not exactly," I said. "It's a temporary assignment. B. J. and I are going to the mounted division for the next ten or so months to ride at the World's Fair," I informed them.

"I didn't know you two knew anything about horses," Gertie remarked, overhearing our conversation.

"We'll be going through a couple months of training," I told her. "Then we'll be patrolling the fair site, French Quarter, and that whole area."

"You guys gonna wear those tight little pants and white helmets?" Gertie asked.

"I am," Wong quickly replied. "He's gonna wear a cowboy hat and assless chaps."

Everyone laughed. I thought to myself that I better lose a little weight or I was gonna look like a dumbass in those tight riding pants.

"Okay, guys, the burgers are ready," the Satisfier announced, placing a pan full of burgers on the table along with the buns and condiments. The gang all got up to serve themselves.

"Steve was gonna turn 'em into hockey pucks. But I saved 'em," Ron said proudly.

"You ain't got to eat them," the Satisfier shot back.

"Oh, I'm gonna eat 'em, mister, 'cause ya still owe me from moving ya," Ron said while fixing a double burger.

Ron's burger was so big that I was afraid the flimsy paper plate was not going to support it. He grabbed two beers out of the cooler and took a seat next to Wong.

"Did you bring that for me?" B. J. said, pointing to the second beer.

"No, that's mine too. I didn't want to have to get up again," Ron said. "So, you two are going to ride mounted at the World's Fair?"

"Looks that way. It's gonna be a big change," Wong said.

"We need a big change about now," I said.

The Louisiana World Exposition, or the New Orleans World's Fair, began May 12, 1984, and ended on Sunday, November 11, 1984. Its theme was "The World of Rivers—Fresh Waters as a Source of Life." It was quite impressive. It had a huge saltwater aquarium as part of the exhibit. The site itself covered more than eighty-four acres. There was a monorail system running through the fair and a gondola lift that crossed the Mississippi River to Algiers on the west bank. The space shuttle *Enterprise* was on display, as well as pavilions sponsored by many countries. It was well received by the more than seven million people who attended.

The expedition site itself ran alongside the east bank of the Mississippi River. A second span of the Mississippi River Bridge system was under construction at that time. When completed, the project would be called the Crescent City Connection. It had an amphitheater that opened on to the river. This project was definitely a shot in the arm for that area. Dilapidated and rundown buildings had been removed, while others were updated and renovated. It was this facelift that brought businesses, hotels, apartments, and condominiums to the renovated central business district. The New Orleans arts district is located there now, along with the National World War II Museum.

The 1984 Louisiana World Exposition turned out to be very beneficial for the city in the long run but not so much for the state of Louisiana or those who invested in it. The fair was over $100 million in debt and declared bankruptcy even before the closing day.

In 1983, the police department took several patrolmen from several districts and transferred us to make up a temporary group for patrol at the World's Fair. Jimmy Sheridan came from the second district, Wong and I came from the seventh, and several others came from the sixth and first districts. One policewoman was also assigned with us. Sheila Wilson was a black woman raised in the heart of New Orleans. She had been on the job longer than I had and worked in a busier district. Our group would be augmenting the personnel permanently assigned to the mounted division.

As members of the police department's patrol personnel assigned to the 1984 World's Fair, we received extensive training in horsemanship and mounted police tactics. We attended informational briefings given by police management. We were told that the crowds would be massive. It would be like Mardi Gras every day. Along with the crowds would come those who would take advantage. Pickpockets, prostitutes, petty thieves, drug dealers, and shoplifters would be intermingled with the crowd each day. It was going to be our job to police this subclass of visitors.

As part of the mounted patrol, we would be in and around the fair site, including the central business district and French Quarter. Anywhere that tourists might congregate, they wanted to have a visible police presence. We would be running two shifts per day, a day and an evening watch. We averaged about four to six mounted officers per shift.

Jimmy, B. J., and I were excited about this new assignment. It was different from what we had been doing and, although challenging, turned out to be a lot of fun. We ended up riding in Mardi Gras and the World's Fair. We no longer had to go to our respective district stations. We came and went directly from the New Orleans Police Department stables, located in City Park off Harrison Avenue and Marconi Drive.

City Park was once the site of the Allard Plantation on Bayou Saint John. It is over one hundred and fifty years old, one mile wide and three miles long, comprising a total of 1,300 acres. New Orleans City Park is one of the ten largest urban parks in the country. The park's board approved the police department's request for the establishment of police stables in 1963. It was completed soon after.

The main structure of the stables had a north–south hallway and an east–west hallway. Horse stalls were positioned along both sides of these halls. Where the two halls converged was the main office, or squad room. A desk was situated against the huge glass windows, where the duty officer could see down both hallways. He had a complete view of the entire building from one spot. When I was there, Dewey was the daytime desk man. Dewey had been in both the mounted and canine units. He was an exceptionally good rider; I had been told this by numerous sources. He also took care of the stable dogs, cats, and chickens. He had a fenced pen on the side of the building that housed his goats and a ram. Dogs, cats, and chickens roamed the stables and assisted in keeping the horses calm and tranquil.

At the end of the stable hallways were large overhanging doors that could be raised or lowered for weather. The main office was one large room with a restroom and shower area adjoining it. Off to one side of the main office, a corner had been walled off to create a supervisor's office that could be secured. The entire complex had a heavy smell of hay and horses. It was not a bad smell, far from it. It was a smell I missed for a long time when my days in the mounted division were over.

At that time, the stables could house about sixteen horses. Every morning the city would drop off three or four trustees. They would muck the stalls and wash the horses. We did all the other maintenance that came along with being in the mounted division. We would brush down our horses as well as maintain our vehicles and trailers and riding tack.

Saddles, stirrups, bridles, halters, reins, bits, and harnesses are all forms of horse tack. Each horse had his or her own stall, and in front of the stall was a large locker to store your tack. I can't tell you how old the saddles were, but they were in very good condition for their age. We did not use a western saddle with a horn in the front. We used a type of McClellan cavalry saddle.

The saddles were shiny black with high pommels and cantles. The pommel is the area at the front of the saddle. The cantle rises and forms the back and is also the back of the seat. It is turned up to help support the rider. The stirrups had a full front that protected the entire front of your feet and shins. These old saddles had been lovingly cared for by many police officers before us. We were expected to keep this saddle and the other equipment in excellent condition. I don't know why they selected the English cavalry style, maybe so officers could dismount in a hurry.

Upon our arrival, we were each assigned a horse. The horse we were each assigned would be our horse. We were each responsible for our own horse's health and welfare. If anything was out of sorts, we should report it, so the matter could be taken care of as soon as possible. We had a farrier who was there nearly every day and a veterinarian on call.

There were one or two thoroughbreds in the stable, but most of the horses were Standardbreds. The Standardbred is an American horse breed. They are solid, muscular horses with good dispositions and are smart and easy to train. Usually heavier built than thoroughbreds, they have thick sturdy legs and powerful shoulders and hindquarters.

The horse I was assigned to was named Sonny. Sonny was large, about seventeen hands. A hand is equal to four inches. A horse is measured from the ground to the top of the highest point of the withers.

The withers are the ridge between the horse's shoulder blades. Sonny was a bay. He had a little tuft of hair between his ears and a large Roman nose. He was afraid of the Ferris wheel at the rear of the World's Fair site, but other than that he was fearless.

Sonny would go wherever I pointed him and would keep going until I stopped him. Whatever was in his way had better move or it would be stepped on. Sonny either walked or Sonny ran. He had no in-between gate. At a trot, he had square wheels. You had to stay in his mouth with the bit because he always wanted to go faster.

He also had one other factory defect. A previous owner had taught him to enter a trailer or stall using an electric cattle prod. He would approach both normally, but once his nose passed the threshold of the doorway, he would leap inside. It did not make a difference to Sonny if you were in the saddle or had a hold of his harness when he did so. If you read his packing directions, you were safe. If you were not prewarned, you were going to get hurt. During the year I spent in the mounted division, Sonny sent four trustees to the hospital.

At the end of a shift, as we rode back to the location where we parked the trailers, we would sometimes play a game we called shove. The object of the game was to force the other rider to the side of the street using your horse. You had to lift your feet out of the stirrups because the horses would make side contact. Your legs could not be in the way. Wong and Jimmy always tried to beat me, but no other horse could beat Sonny. Sonny was like a bulldozer with a walnut-sized brain. They would come and try to push Sonny from the middle of the street and he would have none of that. All I had to do was steer slightly in their direction and Sonny would push them like a tank as far as I wanted. He was never beaten in the game of shove.

On a typical day watch, we would roll into the stables at about seven thirty in the morning. There was always a pot of coffee going, and someone always stopped and bought doughnuts. The entire group would drink coffee, have breakfast, and talk about what they were going to do that day. No conversation was off the table. Politics, city management, family problems, buying and selling property, fulfillment of debts, and storytelling took up a large chunk of our breakfast time.

Out of an abundance of caution, I will not name all the attendees at the following incident. It happened during coffee time one morning. Our horses had been washed and were outside drying in the early-morning sun. Sheila had gone into the sergeant's office and closed the door to make a personal phone call. The rest of the group was drinking coffee and planning where to meet up for lunch. Kevin had gone outside and several moments later returned with a 12-gauge shotgun.

He walked over to Don and handed him the weapon. Unbeknownst to us, they were in the middle of a firearm transaction. The only thing left now was haggling on the price. When you are in the room while two monkeys are fondling a shotgun, it gets your attention and you tend to observe.

"Is it loaded? Don asked.

"Stupid ass. Do you think I would hand you a loaded shotgun?" Kevin said.

Don pointed it at the office wall and blew a hole in it.

Coffee and half-eaten doughnuts flew everywhere. We were all surprised and shocked, but none more than Kevin and Don. The smell of gunpowder was heavy in the air, soon to be replaced by that to-the-core feeling of *oh shit*. The wall he had shot was the wall to the sergeant's office, the office that Sheila had gone into for her phone call, the office that Sheila had not come out of. We knew we had to open that door and face the consequences of what had just happened. We crowded at the door, took deep breaths, and opened it slightly.

"I don't know what you assholes are doing," Sheila said while covering the phone receiver with her hand, "but you better cut it out. I'm on the phone. Now close the door!"

Everyone breathed a collective sigh of relief.

"We have to get this fixed before the Big Iron gets here," someone warned.

Big Iron was what we called the supervisory sergeant who pretty much ran the mounted division. It was a good thing we worked at the stables because there were always tools and lumber lying around. The hole was in a spot that was easily covered by a piece of wood made to look as though it was an extension of the wall's frame. We were admiring the handiwork when Big Iron walked through the front door. As he poured a cup of coffee, the parties with the most guilt slowly made their exit. The sergeant saw Sheila in his office on the phone but paid her no mind. He left the squad room to go check up on the trustees to be sure they were doing their jobs correctly. That was our cue to trailer up and get out of there.

B. J. and I loaded up our horses and headed toward the World's Fair site. B. J.'s horse was named Jorge. Jorge was much older than Sonny and had been on the job a long time. He was a legend. Several old policemen on several occasions told us that they had seen him jump over a Volkswagen. They also told us stories of how they would back him up to a door they wanted knocked down and pat his chest. He would then kick in the door. We knew this was true because we had to watch Jorge when we put him in a trailer. When his chest touched the front restraining bar, he kicked. He almost put my lights out once. I swore to B. J. that I could read his horseshoe's manufacturer's lettering inches from my face.

We always parked on one of the back streets near the fair. Then we would take the horses from the trailer, secure all vehicles, and ride to the front gate of the World's Fair site. There we would stand off to one side and watch the visitors arrive. Many people came up to us to take photos with us. We talked to people from all over the world. This was a welcome change for all of us. We were used to only dealing with people who had called for help or people we were arresting. To have a regular conversation with normal people was a rare pleasure.

We worked that entire summer in the sun and heat, but I don't recall that being a factor. Maybe it was because I was so much younger then. I hate the heat here now. When it's ninety-four degrees and 70 percent humidity, it is miserable. There's something to be said when people talk about a dry heat. I've been to the desert. I can take that heat much better. Perhaps it's because sweat evaporates in the drier conditions and keeps you cooler. Sweat doesn't evaporate quickly in 70 percent humidity. If you want to know what it feels like here, next time you take a hot shower, place a wet towel over your entire head. Then try to breathe. Welcome to summer in New Orleans.

Another bit of lost history. When B. J., Jimmy, and I were in the mounted division for the World's Fair, we came up with a little addition to the New Orleans Police Department's uniform. The three of us started to wear a crossed cavalry swords emblem with a chrome finish above our name tags. This caught on very quickly with the members throughout the mounted division in 1984.

I remember that the three of us were in headquarters because we had to take care of some administrative duties. We were in the elevator, going up to the third floor. On the second floor, Superintendent of Police Henry Morris got into the elevator with us.

As he looked us over, he asked, "What the hell is that?" and pointed to the crossed-swords pin on our uniforms.

Without missing a beat, B. J. told him it was the mounted qualification pin.

He said, "It looks good," and we got out on the next floor.

That pin is still being worn today, but there are only a handful of individuals who know the actual history. To those old NOPD cops who think I'm full of shit, go find a photo of a mounted officer before 1983 wearing that pin on his or her uniform. You won't. You are welcome, my mounted brothers and sisters.

As I previously mentioned, Sonny either walked or ran. He had no gait in between. When trotting, he landed flat; with each step, I got a powerful shock. I would compare it to when you were a kid on a seesaw and the other kid mischievously jumps off when you're up in the air. You land with a crash. I was constantly telling the other guys to slow down as they began to trot and Sonny wanted to do likewise. You had to, what they call, stay in his mouth. That means you had to apply a little pressure with the reins to the bit because Sonny always wanted to speed up.

On this afternoon, we were at our usual position at the entrance to the World's Fair site at Fulton Street. Jimmy, B. J., and I, along with Spanky, another mounted officer, were in a group watching the people come and go. It was about three o'clock in the afternoon. The day was hot, but it had not rained, so the streets were dry.

The afternoon had been proceeding normally when we heard a woman yelling. She was then joined by other voices hollering and pointing to a man running toward Poydras Street. We could see him from our vantage point. He was running with a purse in his hand. The woman had been the victim of a purse snatching. The four of us immediately began pursuit of the perpetrator on Fulton Street. The other horses were getting ahead of Sonny. I then did what I had never done previously: I released all tension on Sonny's bit and gave him a kick on both flanks.

I was totally unprepared for what would happen when I released control of the throttle to Sonny. As I kicked his flanks, a fifteen-foot flame shot out of his ass. We then went into hyperdrive. I watched people and buildings go by in a blur. We flew past the other horses. We flew past the running purse snatcher. We were heading toward the traffic on Poydras Street. I was pulling back on the reins, but the brakes had failed. Sonny had been given permission to run. In his mind, there was no taking that back.

We were in a full gallop. Sonny was not responding to controls. I figured we were going to stop when the vehicles moving on Poydras Street ran over us. Sonny went right into traffic. Thank goodness he turned with them, going in the same direction toward the river. We were coming up to the Hilton Hotel at Poydras and the river. We were twice as fast as the cars and trucks and passed them with ease. He veered to the right of the front of the hotel and blasted into the breezeway running alongside the building. When we exited the breezeway, I could see that B. J. and the other mounted officers had the perpetrator against a fence, placing him under arrest. Sonny saw them too and headed straight for them, never missing a beat. As we passed them, I shouted directions to my fellow officers.

"Shoot this fucking horse!"

I knew I had to do something quick. My luck had to be running out. I went down the right side of his neck and grabbed the reins as closely as I could to the bit. I then threw my weight back with all of my might. I knew this would turn his head and he would either stop or we would take a gigantic spill. I thank the good Lord that we jackknifed to a stop. The other guys were killing themselves laughing. That damn perp was even smiling and laughing too. They could not wait to tell anyone who would listen the story of my misfortune.

Mardi Gras in the mounted division was the best Mardi Gras I ever spent on the police department. Unlike my other assignments, Mardi Gras on horseback was a lot easier. Our duties included riding in the parades, crowd control, and French Quarter assignments. Riding in most parades was easy. The day parades did not have the crushing crowds of the mega-parades rolling the weekend before Mardi Gras day. The crowds during the mega night parades were a bit more boisterous. They had more intoxicated idiots than the day parades. The majority of the crowds at any of these parades were just out to have fun. But there was always an element that carried things too far and was just out looking for trouble.

When riding in a day parade, we rode side by side in the middle of the street, usually behind one of the bands. But when the crowds were heavy like in the large night parades, we would ride on each side of the street to keep the crowd back so the parade behind us could proceed. You would be surprised what assholes will do when they think they can remain anonymous. Some would just do stupid things like throw ice at us. When we could identify one of them, we would let the cops on the street know where they were so that they could deal with them. We had one drunken lummox step out into the street and punch one of the horses in the face like in the movie *Blazing Saddles*. He swiftly discovered that two officers wielding three thousand pounds of horseflesh in a crowd could quickly isolate you. Let's just say his Mardi Gras revelry ended for the year right then.

Before I can proceed, I must explain to you what a Mardi Gras Indian is. If you're not from New Orleans, you probably don't know. The Mardi Gras Indians are made up of black folks from New Orleans's inner city. Their walking groups have paraded in Mardi Gras celebrations culminating on Mardi Gras day for well over a century. Each organization of Mardi Gras Indians is called a tribe. These tribes have names like Wild Magnolias, Creole Wild West, Yellow Pocahontas, and the Fi Yi Yi. Today, there are more than thirty recognized New Orleans Mardi Gras Indian tribes.

These tribes have long-held traditions. They must create and sew their own elaborate Indian costumes. These costumes can cost more than a thousand dollars to make. Each is an individual work of art. They are usually covered with feathers and other decorations. The higher-ranking Indians usually have huge headdresses. Some of these costumes can easily weigh more than fifty pounds. A real New Orleans Indian costume cannot be purchased.

There is a membership hierarchy in each tribe. The tribe's leader is called the big chief. There are usually one or two secondary chiefs. Each chief has a queen. The big chief is always accompanied by the wildman, who carries a symbolic weapon, usually a spear. It's the wildman's job to advise and protect the big chief. The trail chief is positioned at the rear of the procession to protect the rear flank of the big chief from attack. Sent ahead of the procession as scouts are the spy boys. It is their job to scout for other tribes they may encounter on their route. Within sight of the big chief is the flag boy. When the flag boy is warned by the spy boys that a rival tribe is ahead, he flags that information to the big chief. The Mardi Gras Indian processions are not well known outside the New Orleans population. Their routes are never publicized. Their processions could change at any time and in any direction at the whim of the big chief.

Why is so much security built into these Mardi Gras Indians traditions? Because in the early days, violence was often associated with these Mardi Gras Indian tribes. It was a day often used to settle old scores, end arguments, and pay back perceived wrongs. The police were often unable to intercede because of the crowd, the confusion, and the fact that most people were masked. In the early days, these tribes' processions were anything but family friendly.

Today's Mardi Gras Indian parades are not violent. Gun and knife fights have been replaced with symbolic altercations. Tribes will meet, and the big chiefs will face each other down. They will verbally assault each other's tribe and costumes. This too is only tradition, as the big chiefs will quietly greet and congratulate each other out of earshot of the crowd. They then both continue their routes.

On the Saturday before Mardi Gras day, we were assigned to parade duty and were in the formation area of the parade. The formation area was the location where all the floats and bands and any other entities that made up the parade were staged. There were not a lot of spectators at this location; they were spread along the parade's route.

Jimmy, B. J., and I had ridden our horses from the stables to this location near City Park. It was a beautiful cold morning. Cold enough, in fact, that we were wearing balaclavas. But the sun was shining. You could not ask for a better parade day.

I was not riding my usual horse, Sonny. Today I was on Jolly. I did not know Jolly very well. I was used to riding Sonny. Jolly was a good-looking horse, light brown with a black mane and tail. He had a black stripe that ran down his back and down to his tail. The horses were happy to be out in this beautiful weather and were jumping around with enthusiasm. A group of Mardi Gras Indians preparing to march in the parade were congregating nearby.

As B. J., Jimmy, and I attempted to hold a conversation, the horses in their exuberance were moving around under us. They were stomping and occasionally taking a bite of the tall clover we were standing in. I know you have been there before, trying to hold a conversation with someone and you have a little kid by the hand who couldn't give a shit less. While you're talking, the kid pulls on you, goes limp to the ground, puts all his or her weight on your arm, and says in that whiney voice, "Let's go …" I'm sure you have either seen or experienced these distracting behaviors before.

After a while, the aforementioned behavior of the horses became very distracting. When Sonny engaged in such conduct, I would simply take my riding crop and give him a smack lightly on the leg. He would then snap out of it and stop fooling around. I'm sure you remember a fact that I had forgotten: this was not Sonny. So, during our conversation, when I'd had enough of Jolly's rambunctiousness, I calmly removed my crop from my boot and smacked him on the leg.

Have you ever witnessed a Saturn rocket lift off? With incredible power and thrust, it launches straight into the air. Jolly did the same thing, only with more smoke and flame. I was like one of those astronauts. All I could do was hold on for the ride. Then he performed one more maneuver I thought to be malicious. As he reached his maximum ascent height, he violently shifted his lower half to the right. So upon descent, there was no saddle underneath me. The ensuing crash was bone jarring. The worst part about it was I carried extra ammunition on my belt in the small of my back. As I hit the ground, that pouch of ammunition was forced into my lower back. The crash knocked the wind out of me, and the pain was immediate.

B. J. and Jimmy observed the event and came over to check on me. When I finally made it to my feet, I saw that Jolly had not run away.

He stayed right there to gloat in his victory. I thought, *Thank God I am wearing this balaclava.* No one could recognize me. Not only was I hurt, but I was also very embarrassed. I leaned against Jolly. There was no way I could get back in the saddle yet; I was hurting too much. I thought, *I know people are looking. There is no way this could get worse.* That's when I heard a voice over my shoulder. It was a Mardi Gras Indian in full tribe regalia.

"Officer, are you hurt?" he asked.

"Just a little," I replied.

"That was a mighty big fall," he said.

"Thanks, I've been practicing."

"Officer, is dat yo gun over dare in da clover?" he asked me.

I looked over to see my duty pistol lying in the clover about three feet away. I looked down at my empty holster. The force of the crash had dislodged it and flung it feet away from me.

"Yes, yes, that's mine," I said while stumbling to retrieve it. I thanked the Indian for his kindness and his concern for my well-being, as well as his sharp eye in recovering my firearm. I also complimented him on his Indian costume.

I finally summoned the strength to saddle Jolly again. I think he knew he had hurt me because he did not give me another problem the entire day. As I joined B. J. and Jimmy again, they asked if I was okay.

"No, I'm not, but I guess I don't have a choice."

I completed that parade in discomfort. When I got home, I took some muscle relaxers and some painkillers I had left over from the time I broke my ankle. I knew I had to get better fast because Mardi Gras wasn't going to be over until Tuesday at midnight.

Mardi Gras is a crazy time. Sometimes you would do things you would not normally do. Such as the mounted fruit salute. I do not know who invented the fruit salute or how old it is. All I know is how to perform it and the incredible reception it always got. It was easy to do, but it had to be done in unison. To execute it, we would stand in the stirrups and take the reins in our left hands and our riding crops in our right hands. Then, waving the riding crop with a limp wrist, we would shout, "Hayyyyyy … hayyyyy."

I remember one occasion during Mardi Gras when we were

relocating to assignments in the French Quarter as a group. There were probably a dozen officers on horseback. We were coming from the lower end of the French Quarter from Rampart toward Royal Street. We passed several balconies of revelers. One could tell very easily by their dress that these folks were gay. We performed the salute. They went nuts. They clapped and shouted and waved to us and cheered us so loud that we could hear them for two blocks after that. The salute was never done as a slight. It was done as recognition. We never had a single misunderstanding or complaint. I know some of you may be appalled. Just get over it. Everyone had a blast, and everyone appreciated the acknowledgment and shared in the fun of the moment.

It was always good to get back to the stables after a long day on horseback. I did not have a lot of experience at backing up trailers before I got into the mounted division. By the time I left, I considered myself an expert. I was driving back to the stables one day—a rare occurrence because I hated to drive. B. J. never really had a problem with driving, so I would always jump in the passenger seat. But if he was tired or didn't feel like driving, the task would fall to me.

We pulled into the mounted division complex and drove around back. We got out of the vehicle, dropped the trailer ramp, and took our horses out. We led our horses to their individual stalls and removed their tack. We gave them a once-over to be sure they hadn't suffered any injuries or scrapes and then secured them in their stalls.

We then proceeded to the vehicle to back the trailer into a designated parking spot. As we walked back to the open area in the rear of the complex, we spotted Dewey's gray ram. Dewey always kept his goats and the ram locked up in a fenced enclosure. We had never observed him as an escapee before. As we passed, he gave us an evil look.

I don't know how many of you have ever spent time on a farm or have personally known any rams. If you have not, consider yourself blessed. A ram is a truly nasty critter. If you knew him, you would understand why the devil is often depicted as a ram. He will piss on himself to produce the perfect malevolent cologne. He has a nasty tongue that is incredibly long, and he will stick it out while making very inappropriate noises. They get to a hefty size. Don't worry about him biting you; he lets his huge rounded horns do the talking for him. In short, he is a formidable little sack of shit.

With B. J.'s assistance, I backed the trailer into its parking spot, and we disengaged it from our vehicle. I exited the car in time to see B. J. with his hands on his hips in front of the ram. The ram was about four feet in front of B. J. The two beasts stared at each other in an attempt to intimidate one another. It was clear that B. J. was out of his league in ornery hatefulness.

B. J. did not ask for my advice or good counsel. If he had, I would have recommended he just walk away. It was a surprise to me to see B. J. take this confrontation to a physical level. B. J., seemingly much larger and stronger than the ram, took him by the horns and pushed his head down to rub his nose in the dirt. His victory now complete, he stood erect again, apparently waiting for the ram to acknowledge that he had been bested.

It is too bad that no one spoke ram, so we could not advise him that he had lost the competition. He poked out his long red tongue and began an inhuman guttural sound, verbalizing some sort of demonic curse. When the incantation was completed, he stood tall on his hind legs and slammed his horns into B. J.'s knee. It was like something off *National Geographic*. B. J. screamed like a kid on a roller coaster. It was a scream that was composed of fear, pain, and surprise. As B. J. began a limping retreat, I charged the ram, hollering at him and waving my arms. Seeing as he was probably contemplating charging me with a head butt, I too retreated for the safety of indoors. I went into the squad room and saw B. J. on the couch with his boots off and his riding pants pulled down, inspecting his now swollen knee.

"Do you want me to get you a bag of ice?" I asked.

"Yeah, that would help," he said.

"That was stupid, man. Why did you do that?" I asked

"He was eye jamming me," he said defensively.

The time I spent in the mounted division was a welcome break in my police career. It's rare when you can say that you enjoyed working so much at a job with the added benefit of really liking all the people you were working with. Everyone got along well, and even if I was paired up with any of the others because Wong was absent that day, I still had a great time. But all good things must come to an end. After the World's Fair ended, those of us who were temporarily transferred to the mounted division were now on borrowed time. We would be heading back to the districts from which we came. It was now time to start politicking to attempt to stay in the mounted division.

It was about this time also that Wong's horse, Jorge, started to get too old to continue his mounted patrol duties. I don't know what other police organizations do with their old horses after they are injured or are too old to continue their police work. But back then, putting a horse down for those facts would be unheard of. It was a shared belief that these animal officers had served the city and the police department well. The least the men and women of the mounted section could do was try to find them a home where they could retire.

It was the Big Iron who found Jorge a home. He loaded him up in a trailer and drove him to a farmer he knew in Mississippi who had several horses on his large farm. The Big Iron took Jorge out of the police trailer for the last time and released him in the field with the other horses. The farmer told Big Iron that he would keep Jorge but he could not guarantee his safety. The man said he did not know how his wild horses would take to Jorge. He was concerned that some of the males might kill him. The Big Iron told him that Jorge would just have to take his chances because this was his last shot.

Two weeks passed before the farmer called the Big Iron. He said he had gone out the week prior to check the horses. He said that Jorge was not only alive but leading the group. He said the mares were following him around and the male horses were trailing with their hats in their hands and one was carrying Jorge's cigarettes.

We spoke to Big Iron about transferring to the mounted division. He said he would do what he could for us. We kept after him, but soon we got the notification that the following week we would be transferred back to the seventh district. Even though the World's Fair was over, we still were on mounted patrol in the French Quarter and central business district. We rode every day right up until the end. I think it might have been Wong who suggested that we go talk to Sergeant Kelly. Sergeant Gerry Kelly was a platoon supervisor of one of the special weapons and tactics (SWAT) groups in the special operations division. He ran tactical platoon two. We made an appointment to meet with him.

Kelly was an old-time policeman. He knew the workings of the police department inside and out. He had friends and contacts in all levels of the department. He had been with the New Orleans Police Department since the 1960s. Before he joined the police department, Kelly was in the navy; he was a submariner. He had been on the bomb squad as one of his many duties on the department. He was hard as nails but had a great sense of humor. If he liked you, you had a loyal and dependable friend who would be there for you no matter what. If you crossed him with any malice, you were damned to look over your shoulder for the rest of your life. From our first meeting, Wong and I hit it off with Kelly. We became very close friends both on and off the police department. We got together socially and kept in touch until his death in 2016.

After our first initial meeting, Kelly was walking us out to the parking lot in the special operations division complex when we ran into the Big Iron.

"So, that's how it's going to be," Big Iron said.

We tried to explain that the lack of movement in a transfer to the mounted division had forced us to explore other options. The Big Iron looked pissed off. He waved us off and wanted no part of our explanation. I felt bad. I'm sure Wong did too, but Kelly seem to get a big kick out of the confrontation.

CHAPTER ELEVEN

While Sergeant Kelly worked behind the scenes to get Wong and me transferred to SWAT, we were both transferred back to the seventh district. We were again riding as partners on the 3:00 p.m. to 11:00 p.m. shift. We were just biding our time and had placed all of our eggs into Kelly's basket. It was a big change from the laid-back year we had just spent in the mounted division. We were tied to the radio and headquarters, running from call to call.

After a taste of what it was like to be out of the district setting, we knew we wanted to move on. There were officers who truly enjoyed district work. My friend Jan Christensen stayed in the seventh district for his entire career, which was more than thirty years. He always thought of the seventh as his home. I'm sure the day he walked out he thought about how much it had changed since the mid-seventies when he had arrived there.

It was during this wait to be transferred to SWAT that on a late Saturday morning, the doorbell rang at my house. I opened to door to find Gert standing there with a box of fried chicken.

"May I come in?" she asked.

"You have never come here bearing chicken," I said. "This must be serious."

"There's nothing wrong. I would just like to run something past you," she said.

She followed me inside and took a seat on the couch. I went to the kitchen and called back to her to see if she wanted a beer to go with the chicken. I joined her in the living room and asked her what was on her mind.

She said Annette and Debbie were driving her crazy. I knew Annette and Debbie were the two women she lived with—two snooty little uptowners who I never much cared for. They always talked down to me whenever we met. They were too good to come to the club. So thankfully, we did not run into each other often.

"I don't know why you live with those two," I said. "It doesn't seem to me that you guys have a lot in common."

"You're right. I can't defend them," she admitted. "I needed a place to live, but now they have gone just too far. You know I've been seeing that guy Kyle? Now they're telling me that I can't bring him to the house. I pay one-third of the rent, but I don't have any say in house decisions. They always stick together on issues of contention. I am always outvoted."

"I don't think those two have to worry about bringing guys home anytime soon," I said. "Perhaps they could find love if they joined a prison pen pal group."

She laughed for the first time since she arrived.

"I don't make much money at the bakery," she said. "I cannot afford my own place. It would take most of the money I make just to pay the rent. I know Tony Amato married Dawn and he is on the state police. They have not stayed here in forever. I was wondering if you would consider a roommate."

I had been wandering in and out of relationships for years. The longest one was with my high-school sweetheart, Aileen. I would like to say we grew apart, but in retrospect, I know it was my fault. I was not a very monogamous person back then. Gertie moving in would strain that and many other relationships that I might have. I stayed friends with the women I'd had relationships with, but that was cold consolation for all the time I spent alone. I knew Gertie needed help. But I wondered how this was going to work because I still had deep feelings for her. I figured I needed to put my feelings aside and help my friend. As it would turn out, it was as helpful for me as it was for her.

"I don't know, Gert. I use that room for my extensive pornography collection. My hope is to one day sell it for tens of thousands of dollars. That room contains my future nest egg."

"Oh really? Let's just go look," she said, standing up and marching to the back bedroom. She flung open the closed door. The room was basically empty except for my Soloflex machine, which I now used to hang clothes on.

"Well, where is this huge collection of yours?" she asked, waving her arms.

"Oh my God, I've been robbed!"

"Stop fooling around, you blockhead," she said. "I need help, and you're the only one I can come to."

I quit joking around and said, "Sure, we can work something out."

She became giddy with excitement. "How much rent would I have to pay you?" she asked.

"I thought I was going to have to pay you to put up with me," I said. "The room is going to be here with you in it or not. It'll be cooled or heated and cost me the same either way. Just help around the house, buy a few supplies, and help with some meal costs when you can. We won't worry about rent."

I could see in her eyes that she had not expected that.

"This is going to be strange," she said. "Strange and a lot of fun!"

It did not take Gert long to move her things in. It did not take me long to get used to her being there. We settled in together very well. Some nights she would cook, and some nights I would prepare dinner. It was usually whoever was home first.

One rainy Thursday evening, we had just cleaned up after a late dinner when Tony Amato showed up. He knew that Gert was living there now, so he was not looking for a room. He said he had business in town and was staying with a relative in Metairie. He figured since he hadn't been by for quite a while, he would stop in to catch up.

We all grabbed a beer and headed for the living room to relax and talk. Tony told me all the things that were going on with the state police, and I filled him in with what was happening with NOPD. He asked how everyone at the club was doing. Gertie filled him in with all the latest details. When Tony was up to speed on all the Dreux gossip, Gert asked both of us what we had done that day at work. She said she had always been interested in our day-to-day lives as police officers. We did not have regular office or factory jobs. Every day had to be different.

Tony and I looked at each other.

"Did you have a good day or a bad day today?" I asked.

"Shitty day," he said. "How about you?"

"Okay all in all," I said. "So tell us about your shitty day."

"I worked a bad accident today," he said. "It was morning rush hour, and it was raining in Baton Rouge too. I get a call of an injury accident on Interstate 10. Poor guy had pulled to the shoulder with a flat tire. While he worked on it, a vehicle sideswiped him. I get there with all my vehicle lights on and stop the right lane of traffic. A Good Samaritan was attempting to help the guy. He had applied about four tourniquets to the victim, but with the kind of trauma this guy had suffered, they weren't gonna do any good." I glanced over at Gert and she had this pained look on her face. I did not tell her graphic stories. It was clear she knew what we did in our jobs, but was not used to hearing the details. Tony continued his story.

"Emergency medical arrived, and they ran over to him. They took one look at him and slowed their pace. I've seen this before," Tony said. "This guy was in the death throes. He would be dead within a minute or two. The tourniquets were about the only things holding him together. When the Good Samaritan saw what he perceived to be a lack of interest from the emergency medical technicians, he started to yell, 'Would someone please help him over here?' I went to one knee next to him on the wet ground. It was still raining on all of us. I put my arm on his shoulder and leaned close to his ear. I told him it was a very good thing that he had done to stop and help. I told him there was nothing he could do for this man and that he would be dead shortly. Then I told him that when a person is dying, the hearing is usually the last thing to go. I thought it best for him not to die hearing the guy pleading to the EMTs for help. By the time I finished that sentence, the guy died.

"I helped the Good Samaritan to his feet and thanked him again. I then asked him if he had witnessed the accident, and he told me he had. I asked him to stick around because I needed to get his information and witness testimony for my report. That was my shitty day."

Gertie gave me a look like she was sorry she asked.

"Now tell us about your day," Tony said.

"Wong and I were on patrol in New Orleans East," I began. "We were driving south on Bullard Road, and there was a small truck in front of us. We came to the four-way stop at Morrison. The truck comes to a stop, and we were waiting behind him. Instead of proceeding through the four-way, he smashes his accelerator and proceeds to do one absurd burnout. The smoke completely enveloped our unit. You could not see past the hood of the car. He then goes through the intersection and proceeds at normal speed down Bullard.

"We get behind him and lit him up. He pulls over without any problem. Wong and I get out of our unit, and since Wong was driving, he walked up on the driver's side of the truck and tells the guy to get out. The driver was a kid, no more than seventeen years old. Wong asked him if he knew why we were stopping him. He just said, 'No, sir.' I could see the passenger was female, and I'm sure Wong spotted that too. The kid was probably trying to impress her.

"Wong said, 'I can tell you two things about yourself right off the bat. One, you're not the one paying for those tires. If you were paying your hard-earned money for tires, you would not be destroying them with burnouts. Two, you ain't the smartest kid in New Orleans East. You didn't even check your rearview mirror to see a marked police unit behind you at the Stop sign before you did the burnout.'

"'What do you think we should do with this guy?' Wong asked me so the kid could hear. 'Should we write him a very expensive ticket to teach him a lesson?' I said, 'Why? He ain't gonna pay it. His poor parents would have to pay it. Maybe we should just put them in the back of the car, lock up his truck, and take them home. I bet his folks take the truck away from him for a couple of weeks.' The kid looked at Wong with puppy dog 'oh please don't do that' eyes."

"So Wong told him, 'I tell you what. I'm going to give you a break. Do you think you've learned a lesson about doing stupid shit?' The kid said, 'Yes, sir, yes, sir. I've learned a lesson. I swear I won't be doing that again.' Wong motioned for the kid to leave. The kid wasted no time in doing so. I knew Wong wasn't going to write that kid. Everybody's guilty of doing some stupid shit now and again. He was just hoping that this scared that kid enough to think twice about it next time."

"I don't know if I could do your jobs," Gertie said. "I know you find it exciting, but the danger aspect would take the fun out of it for me. Don't you worry about getting hurt or worse every day?"

Tony looked at me for a moment. I just rolled my eyes and took another sip of my beer.

"To do this job well, you just can't think about that," he told her. "You put that aspect out of your mind. If you went to work every day worrying about if you would come home, you could never do the job, much less be any good at it. I'm not saying it doesn't enter your mind. Sometimes caution is a good thing. It keeps you on your toes. You're going to pay a lot more attention to what you're doing if you are working high up without a net," Tony said.

"He's been hurt a couple of times," Tony remarked, pointing his longneck bottle of Dixie at me.

"Not as bad as you," I said. "Tell Gert about the time you got shot, Tony."

"Wait, wait. You got shot?" Gertie asked. "How come I don't know anything about this?"

"Because I told him not to notify any of you guys when it happened. I was in the hospital already being inundated by state troopers, friends from Baton Rouge, press people, lions, tigers, and bears. My hospital room looked like a flower jungle. They all just wanted to give me their well wishes. I was touched and understood, but I needed rest to get better. So he kept the incident quiet around here just like I asked him to," Tony explained.

"How did it happen? When did it happen? You can tell me about it now, right?" Gert asked anxiously.

Tony looked at me and smiled. I stood up and began walking to the kitchen.

I said, "I better go get us new beers. This is a good story, and I don't want to stop in the middle of its telling."

"It was this past July," Tony started. "I was working a federal speeder grant on Interstate 10 between Baton Rouge and Lafayette. I was on I-10 East, driving a 1996 Chevy Camaro that was the fastest state police unit I've ever had. It had the police package in it. It did not have bar lights, but the rest of it was painted as a state police unit. A few days before, I had gotten into a chase with one of those fast Japanese motorcycles. I got it up to 155 miles an hour.

"I had already written twenty-two tickets that day. I got behind a white van with Texas license plates. It was all white except for blue lettering, signage for some sort of catering joint, on the sides and back. I turned my lights on and hit the siren once to alert him to pull over. He did not. Instead, he accelerated and started to gain speed. I was pulling him over for doing seventy-six in a sixty zone. He ran for a minute or so, but he was never going outrun the Camaro. I was on his tail the whole time."

Tony continued, "He exited at the Ramah off-ramp. He then stopped between the off-ramp and the cross street ahead. This is truly out in the middle of nowhere. If he had gone to the end of the off-ramp, across the road is a bait shop. Other than that, there is nothing at that exit. I pulled in behind the van and made my first tactical mistake of the day. Because the off-ramp road was narrow, I lined up straight behind him. I did not cock my unit to put the front end between him and me.

"I had called the troop and gave them my location, the description of the van, and the Texas license plate number. I got out of the Camaro and closed the door. Closing the door was my second mistake. I remember clearly how quiet it was. It was just a few minutes after high noon. *Damn it's quiet. It's too fucking quiet,* I thought to myself. I heard no birds chirping. I heard no bugs in the swampy area that surrounded us. As I observed the van, I had my ticket book in my left hand. I looked at the driver's side mirror, and I could see him looking at me. The driver's window was down. I thought this strange, since this was July in Louisiana and it was hot. I could clearly see the driver's face. He looked to be Hispanic, about eighteen years old. After this was over, I figured he had rolled down the window while stopping, hoping I would walk up and place myself in front of it. He probably had already decided what he was going to do before he pulled over.

"I motioned for him to exit the van. I watched the door open, and he stepped out. His head was down, and his shoulders were rounded. I used to think that this was the body language of someone who had been caught and had now given up. I walked to the front of my unit and had no cover. I was still sizing him up when he slowly raised his right hand, giving me the first glimpse that he had a weapon and was about to shoot me.

"When I saw the weapon coming up, a voice inside me screamed, *Move!* My mind started racing a million miles an hour. *Get out of the kill zone … Draw your weapon!* Then I saw the flash of the first round. The first shot missed me and cut into the driver's side fender of my unit. I could not back up. The average car is about seventeen feet long. If I tried to make a run for the back of the unit, I would still be in the same line of sight. He could shoot at me several times on the same line before I made it to relative safety. The tree line was too far away to make moving toward it an option." I lit a cigarette and looked over a Gert; she was mesmerized. Tony went on.

"I spun across the front of my vehicle, turning 360 degrees. I thought if I could only get to the passenger's side of my unit, I would have substantial metal between him and me. Then I could get to the back with cover and possibly return fire. As I executed my spin and moved across the front of my unit, he fired again. This time I wasn't so lucky. The second round hit just under my bulletproof vest on the right side. If you drop your arm to your side, the bullet entered just where your elbow would touch your body. I know it's cliché, but it felt like a hot poker had just stabbed me. It burned, and it hurt. I told myself, *Fuck, that bitch shot me.* I was still moving across the front of the unit when he fired again. This bullet struck me in the left thigh, four inches above the knee. I thought, *Motherfucker, he got me again! How many times is this fucker gonna hit me? If he has a 9 mm or some sort of automatic, he's got rounds beaucoup. He can shoot at me all day.*"

Tony continued, "When the third bullet hit just above my knee, it buckled, and I almost went down to the ground. The pain was incredible. I thought, *Is this it? Am I gonna die on the Ramah off-ramp on I-10 East?*" Tony looked at us and said, "This may sound crazy, but I felt my dead father's presence. For a fraction of a second I thought about just giving up. If I dropped, I'm sure he would have walked over and finished the job. I was not afraid. There wasn't any time to be. I guess that's when all my Marine Corps training and will to survive kicked in. I said to myself, *No. Fuck no. Not today. Push through the pain and fight!* He shot at me again, and at the time I thought he had hit me in the middle of my stomach. I thought, *Oh shit, this is bad. Now I'm gut shot.* It hit me then that I was in a dire situation. I wanted to kill that motherfucker with every fiber of my being. But I knew I had been wounded and wounded bad. I had to settle on survival as my first mission. Although I would have loved to put fifteen rounds into that sack of shit."

Tony explained, "It turned out that that fourth shot had missed me. I was not shot in the stomach after all. The unbelievable pain was only sympathetic pain transferred from the two wounds I'd already suffered. When I hit the passenger's side of the unit, I went to the ground. I shoulder-rolled all the way to the back. When I got to the trunk area of the police unit, I drew my weapon and got into a firing position on my back. My plan was if he walked around the back of the police car, I would unload on this shithead. I looked under my vehicle for feet. My head was on a swivel. I saw his feet, but they were not coming for me. He was running back to the van.

"I'm Italian," Tony said, looking at us. "The Italians and saints are like this." He held up his right hand with his index and middle fingers crossed. "I asked Saint Michael the archangel to give me one chance to kill this motherfucker. But that coward little shit jumped in the van and took off. It may sound fucked up, but I was thinking that my only chance of killing this bastard was driving off with that van."

"Why Saint Michael?" Gertie asked.

"'Cause Saint Michael the archangel is the patron saint of police officers. And you call yourself a Catholic high school girl?" I scolded.

"We never had to learn the patron saints," Gertie said. I could see everyone needed another beer. I got up and walked to the kitchen for three more as I knew the story well; I would not miss any details.

"I knew I had to call for help," Tony continued. "I was wearing a lapel mic and handset on my shoulder. I called to the troop and calmly told them I was shot and my location. I specifically attempted to be as calm as possible in my communications. I have heard officers screaming into the microphone and they have to repeat themselves several times because no one can understand them. I wanted to be short, clear, and concise. I knew then that help was a distance away, but at least they were coming.

"I'd had breakfast that morning with several Iberville Parish sheriff's

146

deputies. Iberville Parish has lots of black folks in its population, and so did the sheriff's office. I had many friends in the local parish departments. When we broke up that morning, one of the deputies who was a buddy of mine said if I needed anything out there to call him. He said, 'I'll be coming for ya.' He said it just like that, in the mid-Louisiana black dialect. I said thanks but didn't give it any more thought at the time."

Tony went on. "The whole shooting incident only took between five and seven seconds. With the van gone, I was now alone, just me and my intense pain. The adrenaline started to wear off. Now I started to worry. I had been shot in the thigh. The femoral artery runs through there. Had he cut it? Had he nicked it? If he had, I would never make it to a hospital. I became more and more angry at the fact that he had gotten away. If I was going to die from this, I certainly wanted to take that piece of debris with me.

"As the guy was shooting me, a vehicle had passed by. It did not stop. I have no issue with that. To intervene in that kind of encounter, you better be well trained and be armed to the teeth. If you're not, the best thing to do is call for help. That's what this person did," Tony said. "He drove to the bait shop that I mentioned and told the owner to call 911 and tell them a state trooper had been shot. The owner did so and then grabbed his hunting rifle and ran to me. He was the first person to arrive on the scene. I told him I was hurt and what the vehicle looked like. I told him that if that white van came back, just start shooting. This guy was scared to death, but it made me feel good that he put that aside and came to help me.

"With this guy and his rifle standing over me, I started to take a self-assessment of my injuries. I rolled my neck; everything felt fine. I ran my hands over my face and head; there was no blood. I could move my hands, I could move my arms, I could wiggle my toes; they all still worked. As I said, I thought I was gut shot. I looked for a hole in my stomach and I could not find one. That was a relief. Then I found the hole in my shirt and pulled the shirt over to see the hole in my side. 'Well that's one,' I said. I put my hand on my leg where the extreme pain was and felt around. My hand was bloody after I found the hole in my pants. I was then sure that I had been shot at least twice," Tony said, going through the act of pulling up his shirt and feeling his leg as we watched.

"I started to worry if I was bleeding out inside. I was in terrible pain. I did what I call a slosh test. I got on my back and rolled from side to side. I was listening for sloshing inside of my abdomen. I thought at the time it would indicate if I was bleeding badly inside. As I had no medical degree, I figured this test made sense. I could hear no sloshing. I was still on my back, and I wormed over to look at the spot where I had been lying. I was looking for lots of pooled blood. If I was bleeding out, it should be there. There was only a minimal amount of blood on the ground. Even if my tests were not medically sound, they did make me feel a lot better. I kept telling myself, *Fight, fight. Do not give in to the pain.* The poor guy watching over me must've thought I was going nuts," he said.

"The next person on the scene was the Iberville Parish sheriff's deputy who told me he would be coming for me that morning. He told me everything was gonna be okay and that EMS was on the way. I found out months later that seeing me in that condition played havoc with his psyche for a long time. I'm sure he was thinking, *There but for the grace of God go I. It could have been me!* After all, he did the same work that I was doing. Same interstate, same exits. He was totally familiar with this entire area. Sometimes, police life's a bitch. But I must say that his being there gave me great comfort. At least now there was someone there that I knew, a brother officer who cared about me. If I was going to die, I would be holding the hand of a friend.

"That deputy and my Good Samaritan stayed with me as we waited for medical help. I was lying on my back on the hot pavement. I thought, *Why couldn't this have happened in December?* Lots of things go through your mind at a time like that. How bad am I hurt inside? Why didn't I react better? Why didn't I use the unit as cover? Has writing thousands of tickets without incident made me complacent? I just tried to shut off, to put the questions out of my head. If I had done anything wrong, worrying about it now wasn't going to change a damn thing. I did think about my family. I knew they would be very worried when they got the news of what had happened to me. That just made me even more furious that I did not kill that motherfucker.

"He had stolen a lot from me and my family, the extent of which there was no way of knowing then as I lay there. While trying to get my mind off the pain, I hoped for a moment that if they did catch him that he would violently resist that a young asshole full of machismo would want to go down in a blaze. I knew all the state troopers between Mississippi and Texas. They would have happily obliged him."

Tony continued, "EMS finally showed up and started cutting off my clothes. They cut off my shirt and bulletproof vest. They cut off my pants and were about to cut off my boots. These were my favorite Danner boots. I told them to not cut the leather. Cut the laces. I want to keep these damn boots. They did as I requested, and I still have the boots today. They called for a life flight helicopter evacuation. Then they started discussing between themselves the best hospital to go to. Baton Rouge General or Our Lady of the Lake Hospital. They were well into this discussion when I asked them, 'Who fills holes the best?' They both agreed Our Lady of the Lake sees more shooting victims than Baton Rouge General. 'Then that's where I'm going,' I told them.

"As all this was happening, the other state troopers working that day started looking for the van. One of my pals who was too far away to offer assistance sat on the side of I-10 West, figuring that the suspect might try to run back to Texas. About forty-five minutes after I was shot, he spotted the van heading westbound. He called it in, advising all the other units that he had the suspect vehicle. He then did a felony stop on the van. Both driver and passenger were arrested without incident. I was disappointed to hear the latter, not because they got arrested without incident but because I wanted to see 'em dead," Tony said.

"I only found out later that the young guy who shot me was quite the little prick. He was from El Paso, Texas, and had been making his money as a male prostitute. He had gotten close to one of his usual Johns and somehow conned the guy into trusting him. He got the guy to bring him to his residence for a trick. After getting into the guy's house, he pulled a weapon on him. His intent all along was to rob him. He forced the guy to take a bottle of sleeping pills and down a half a bottle of vodka. His intent was to kill this guy and make it look like a suicide. When the guy passed out, he ransacked the home. He found the victim's .357 Magnum handgun. It was a Colt Python, a very valuable weapon. The victim liked it so much that he had his name engraved on it—a fact that the little asshole didn't notice. When he was arrested after shooting me, he had dumped the spent shells but kept the gun as a trophy. The aggravated burglary victim did not die. He got to the hospital just in time. But this little shit now faced two counts of attempted murder."

"Where is he now?" Gert asked.

"Oh, he's in fuckin' jail," Tony said angrily. "The jury had been picked and seated. We were moments away from starting the trial. Then that little pissant tells his lawyer he wants to plead out. This was in Iberville Parish, Louisiana. The jury was made up of five farmers and seven older black ladies. You should've seen the way they all were looking at him. They knew why they were there and what kind of trial this was. They were not going to leave an ounce of meat on his bones. He must've seen those icy stares too. As he started shittin' his pants, that little coward pled out. During the victim impact statement, right before he got sentenced, I got a chance to talk directly to him in open court, before God and everyone. I told him, 'I don't regret the fact that you shot me. My only regret is that I did not get the opportunity to kill you!' That little asshole got forty-five years. Not enough as far as I'm concerned," Tony concluded.

"How can you guys do that shit?" Gertie asked. "It's all bad. You're swimming in the bottom of the barrel of humanity."

"No, you guys never hear about the good stuff. You guys only get the stories about the funny, the macabre, the gut-wrenching. You guys never hear the stories about the people helped, tragedies avoided, and lives saved. Because the good isn't interesting. Nobody wants to hear boring stories with happy endings. They only want adrenaline, fireworks, blood, and guts," Tony said regretfully. "I know that clown over there, he tells you tons of stories," he said, motioning to me.

"How long have you known him?" Tony asked Gert. "Has he ever told you what that little metal in that frame on the wall is? That's the New Orleans Police Department's Class B Medal of Merit, the second highest award you can get on the police department. He didn't tell you the story behind that, did he? That's because it wasn't funny. It wasn't entertaining. It was just him and his partner going above and beyond. I will bet you ninety-five dollars he never told you anything about that, did he, Gert?"

"No. Until you pointed it out, I never noticed it," Gert said.

"My point exactly. Everybody wants to hear amusing stories. He likes to tell funny stories; so do I. You said you would never do this job. That's because you never hear all the good things. Because the bad things are so very interesting. He got that because he and his then partner Duffy pulled two women out of a burning car after an accident occurred right in front of them. The women were badly hurt and semiconscious from the accident. They saved their lives that night," Tony said.

"But you never hear those stories. You only hear the sad or amusing tales of this job. I know that cretin; he is never going to tell you a story that makes himself look good. He is gonna only tell you stories that will entertain you. He will always sell himself short. That is the personality trait I met in high school. And that is the personality trait I cherish today. He is one of my very best friends. He is always asking, 'What can I do for you?' I have never known him to be about himself," Tony said.

"Don't believe any of that shit, Gert," I said. "I got that medal outta one of them claw machines at Pontchartrain Beach. It was around the neck of a stuffed turtle. The little bitch I was with didn't like turtles. So screw her … I kept the medal," I said, desperately trying to change the subject.

"If you got it out of a dumb machine, why would it be framed on your wall?" Gertie asked.

"'Cause the damned bedroom camera malfunctioned!" I insisted. "I would have a whole mural of that turtle-hating bitch and my incredible Kama Sutra gymnastics poses lining that hallway if my plans would have come to fruition!"

"What was her name?" Tony asked.

"Aphrodite," I replied.

"I rest my case," Tony said.

CHAPTER TWELVE

Politicking with Sergeant Kelly paid off. I was soon transferred to the special operations division, special weapons and tactics (SWAT) tactical platoon two. I was transferred first without Wong. Kelly told me to wait and that Wong would be transferred on the next list. He said he had worked that out and could not take both of us at the same time; there were issues that he could not let me in on. But he assured me it was going to happen. All these years later, I can tell you that Gerry Kelly never told me anything that he was going to do that did not happen. Gerry was a man of his word, and he kept it. Wong was transferred on the very next Friday.

Besides the mounted division, this was my first taste of law enforcement on a citywide level and not confined to the seventh district. The special operations division was in the complex on Bayou Saint John on Moss Street. We shared the complex with emergency medical services and the traffic division. I still remember early mornings when the personnel from EMS placed the spine boards and other equipment from the emergency units against a brick wall and hosed them off to clean them from the bloodshed of the night before. Tactical platoon one and tactical platoon two were housed in the tactical unit's offices. Our working hours were from 10:00 a.m. to 6:00 p.m. and 6:00 p.m. to 2:00 a.m. If a SWAT call for service happened after 2:00 a.m., the 10:00 a.m. to 6:00 p.m. shift would be called out.

We had a good, although diverse, group that made up our platoon. There was Sam; Bubba; John Frost, who I mentioned earlier in the story about how he jumped into the Industrial Canal to save Johnathan;

Johnny's partner, Dennis Bond, Debbie, Ben, Sam, Harold, Fitz, Conrad, Ronald, and Haydel. We were a very close group. Our platoon sergeant was Gerry Kelly, who was backed up by Buddy, the other sergeant on our platoon.

The platoon had a ritual of always meeting for breakfast or dinner, depending on the shift, at the Rocksford Grill on Saint Charles Avenue. Sam, Ronald, and Haydel, the three black officers on our platoon, refused to eat there. It was not a white-and-black thing. I think you will understand why after I give you a little more in-depth information about the Rocksford. The Rocksford Grill was a hotel restaurant for the Rocksford Hotel. It was opened in 1936 and was a twenty-four-hour grill. I don't think they had cleaned anything since 1936. It was located very near the corners of Camp and Julia Streets.

In the mid-eighties, Camp and Julia was skid row ground zero. How the Rocksford was never closed by the Louisiana Department of Health, I will never know. All kinds of people ate there, from all walks of life, all hours of the day or night. A bum could be sitting on a stool at the bar next to a guy in a tuxedo and you wouldn't even have thought it strange.

As you walked in, there were about twenty tables in the main room, which also had a long bar to serve customers. Behind that was the kitchen. The cooks worked nonstop. The place was always crowded with people who didn't care what it looked like because they liked the food.

Kevin was our favorite cook. The only problem is, like most of the cooks, Kevin and the law did not see eye to eye. I think he was doing life sixty to ninety days at a time. Every time we came in, we would ask if Kevin was back. The waitresses who were closer to him would tell us how many days until his return. When Kevin was back, it was truly a holiday, for as long as he stayed out of trouble and was sober.

Kevin knew us all well. We would exchange waves and give Kevin the high sign. When we ordered a bacon and cheese omelet, it would have a half pound of bacon, about six eggs, and a quarter wheel of cheese. The plate would take two waitresses to carry it to our table. When Kevin was cooking at the bird, we ate like kings. We were always led to an overflow backroom, away from the main dining room, separated from the main crowd.

There were a couple of other small problems with the Rocksford

Grill. It was infested with German roaches, but you just had to get over that. At least you weren't staying in the hotel, where they would crawl all over you at night. A lot of European backpacking types stayed there. I guess because it was a multistory flophouse. They could stay there for next to nothing. I'm sure many of them checked in and when they turned on the lights in their room had second thoughts. But they could not find a room anywhere in central New Orleans for that kind of price.

When I first got to SWAT and was introduced to the Rocksford, we were led to our usual back room. I remember that it had four four-man tables and two two-man tables. In the corner on the back left wall, there was a square pat of butter sticking to the wall at about eye level. I spent the next three years in SWAT, and I saw that pat of butter migrate from eye level to about four inches above the floor molding. It naturally moved faster in the summer and slower in the winter. I can't tell you if anyone saw it but us. But no one ever thought to remove it. I guess it was like the hourglass in the *Wizard of Oz*—an incarnation of time and destiny. Now you know why Ronald, Sam, and Haydel refused to eat there.

I enjoyed my time on the SWAT unit. After some initial training and some specialized weapons training, we were good to go. Our job was to come to work, hold roll call, eat at the Rocksford, and then hit the streets. The entire city was our hunting ground. We concentrated on felony arrests. Narcotics, weapons, and fugitives were our main sources of arrests.

Later in my law enforcement career, when I became a federal agent, I used a line that would crush any disagreement over experience with any federal agent I worked with. I would tell them, "The last month I served on the tactical unit of the New Orleans Police Department, I made thirty-two felony arrests." Most federal agents don't make thirty of their own arrests in their entire careers.

My primary job on a SWAT call for service was as one of a four-member assault team. I carried a Remington 870 shotgun as my main SWAT weapon. It had an extended magazine to accommodate more shells. The stock had also been modified with a flashlight. Wong carried a Heckler & Koch 9 mm MP5 submachine gun. He nicknamed it the crime stopper. The MP-5 was a nice weapon, but my 12-gauge was a devastating one. It had incredible knockdown power, and the slugs could go through doors or walls if need be. You must remember that this was 1985. We did not have the kind of gear that special operators utilize today. The evolution of tactics has come a long way in the last thirty years.

Every other Thursday was a SWAT training day. We trained in all the aspects of tactical special operations. After I gained more experience, I was often picked to play the bad guy in these training scenarios because I gave all of them, including the hostage negotiators, a run for their money. Sam and Debbie were the two hostage negotiators. It was the crappiest job on the SWAT team. It came with all the obvious problems of trying to negotiate with desperate and sometimes crazy individuals, and they were responsible for completing the written report of the incident. That's why when Kelly told me I had to be trained as a negotiator, I went kicking and screaming. I begged him not to do me like that, but he just told me he thought I would be good at it, and we had to have someone qualified to do it if Sam or Debbie wasn't there.

Thank God that for most SWAT rolls Sam and Debbie were there. But there was one SWAT call when they were absent. I think one was sick and the other was on vacation. I knew I had been handed the shit stick without anyone having to tell me. Instead of changing into my SWAT gear, I went to the armory and got a negotiator's jacket and my ballistics vest. There was no use whining about it. Somebody had to do it, and this time it was going to be me. I had completed all the necessary negotiator's training and was now a certified hostage negotiator. It wasn't the actual negotiations with the suspect that concerned me. Hell, I knew I would be good at that. I dreaded the complicated report that would be my responsibility to write. I hated writing reports.

I guess the Lord was just testing me, because just as we prepared to leave the compound, they called from the scene and told us we were no longer needed and that the individual had given up. As I went back to the armory to hang up the negotiators jacket, Kelly met me.

"I'm really proud of you," he said. "You didn't cry or bitch. You knew what needed to be done, and you did it. That's the kind of team guy I knew you were."

That made me feel good. And, considering I did not know how to type then, not having to write a complex SWAT report made me feel even better.

SWAT calls were so much better in the winter. The cooler temperatures made it easier to tolerate, considering all of our tactical gear. The helmet, balaclava, goggles, undershirt, ballistics armor, and heavy black battle dress utility boots, as well as an outer utility vest full of extra magazines and communication equipment, were so much more comfortable in cool temperatures. That said, it was a living hell when it was ninety degrees.

We had a SWAT roll in midsummer across the river in the fourth district. Some nut had tried to rob an insurance company office. Many criminals are not very bright. These offices do clerical work. They're not chock-full of cash. He attempted to rob it all the same. During the robbery, all the office personnel managed to escape the building. But they all swore, as in so very many instances, that the perpetrator was still inside. We set up a tactical perimeter around the office front at about two o'clock in the afternoon in ninety-five-degree heat. Then we started our fruitless attempts to make contact and negotiate with an empty building. Wong and I were assigned to cover the front of the structure.

Several vehicles were still in the parking lot because everyone in the building had run away in haste. Wong and I low-crawled to the closest vehicles that afforded us observation and cover of the front entrance. I was on the right side of the parking lot and Wong was on the left side.

We lay in a prone position with our weapon sight fixed on on the front door, utilizing the vehicle's front wheels for cover. The sun was shining down and baking us. You could have probably fried an egg on that concrete. We were both hot as hell. I was concentrating very hard on the front door when I noticed an officer standing behind me. He seemed oblivious to any tactical threat mitigation. He then addressed me.

"Man, you gotta be hot as hell down there," the fourth district officer said.

He was standing in the open just behind me. It was Glenn Smith. Glenn Smith, the officer who got stabbed in the ear with a pen by a meter maid he was arguing with for writing a parking ticket on a marked New Orleans Police unit parked in a law enforcement zone.

I said, "Yes, I'm dying out here."

Unable to recognize me in my SWAT uniform, he said, "Dave, is that you?"

I said, "Yeah, Glenn, it's me." I had known Glenn since I started as a cop. He and I had gone to the academy together.

"You want me to get you a Coke?" he asked.

"Man, that would be great," I replied.

He walked off like he was sauntering at a parish fair. He soon returned with a cold Coke and bent down and gave it to me. I took a great big swig. Then I looked over at Wong, who was no longer covering the front door but looking at me and panting like an overheated Rottweiler. I then removed my helmet and rubbed the cold Coke on my forehead.

"Is that Wong over there?" Smith asked.

"Yeah, that's Wong," I said.

He stood back up and walked over to Wong. I could hear them talking, and then he walked off. He soon returned with a cold Coke for Wong too.

"They're getting pissed at me for going back and forth," he told Wong. "I guess they better figure out that the place is empty before you guys die of heat exhaustion."

Smith strolled out of the forward perimeter and back to the rear area. Thank God they decided to assault the building twenty minutes later only to find it empty, just as Glenn Smith and all of us had figured all along.

As I have previously mentioned, John Frost was assigned to SWAT tactical platoon two with Wong and me. Johnny Frost was a great guy. He had a big heart and would help anybody. John was too smart for his own good sometimes. I don't know how much formal education he had, but it seemed like he knew something about everything. He was a big guy, about six foot four and 240 pounds. He was as strong as an ox. His grip could easily break bones in your hand. He wore thick black glasses that gave the mistaken impression that he was a big doofus. He was not, but Johnny did have bad luck. Whenever his bad luck put him in an unfortunate situation, I was always there to aggravate the living shit out of him. That's how I know he was such a nice guy. On countless occasions I'm sure he considered beating me to death. We called him Big Moe after Moe Howard of the Three Stooges.

As I said, Moe was very smart. Gerry Kelly once told me a story about him and one of the bomb squad technicians. Johnny and the technician were talking shop, even though Johnny was not on the bomb squad and had no formal bomb training. He challenged the technician that he could build a device that the technician could not defeat.

About a week after issuing the challenge, John brought in his device. Kelly said he had rigged the device with a lightbulb. If the lightbulb lit up, that would indicate that the device had gone off and your day was over. Their bet was that the tech had to disarm it manually, not blow it in place, which would have been the preferred fix. The technician, whose name I shall not mention, looked Moe's box over for quite a while before coming up with a plan of action. He began his attempt and the light came on within five seconds.

As I said, every other Thursday was a SWAT training day. We did classroom and physical scenarios. In the mid-1980s, the New Orleans Police Department did not use wax bullets or marking cartridges in specialized force-on-force training. I don't know if they were too cheap to buy them or if they were not available then. Wax bullets had been around a long time. They were used in different applications by illusionists and magicians, as well as for other uses. But I do not think they were widely available as training aids. So Big Moe figured he would spice up training day by making some at home.

Wax bullets are relatively easy to make. I am not going into the recipe; someone somewhere might attempt to do it and screw up, with possibly deadly side effects. One should never point a loaded gun at anything they do not have specific intent to kill. We always exercised great care when using these sorts of tools.

During training, a training officer was always on the scene, and all weapons and ammunition were visually inspected before and after the training scenarios. Live ammunition was downloaded and removed from all weapons, storage vests, and ammo pouches. This ammunition was relocated to a separate place, away from the training area, before the commencement of any training that utilized these types of aids.

Moe was right; it did add a realistic dimension to the training. When a wax bullet hit you, it stung like hell. We wore ballistic helmets, gloves, vests, and goggles, but if one hit you anywhere, you knew it.

On one particular training day, it was very hot and the wax had started to melt in the practice ammunition, so we decided to call it a day. Moe took one of the wax shells and put it in front of the air conditioner in the office. He figured he would let it stay there long enough to solidify, enough to pay me back for some of the aggravation I had been giving him. When we ended our training debrief, we had not yet changed out of our SWAT gear, so I still had my heavy boots on when he shot me in the foot.

The air conditioner had done its job. It had solidified all right; it was solid as a rock. That thing stung the shit out of me. He could tell immediately by everyone's reaction, as well as my own, that he had possibly gone too far. There were no training personnel or rank in the room, which was a good thing because they probably would have had to take some sort of action against Johnny. He apologized to me profusely and explained that he had not realized the wax had gotten that hard.

I pulled off my boot and sock and inspected the area. It had not broken the skin. As I was rubbing my foot, I told Moe no worries. He had made a mistake, and it was over. When everyone present realized that I was not hurt, it was then okay for them to laugh at me. I didn't even try to think of a comeback. I'd been messing with Big Moe so much and for so long that I'm was sure I deserved this and a lot more.

Life in the tactical unit was quite different from anywhere else I had worked in the police department. When we were not SWAT training, we were out on the street in two-man units. Sometimes we would work as two teams if we were going to a high-crime area. We could work anywhere in the city; that was entirely up to us. We might be uptown, in the French Quarter, in New Orleans East, or in the Lower Ninth Ward. We had a lot of freedom, but we were expected to produce. We mostly worked in uniform, but our units were unmarked. I would like to take full credit, but catching bad guys in the bad areas of New Orleans wasn't that hard to do.

Sometimes during large events hosted by the City of New Orleans, we were assigned perimeter security duties. The events included things like the annual Jazz and Heritage Festival, Saints games, or the NCAA

Final Four basketball tournament. Many events choose New Orleans as a venue. The city is nationally known as a place to have a good time. You would be surprised to learn just how many events and conventions are held in the city each year.

The tactical unit patrolled the outer areas of these events, protecting people walking back to their cars or leaving the event and going to the French Quarter. It was easy to discern the sheep walking to their vehicles from the wolf loitering in the area for no apparent reason.

B. J. and I were on such an assignment for a New Orleans Saints NFL game. It was around halftime, and things around the outer area were quiet. We were parked in an area several blocks south of the Superdome. The day was comfortable, and we had our windows rolled down. It was early afternoon, and we had not eaten lunch yet. We were trying to decide where to go when we heard several gunshots close by. We looked at each other, knowing lunch was probably going to be delayed. Within a minute, the radio sounded the alarm of a priority call, a shooting, and the location. Because we were not members of that district and they had no knowledge that we were even in their area, it was not our responsibility to answer the call. But this shooting was only about two blocks from our location, so we started that way.

As luck would have it, we were the first ones on the scene. The location was a high-rise public housing complex. Part of the Melpomene Projects, its two high-rise buildings were twelve stories tall. It was also one of the most dangerous housing projects in uptown New Orleans, along with the Magnolia and Calliope Projects.

There was a breezeway between the two high-rise buildings. This opened to a huge courtyard area at the rear. A crowd had gathered around a male subject on the ground. While still under the protection of the breezeway, we observed a loaded pair of Pampers that had been thrown from a much higher floor strike a male teenager in the crowd with a loud smack. The shit bomb exploded on impact. The crowd roared with laughter, but the target did not appreciate the humor and screamed and cursed. Our victim was far enough away from the buildings to hamper accurate fire of any additional baby crap missiles.

We quickly jogged to the victim, running from under the breezeway cover to traverse the danger zone. Upon getting to the victim, we found him lying on the ground, quite conscious, with a gunshot wound to his buttocks.

"You want to tell me what happened?" I asked him.

"No," he replied.

"Do you want me to tell you what happened?" I asked.

He gave me a confused look. "Okay, you tell me what happened," he said.

"You went to see someone up there," I began. "When you were coming or when you were leaving, you ran into little Dukey. You and Dukey been having a humbug. You turned ass and ran, with Dukey shooting at you from behind. Something like that?"

"Yeah, something like that," he admitted.

"You want to tell me who he is so I can arrest him for you?" I asked.

"No, I'm gonna take care of it when I get out," he said.

"I don't think you understand me. You ain't gittin' out. He killed ya."

"No, I'll be okay," he said.

"No, you ain't. If you tell me who he is, I can arrest him for killing ya."

"Thanks, Officer, but I got it," he said.

Just then, the emergency unit personnel showed up. They gave him a quick once-over and threw him on a stretcher. As they were rushing him to the emergency unit, I asked him one more time for the name. He again refused to give it to me. About fifteen minutes later he was dead.

Old movies depict a gunshot wound to the ass as a comical injury. It is anything but. Major arteries run through the buttocks. A gunshot wound or deep stab wound in that area can easily be fatal. If one of the arteries is nicked or severed, the result can be catastrophic. These arteries are located deep inside the muscle, making them surgically difficult to get to. I had not been playing with that victim. I knew the odds and was attempting to use the short time we had to make an identification of the person who shot him. I was aware how serious a wound in that area could be. To my knowledge, no one was ever identified or arrested for that murder.

Working in SWAT was not all serious incidents like that shooting. We tried to have as much fun as possible between those kinds of events. One of those times occurred when Wong and I were working the second shift on the tactical platoon, 6:00 p.m. to 2:00 a.m. We had broken up the night before about two thirty. We were sitting around the office the next evening, waiting for Kelly to come out and hold roll call. Big Moe arrived last. Big Moe drove a fire-engine-red Chevrolet dooley truck. We all called it the Coke truck because if it had Coca-Cola logos on it. You would never be able to tell from the color that it was not an official Coca-Cola vehicle. Moe came in and plopped down on the couch under the air conditioner. He looked upset about something. As we bantered back and forth. Moe sat there in silence.

Finally, Big Moe spoke up. Everyone on the platoon was present when he recounted a distressing story. Moe said he had left with the rest of us the night before and headed home. He took his usual route and got on Interstate 10. He had gone about five miles when another driver pulled alongside him waving and beeping his horn. He was attempting to get Moe to pull over. Moe complied with the request. He said the other driver was really pissed off. Moe was taken completely off guard.

The driver told Moe that he'd been following behind him at highway speed when a huge banner came from under Moe's truck and struck his vehicle. He said it was a Coca-Cola banner about twelve feet long and that one of the steel grommets had cracked his windshield. Moe said the guy started to settle down a little. I guess it might have been because of the fact that Big Moe was in uniform and towered over the guy. Moe told him he must have kicked it up off the road. He explained to the guy that he hadn't seen anything in the road and hadn't run over any obstacles.

Moe told us the whole damn thing was a mystery. He said that, at the time, he had no reason to doubt the guy. The guy acted like everything he said was true. Though the supposed banner was a mile back and Moe said he had not seen it, he had no reason to doubt the guy. He said the guy stormed back to his vehicle and took off.

As Big Moe recounted the story, everyone was laughing. But no one more than Bubba. Bubba was killing himself laughing so hard. When Big Moe saw how much Bubba was laughing and enjoying the story, he started laughing along with him. When the story was over we all thought this could only happen to Big Moe. Then Kelly came out, and we held roll call for the evening.

When we broke up, we all went downstairs and walked to our vehicles. Bubba quietly asked B. J. and me to hang around as we watched

Moe and Dennis drive off. Then Bubba started laughing uncontrollably again. Bubba confessed to us that he had gotten the Coca-Cola banner from a detail on Bourbon Street. He said before we broke up the night before, he had tied it underneath Moe's truck. He'd wanted Moe to have a real Coke truck. He had not anticipated what ended up happening. He'd just been messing with Moe.

We decided as a group that it was best not to advise Moe of the story behind the banner. It would only serve to piss him off. I guess Bubba was lucky that he got away without Moe finding out it had been him. Moe would have been determined to get his revenge, and Bubba would certainly have been in peril.

# CHAPTER THIRTEEN

Gert and I had been living together for a couple of months. It was fun. However, there were some difficult times. Like when she would have Kyle come by or when she would have people over who I did not know. On these occasions, I felt like a third wheel. But all in all, it was working out good. It was nice to come home to someone. It was very comforting to have someone else in the house, someone to talk to over dinner, someone to cook for who really appreciated it, someone to have a beer with at the end of the night.

I was working the tactical unit shift of 6:00 p.m. to 2:00 a.m. Gert was usually asleep by the time I got home. So one night when I got to the house at about a quarter after two and found it dark, I was not surprised. As I stepped inside and secured the front door behind me, I saw Gert was sitting on the couch with just a single candle lighting the room.

"What are you still doing awake? It's late," I said.

"I couldn't sleep." She sniffled.

This was my first indication that she had been crying. I took off my gun belt and set it on the dining room table. I then sat on the loveseat and put my feet up on the coffee table.

"What's the matter, Gert?" I asked.

"I had a big fight with Kyle," she replied.

"Did you guys break up?"

"I really don't know," she said. Her voice broke a little when she answered.

"What did you guys fight about?" I asked.

"We're not going to talk about that, Dave," she said.

I could tell by the way she said it that I had better not ask any more. The sign said bridge out, so I figured it best to just turn around.

We sat there looking at each other in silence for a while. Then I got up and walked in the dark to the kitchen. I asked if she wanted me to get her beer.

"No, make me a gin and tonic, please."

I always kept hard liquor in the house. I had whiskey, gin, vodka, tequila, and all the mixers. But I kept it on hand mostly for company. I only drank the hard stuff on occasion. It wouldn't be until many years in the future that that monkey climbed on my back. But since I was making her a gin and tonic, I figured I would have one too. I always drank Bombay Gin. It had been my favorite since I was about fifteen years old. Maybe it was the picture of England's <u>Q</u>ueen Victoria on the bottle that gave it its classical mystique for me. I made two stiff ones and brought them out to the front room.

I set one in front of Gert as she dabbed her eyes with a Kleenex. I then took my position again on the loveseat.

"Damn, that's strong," she said. "But I guess that's just what I need."

They were strong, but I had never been accused of making light drinks.

"Whatever it is, Gert, it's gonna work out," I told her.

"I know," she said. "But it doesn't stop it from hurting now."

"Things always seem to look better in the light of the morning," I said.

"Yes, maybe so. We'll just see tomorrow." She sighed heavily.

We sat silently in the dark over that drink and into the next.

"Can I say something that's been on my mind for a long time?" she asked.

"Sure, kiddo. You can tell me anything."

"You might get mad," she warned.

"I don't get mad, Gert. I just seethe quietly inside, plotting revenge," I said.

"I know you're joking, but I am trying to be serious," she admonished.

"I'm sorry. What's on your mind?" I said.

"I think I know you pretty well," she started. "You say a lot of stuff about a lot of things, but you never say anything about yourself. You give a lot of sage advice to friends in need, but you never ask for any from anyone. You never ask for any kind of help. Sometimes when I look at you, you seem thousands of miles away. It's those times when I feel like I'm only talking to the answering machine.

"I remember what you were like as a kid. I also remember when you first joined the police force. You were a different person. Please don't take this wrong, but now you seem so sad. Your relationships never seem to work out. Sometimes I think you sabotage them because you don't want anyone to get close.

"I think I know you better than anyone else. It hurts me to see you that way. I could kick myself because I have always had a love for you. You were my first love. I think I was yours too. You were older than me. You seemed more mature than most guys your age back then. I'm sure you felt love differently from the younger me. When we came of age, old enough to really love each other, I wanted a new love, not an old reliable true love."

She continued, "I remember your attempts at wooing me my senior year of high school. You even kept it up several years after. But I always kept you at arm's length. You were already mine, at least in my thoughts. You were not a challenge for me. I wanted to capture and break my own wild mustang, not sit on the porch with my loyal and faithful dog. I had grown accustomed to you loving me. I took it for granted. How stupid we are when we are young.

"That night on the phone, when I was talking to you like you were just one of my girlfriends, I told you I had lost my virginity to someone I hardly knew. Your silence spoke volumes. I did not know it then, but I had driven you away forever, the only person who had unconditionally loved me as a friend, as a teenager, and into adulthood. I know that forever changed us. You became distant, and then you dropped off the map for a long time until we met again at the Dreux.

"I got mad the first time I went there. Barry informed me that you were a regular. He warned me that night. He told me if I hurt you in any way, I would never be welcome at the Dreux again. I was really taken aback. I did not know Barry knew anything about us. But Barry is a lifelong friend of yours. Now, these many years later, I know Barry is so much more. I swear he can see into your soul, as long as you pay your tab."

She stopped talking and just looked at me. I did not know what to say. What could I say? She was right in everything she had told me. This was the first time I realized that she had been aware of everything that happened and how it made me feel, how she had broken my heart so long ago.

"Well, Gert, no good in thinking about those things now," I said quietly. "I don't want to dig up that pain again. It's getting late, and we should probably be getting ready for bed."

I drank the rest of my drink and set the glass down gently. Gertie blew out the candle but did not get off the couch.

"Don't worry yourself about it, Gert. Life isn't fair. Take it from me. That is one undeniable truth that I have learned the hard way," I said in a hushed voice. Then I stood up and walked into the dining room to pick up my gun belt and put it over my shoulder.

I heard her whisper, "I am so sorry, Dave."

I didn't say anything back. I just walked to my bedroom with what felt like a golf ball in my throat.

The next morning, she acted like nothing had happened. I never brought it up again. Nothing could be changed. The past was nobody's fault. Life plays out and you make your choices as you go along. We all wished we could go back in time and change some of the choices we made in our youths or in haste. But that was never going to happen, not in this life. The only thing we could do was try to learn from the past, so we didn't repeat the same mistakes.

It helps me to remember, even now, that no matter how bad things get, there is always somebody out there suffering ten times more than me. In any personal suffering, there are always things to be thankful for. I thank God every day for all the blessings he has bestowed upon me, my family, and my friends. Even in the worst of times, if you take a moment and reflect, things could be a lot worse. Just ask God for the strength and courage to push through those times, but always remember to include those going through much worse suffering in your prayers.

I was always very thankful of the blessings I had, especially my friends. Until I got to the SWAT team, I had liked many of the people I had worked with. But the people I worked with in SWAT became very close friends. We had parties and even went on canoeing trips together. We were a very tightknit group. I guess when you're working in very high-stress environments, you tend to be close with your comrades. I have seen every one of them on dangerous SWAT rolls. They were all professional, well-trained tactical officers. You never had to worry because they were going to be there with you through thick and thin no matter what.

One Sunday we had just broken up from a huge meal at the Rocksford. Wong and I decided we would cruise around the central business district looking for any criminal activity. We really did not expect to find any on a Sunday afternoon. As we passed the LL&E tower, a thirty-six-story office building at 909 Poydras, we found some. We observed a male subject take a heavy metal bench and smash it through a plate glass window in the building's foyer. The subject then leapt into the building and out of sight. Wong and I quickly made a U-turn and pulled up in front of the building. We made a call to other SWAT units who were still in the area, advising them of our situation. Dennis Bond and Big Moe, who had been with us at the Rocksford, radioed that they were only moments away.

Wong and I entered through the same smashed glass window. The subject had cut himself upon entering, and there was a blood trail on the floor. Since the elevators were turned off, the subject had entered a stairwell. There was blood on the handle of the door, so it was safe to assume he had gone in. We found the blood trail again in the stairwell, leading up. As we were in pursuit, we found blood on the door leading out of the stairwell on each landing. The subject was trying each door, and when he found it locked, he continued his ascent. I heard Dennis and John enter the stairwell and call up to ask what floor we were on. We called down our location and pressed on.

I was an avid runner at that time. I ran three miles a day, five days a week. Wong was not into cardiovascular training and began to lose steam around the eighteenth floor.

"Go," he told me. "I'm right behind you."

I made a little time on Wong and reached the thirtieth floor. There was no blood trail on the landing and no blood on the door handle. I called down to Wong that the suspect had made entry on the twenty-ninth floor. We called down to Dennis and Johnny that we were going in behind him.

When we made entry, we found ourselves in a large office area with many desks. The desks were close enough together that you get on top of one and jump from one to another. At the far end of this large room, we spotted the suspect. He had a small copy machine over his head and was attempting to smash out the window. We were on the twenty-ninth floor. I seriously doubted his ability to fly, so I needed to reach him posthaste.

I jumped up on the nearest desk and then leapt from desk to desk in a straight line toward him. When he saw me coming, he stopped smashing the copier against the window and was getting ready to throw it at me. As I reached him, I simultaneously pushed the copier he was holding above his head and struck him with one punch. He dropped the copier and went down. By that time, Dennis and Moe had reached us. We wrestled a bit with him until we could get him handcuffed.

We then waited for an emergency unit and representatives from the office space to arrive. After we got him handcuffed, he began to settle down. This man was in good shape, clean-cut, and decently dressed. I asked him what he had planned on doing if he had smashed out the window. He told me he really could not say. Then he told us a story that was very surprising.

He told us he was in the French Quarter because he was staying at one of the major hotels. He had stopped in New Orleans overnight on a trip to Pensacola, Florida. He was driving there to begin navy flight school. He was an active duty member of the US Navy. He said he had stopped at a famous New Orleans bar. He had one large drink. The next thing he knew, he was receiving a punch in the face from me. He said the rest was basically a blank. Emergency medical showed up and checked him over. The cuts he had received going through the window were superficial. He was taken to the hospital, treated, and then brought to central lockup. There he was booked on several charges. The incident was over as far as we were concerned.

About two weeks later, several tactical team members were patrolling the French Quarter. A call came out that a naked man had somehow gotten to the top of a French Quarter structure and smashed an upper window of the Cabildo Museum next to the Saint Louis Cathedral. He went through the window and into the museum. First district officers had followed and captured him.

It turned out that he was a salesman in town for a convention. He had no criminal record. He had no history of mental illness. He was just a typical tourist. The strange thing was that he had just had a drink at that same bar that the navy officer had been drinking at before his high-rise rampage. It seemed that these two men might have been victims themselves. Someone had spiked their drinks with some unknown powerful drug, perhaps to render them helpless to an impending assault or robbery. It was too much of a coincidence not to take some sort of action.

We got ahold of the district attorney's office and advised them of our suspicions and findings in these two events. It would have been tragic to destroy the reputations and future careers of a navy pilot and an innocent salesman. They had been under the influence of some unknown substance when they acted as they did. They had not ingested that substance willingly or knowingly. It was our opinion that the charges on the two men should be dropped. The DA's office did indeed drop the charges. I believe the first district follow-up unit paid a call to the bar and made them aware of the two events. They could instruct their personnel to be on the lookout for suspicious persons near other patrons' drinks.

As my time on tactical platoon two increased, so did my fondness for the personnel there. I could not have asked for a better group of people to work with. As I said before, our personalities were diverse, but everyone got along well.

Every couple of months on a Saturday of our working weekend, we had a potluck lunch at the office. We called it a pig out. Everyone brought a dish. Appetizers, entrées, desserts, and drinks were divided up according to who could and could not cook. Those who could cook were assigned entrées and desserts. Those who could cook a bit were in charge of appetizers. Those who lived by themselves and ate only TV dinners oversaw the sodas and iced tea.

These pig outs were large affairs with plenty of food. Since we were all native New Orleanians, the menu often reflected the diverse culture of the city with Creole, Soul, French, and Spanish dishes. There is one thing that has always stood out for me about New Orleans. The food here is fantastic. I do take issue with some of these new metropolitan restaurants popping up in the city. The millennials seem to favor them. I am a little concerned for the culinary future. Many of these millennials came after Hurricane Katrina. I am skeptical that they have even tried or know of the historical foods of New Orleans. Yogurt cucumber mint chutney over unknown whitefish sitting on a bed of sautéed asparagus is not New Orleans. In the past, there were very few bad restaurants. New Orleanians would not suffer them. They would close within a year. Now, with the new influx of clueless transplants, I have my doubts.

At the pig outs, we ate like royalty. Overindulgence was the practice of the day. Of course, a couple of times we paid for it. After one such pig out on a summer holiday weekend, we got the call to assist on a drowning in City Park. Remember that the SWAT complex was on Moss Street right across from City Park. On weekends like the Fourth of July, the park was packed with people celebrating. As it goes in New Orleans, this summer day was hot. One of the folks enjoying the day decided to cool off by jumping into one of the many lagoons that snake through the park. He got into distress, went under, and did not reappear.

Responding district officers do not have the special equipment needed to do a water recovery. In those instances, they call the special operations division for assistance. About six of us relocated to the scene in the park. Big Moe removed a grappling hook on a length of line from his trunk. We asked witnesses where they last saw him go under. They indicated a spot about fifteen feet from the bank.

In a body of water without a current, the person you're looking for should be very close to the spot where you last saw him go down. Moe took the grappling hook and tossed it past the spot where the victim went under. Then he allowed it to sink and slowly pulled it back in. He located the victim on about the fourth attempt. He knew right away by the weight on the line that that attempt had been successful. There was also an emergency medical unit at the scene. We got a sheet from them. As Big Moe brought the victim close enough to grab, we pulled him up onto the bank and simultaneously covered him with the sheet. The crowd waiting around seemed to feel cheated that they did not get a chance to observe him, but I'm sure the family felt appreciation at our small act of sensitivity.

Big Moe told us that he regretted eating so much because he felt very uncomfortable. We all agreed, but that was the chance we took on a pig out. That was one of the things I liked so much about being in the SWAT unit. You could be doing one thing at one moment and something completely different fifteen minutes later.

As luck would have it, after another of our community dinners, we got a SWAT call for service. We changed into our tactical gear and relocated to the scene. It was for a barricaded subject down in the fifth district. The houses there are stereotypically smaller than houses in the rest of the city. Many were what are called shotguns or camelbacks.

Shotgun houses are long, narrow one-story houses. This architecture is closely associated with old New Orleans. You could open the front door and walk straight through. Each room leads into the next. There was an old saying that you could fire a shotgun through the front door and out the back door and not hit anything. A camelback is a shotgun house with a second floor. The second floor usually begins about halfway down the roofline of the house. A camelback house is higher in the back than in the front. Most of these homes are on long, narrow lots and have chain-link fences around them. Block after block of these narrow homes make up the neighborhood. Long, narrow alleys separate the houses.

We arrived and went into the usual mode of establishing a perimeter around the residence, evacuating neighbors who might be in harm's way, and setting up a command post. The negotiator got all the information on the incident from the officers who were already there. B. J., Moe, Dennis, and I were sent to the rear of the suspect's dwelling. We had to go down a house or two, go into that backyard, and jump fences until we got to the rear of the suspect's house. It would have been foolhardy to walk down the narrow alley to the rear of the suspect's home because he could easily shoot us as we went past a window.

We had already gone over several fences and were now close to our target when we heard Dennis request us to turn back. B. J. and I turned around to see Dennis covering the rear of the suspect's house with his MP5 and Big Moe stuck on a fence behind him. Moe had attempted to do a tactical roll over the top of the fence but his loadbearing vest had gotten caught. He was dangling by his vest. He was hanging low enough that he could not get a leg or arm over to free himself. He was struggling like a turtle on its back.

As Dennis covered us, B. J. and I went to free Big Moe. He was pretty much dead weight. We had to pick him up and free his vest from the top of the chain-link fence. He stopped his thrashing and patiently waited until B. J. and I freed him. I could tell by the expression on his face that he was waiting for me to say something. But this was not the time to ride Big Moe. We had a job to do, and there would be plenty of time for that later. Dennis was still covering for us when we passed him. I could hear him laughing as I went by.

Big Moe knew all the aggravation I gave him was out of friendship, though I'm sure he sometimes had his doubts. But deep down he knew the truth. He knew I never played or kidded with people I did not like. Quite the opposite. I treated people who were unproven or who I did not like with silence. I did not play with them, joke with them, or talk to them. I would be cordial but cold. I would answer questions or reply in as few words as possible. If someone came certified by another friend, I tended to act a little more open. After being on the job for as long as I had been, I was skeptical of almost everyone I met. If you know many cops, you likely know that my behavior upon first meeting people is the norm, not the exception.

These personality changes come gradually. You don't see them happening. Others close to you might, but sometimes it is so gradual that they don't even notice. I don't know which is better, the way I was then or the way I am now. Now, more than thirty years later, I find myself to be far too trusting. I used to be razor-edge sharp. Now I think sometimes I'm more like a McDonald's spork. I don't live in that world anymore. I must constantly remind myself to be more tactically sound. Don't get me wrong; I'm more tactically cognizant than your average suburbanite, but far from what I used to be. That SWAT officer has become an old man. I am thankful that after I left the police department, I put in another twenty-two years in a federal law enforcement agency. I retired with a commission to carry a weapon anywhere in the United States.

I can't physically fight a threating hooligan as I could in the old days. Now, I guess I just have to shoot him.

On the tactical unit, a SWAT roll could happen at any time. When a situation got out of control or became too dangerous, by policy, the police officers would secure the perimeter and call SWAT. You can imagine that in a large metropolitan city like New Orleans, the police department stayed busy. Tactical platoon two was assigned dayshift. So when a call came out at 6:00 a.m., we were the ones to receive it. After-hours callouts were made through police dispatch. They had a list of all personnel on each platoon. They would not call the guys who had just gotten off at 2:00 a.m. They would call the guys going on at 10:00 a.m. to respond. The thought process was that the officers on the next shift were well rested. That early morning, I got the call and proceeded to the SWAT office on Moss Street.

I arrived to the usual hustle and bustle of everyone readying equipment. Vinny and Sergeant Roy were loading up the SWAT van with specialized tactical equipment that was kept in the armory. I had seen this show before, and it worked like a well-oiled machine. They had done it so many times that it only took a few minutes. Then all personnel were en route to the scene. We did not ride in the SWAT van. That's more like the stuff you see on TV. The SWAT van was chock-full of equipment. We took our own vehicles, in which we placed all of our personal gear. We each carried around our uniform, ballistics vest, extra rounds, gas mask, elbow and knee protectors, communications gear, loadbearing vest, and ballistics helmet in a huge heavy bag. On a roll, we would just throw this bag in the trunk, along with our heavy weapons. It made life simple.

We rode out to the location, which was in an affluent area of New Orleans. There we got a brief from the district rank on the scene, as well as the responding officers. Dawn had broken by the time we arrived on that misty summer morning. It was muggy but still comfortable. The sun would soon be out and, like any summer day in New Orleans, it would be hot. We were thankful to get the roll early in the morning.

Unfortunately, since this was an affluent area of the city, residents coming out to get their newspapers observed the SWAT team and our support vehicles, as well as the district units all over the street. They had probably never experienced this kind of event in their neighborhood. Naturally and understandably, it drew them out as spectators. We had a growing crowd of neighbors forming across the street. As in most New Orleans neighborhoods, everyone knew everyone else. They were concerned about the well-being of the people in the home we had surrounded.

I never had any anxieties going on a SWAT roll. After all, back then I was totally indestructible. When we arrived, we were there to win, to put a stop to that situation and to arrest the guilty and rescue and remove the innocent. I did not have much compassion or care for the criminals. They knew full well what they were doing. They cared nothing about their victims or the many people they'd hurt. Most were sociopathic sacks of shit. I could not care less whether they went to jail or the coroner's office. The choice was usually up to them.

This roll would be different.

We gathered two houses down from the suspect's residence. There we got the details of this roll. Our suspect was an elderly professional, a man who had faithfully served his community for more than fifty years. His wife had become very ill with cancer. In this advanced stage, she was not long for this world. He knew she would spend the final weeks or month of her life in pain or heavily sedated. She told him she did not want either. She begged him to put her out of her misery. Since she was the only woman he had ever loved, he knew he could not face life without her. So they made an agreement, a pact, to go together that day.

He had telephoned their only son, who lived out of state. They both told him how much they loved him and that this was their wish. Then they told him to be strong and that they would see him again in heaven. The son called the police to advise them of the phone call he had received. The district officers got there just as one shot rang out. They kicked in the door, and now they had the old man trapped in his bedroom with his now dead wife at his side. That was where the officers stopped and secured the area and called SWAT.

Sam was the hostage negotiator that day. As we took positions on the perimeter, he went inside and took a position just out of sight of the bedroom door. He then started a conversation with the man. I was positioned in the rear yard, just off the bedroom window. I knew this old guy was not going to climb out that window. I knew in my heart that he was not going to hurt any cops that day, but we could take no chances.

The man told Sam that there was no way back. He was ready to go, but he was still afraid. He told Sam that he could not break the pact, and he didn't want to. But the final act was giving him great trepidation. He told Sam he was not going to force the police to do what he needed to do and that he wasn't a threat to them. He asked Sam to please pray for him and his wife. Then he shot himself in the chest. He knew exactly where to place the gun. He was dead immediately.

I was under the window when I heard the shot. I just stood up and walked out toward my vehicle. I did not need a debrief. I knew exactly what had happened. I felt so bad inside. I wished this thing could've ended some other way. But once they made the pact, the course was set. Before I reached my unit and Wong, I saw Kelly with Sam by the arm, quickly moving to his vehicle. I learned later that Kelly got Sam out of there to counsel him. He wanted to be certain that Sam understood that there was nothing he could have done in that situation. Kelly told Sam he had known it was going to go that way before they stepped into the house. He wanted to be sure that Sam did not somehow blame himself or worry himself with what-ifs.

It was over and done. It was nobody's fault. He summarized by telling Sam that life was not fair—a fact of which I was already painfully well aware.

Kelly liked B. J. and me. He often confided in us. He never let on that he was looking for our opinions to help him make a more informed decision. He just asked us what we thought about certain circumstances. When we gave him our opinions, sometimes he would sit back and reflect on it. Other times he would tell us that we thought that way because we didn't know shit. I figured he was right on both accounts. It still felt good that he gave a crap about what we thought. The three of us were close.

Gerry died in 2016. He had been at my house just three weeks before. He'd had dinner with my wife and me. He told me he had been having some health problems but did not elaborate. Typical Kelly. He kept his business close. He did not want to trouble anyone with his problems. I miss him. Even now it's hard to write about him.

Years before, we always got together with the entire team to go canoeing or have a party at his house. Everybody brought food, and we would eat until we were stuffed. Then of course we played two hours of volleyball. At one of these get-togethers, Big Moe boiled thirty pounds of shrimp. It tasted great. We all ate as much as we could and washed the food down with beer. What Moe did not realize was you couldn't put hot shrimp in an empty ice chest and close them off. After you boil shrimp, you must ice them down or else they will go bad. It did not hit any of us until we got home. Moe put the entire New Orleans Police Department's tactical platoon two on the crapper for the next fourteen hours. He had single-handedly hobbled half of the City of New Orleans's tactical response forces. None of us bugged him about it because he had been trying to do the right thing. After our stomachs settled down, we actually laughed about it.

During these get-togethers, we often sat around and talked about our police experiences. These conversations were good for everybody because we were exposed to how people handled different situations. You could put much of that information in your toolbox to use when you needed it. Sometimes the stories were just for entertainment. It was a way to get to know the people we worked with so closely.

On one such occasion, it had gotten late and it was dark. We lit a fire in the fire pit at Kelly's house and moved our chairs around it. It was late fall, so thank goodness there were no mosquitoes or gnats. South Louisiana is only comfortable when the weather turns cooler. In June, the mosquitoes could easily drain you of all your blood if you stayed outside too long. If you made it inside, you would look like one of those Egyptian mummies you see on the National Geographic channel.

Kelly had been in the SWAT unit a long time. He was trained as a bomb technician and an emergency medical technician. He had been there before there was a SWAT concept on the police department. They just called it the tactical unit before that. The city evaluated the tactical response operational procedures after the downtown Howard Johnson sniper incident in January 1973. If you are not familiar with that incident, just plug the above phrase into Wikipedia. It was a shit storm. They had Mark Essex's .44 Bulldog rifle on the wall in the crime lab at police headquarters. It was above the firearms forensics station. I had seen it many times as a homicide detective.

As we sat around the fire, Kelly recounted an incident, one that he had told me several years before as we were riding together covering Pope John Paul the Second's trip to New Orleans.

Kelly was the sergeant of tactical platoon two even then. They had gotten a call of a domestic disturbance that had gone so bad that they needed the SWAT team. They arrived on the scene in the morning on a sunny day. It was in an old New Orleans area where the houses were close together. Since it was early spring, many residents had their windows open. Most of the windows back then were covered with screens to keep the mosquitoes out. But that did not stop people from hearing and seeing what was going on on the other side of the windows.

They had evacuated the homes on each side of the suspect's residence. This had become a very dangerous situation. The suspect had a wife and seven-year-old son. He had already shot the wife. She was down and out. They had no idea if she was alive or dead. Kelly took a position with a long gun (a rifle) in the home directly beside the suspect's house. He could hear the hostage negotiator talking to the suspect. He could clearly hear the suspect's responses. He knew he was very close. The windows in both the home Kelly was in and the suspect's home were open. Only a few screens separated them.

Kelly said he could see the kid coming in and out of the bedroom across from which he was positioned. The kid looked frightened and confused. The suspect was screaming profanities and threatening to kill himself and the child as he walked around the house. Kelly said as he listened to negotiation going on, he knew the incident was not going to end well. Gerry said he heard a silence that lasted for about four minutes. After all the yelling, he figured negotiations had reached an impasse.

He still had a clear view through the window. Suddenly, the suspect and the child appeared in the bedroom across from Gerry. He could see the subject clearly; he was still armed with a pistol. The kid was right next to him. He said the guy never looked out the window. If he had, he would've easily seen Gerry aiming the rifle at him. They were only about twelve feet apart. The suspect then spoke to his son. Gerry said he could hear him clear as day.

"This is only going to hurt for a second," the suspect told the child.

Gerry fired once, killing the suspect. He yelled to the others outside that the suspect was down. Officers breached the door and went inside the residence. The woman was not dead, and EMS transported her to the hospital. The child was taken and given over to social services.

After telling us the story, Kelly cautioned us that you never know what is going to happen on a SWAT roll and that we needed to be flexible. He said when we saw a situation that we had to act on, there would be no guidance from management. In that type of situation, you had to depend on everything you knew—all the facts you had gathered and the voice inside telling you what was right.

"Don't hesitate when someone's life is in danger," he said. "There will always be Monday-morning quarterbacks taking days to critique the actions that you took in a fraction of a second. Fuck 'em. They weren't there. If you save a life, it's all worth it. I'm not saying you won't get screwed over by doing what is right. But you will be able to stand up before God and all those assholes and hold your head up, and no matter what they say or do, you know you absolutely did the right thing."

CHAPTER FOURTEEN

Gertie and I had lived together for about eight months. Those were some of the happiest times I had spent in many years. She did not break up with Kyle after their big argument. In many respects, I wished she had.

She moved in with him in the fall. So, it was just me again rattling around the big old house. I truly missed having her there. The place was quiet and lonely again. I had no desire for another roommate. Gertie had been the exception. Work was going well, but my social life sucked. If it weren't for my good friends at work and the Dreux, I would have gone crazy.

Gert would show up at the club either Friday or Saturday nights but usually not both. I could only go there on my weekends off. Sometimes we missed each other. The good thing was that Ron, the Satisfier, Greg, and Barry were always there. Jerry's relationship with his girlfriend became very serious, and he was not usually in attendance. Then we all got invitations to his wedding.

The ceremony was held at Saint Frances Cabrini Church on Paris Avenue, with a reception that followed at the Walnut Room at Lakefront Airport. Lakefront Airport was constructed in the mid-1930s under then Governor Huey P. Long. The terminal building is in the art deco style, and the interior retains much of its original lavish 1930s ornamentation. Lots of marble and grandeur. The *Fountain of the Winds*, a sculpture by Enrique Alferez, stands at the entrance to Lakefront Airport. It was the first view of a nude woman that I saw as a child. It is an incredible piece of artwork from the art deco period.

Jerry's wedding ceremony was a beautiful event. It was strange to see Barry in a tuxedo as one of his groomsmen. The crew from the Dreux and I were sitting in the rear of the church. We did this to give his relatives better seats. Every now and then, Jerry would turn to look at us. At first, I figured he was just seeing if we were enjoying the day's proceedings.

When we got to the reception, things turned more peculiar. As he introduced us to his relatives, especially his new wife, he always followed our names with a caveat.

"This is Dave … from the club."

"This is Ron … from the club."

It was as if he had already briefed his wife and his relatives for some impending calamity. I remember when I met his wife, she was smiling until the cautionary "from the club" phrase was added. She stopped smiling and gave me a dead-fish handshake. If this had been the 1700s and we were being introduced by a butler crier he would have said, "Ladies and gentlemen, I present to you Lord David McAllister hailing from Manor Dreux of Gentilly Dreux. Gentle ladies, please secure your grip upon your purses and chastity."

I assure you that no shenanigans were planned or even discussed. We would never do anything to harm or interrupt Jerry's wedding. It was like he had a ready excuse in case we were caught poking our dicks into the wedding cake. That must have been why he was looking at us in the back of the church so often. When you are a serial practical joker like Jerry, you could trust no one. I wondered why we had gotten invitations at all. I guess he figured if he did not invite us and take the chance, he could have lost five friends in one fell swoop. The rest of the gang spoke about it over drinks at the reception. We all had felt it. We were all a little let down that Jerry had not trusted us more. I guess he felt if you live by the joke, you die by the joke.

No matter what, we were determined to have a good time. We talked, drank, and danced until the reception was over. As I was slow dancing with Gert, I asked her where Kyle was. She said he told her that since he did not know Jerry, he did not want to go to the wedding.

What a selfish fun-killing douchebag, I thought. But I said that, "That's okay, Gert. You can have fun with us."

After our dance, I excused myself and walked through the exquisite marble-and-granite lobby to the front of the airport. There I saw Barry standing outside with his hands in his pockets. As I approached him, I lit up a cigarette.

"You clean up well, my friend. That tuxedo looks good on you," I told him.

"Thanks," he said. "It's a rental."

"Well, it fits you to a tee," I complimented. "Beautiful day for a wedding."

"Yeah, you couldn't ask for better," he said.

"What are you doing out here by yourself?" I asked.

"I just wanted to get some fresh air and sunshine," he said. "So you haven't stolen any silverware or soiled any bridesmaids?"

"Oh, so you saw it too?" I asked.

"Hard to miss," he said. "I told him that you guys weren't going to do anything. But he was still scared shitless. I think his wife drives the car more than he does."

"I guess you're right. I never noticed," I said.

"I saw it coming," he said. "When they became serious, he quit coming to the club. He blew us off all of a sudden. That wasn't Jerry. That was someone else's influence. He's had girlfriends before and never did that.

"I tell you, David," he continued, "don't allow anyone to run your life. Love should be shared, not sequestered. If you both don't love and care about the same things, you shouldn't be together. Don't settle on someone because it's comfortable. Comfort is not everlasting. I saw you and Gertie dancing together. I wish things had been different for you two. I know you love each other very much."

"Things are what they are, Barry," I said. "I can't wish for things past. Look at this cigarette." I held the still smoldering butt up for his inspection. "I can wish that this cigarette was as it was moments ago before I lit it. But that will never happen. Should I lament the fact that it's gone? What good would that do? Or should I just put it out and remember the fact that it relaxed me and I smoked it in good company with you? I guess what I'm saying is, it's all a matter of how you look at things."

"That's very profound, but where do come up with that stuff, David?" he asked.

"I watch old cartoon reruns of *Tooter Turtle*," I said.

"Can I get one of those cigarettes?" Barry asked.

"Sure, but you don't smoke."

"I do today, only today, with my best friend."

I gave him one of my cigarettes and a light.

"You're a good man, Mister B." I exhaled. "A good man."

"You too Mister Wizard. You too." He coughed.

"Buy gold." That was one of Johnny Frost's pieces of advice that became his identifying catchphrase. He advised us of that fact in a long conversation on national finance and the stock market while he ate meatloaf and mashed potatoes at the Rocksford.

During the dinner, he tried to explain where he felt the market was heading in the long run. Then he explained to us all that we could protect our savings by buying gold. He told us that in times of uncertainty and market volatility, gold would most always increase in value. He said he owned gold, but he refused to tell us how much. We all listened to Big Moe, but to my knowledge nobody bought gold.

Sergeant Kelly would tell us at least once a week to buy gold. I think Kelly did this just to get under Johnny's skin. We would be eating at the Rocksford or leaving the office at two in the morning, and instead of saying goodbye, he would just yell out to us to buy gold. Big Moe never took offense to any of that. Now that I look back, the average price of gold per ounce in 1986 was $325. As I sit here writing today, the average price per ounce is $1,250. I wish I had listened more to Moe.

Big Moe was right about a lot of things. But that never shielded him from making simple mistakes that placed him in the spotlight for our jokes. I used to love to mess with Big Moe. I'm sure it drove him crazy, but I only did it because I liked him.

Moe was always trying to take a situation and make it better. Like a lot of cops back then, Moe lived in a city to the east of New Orleans called Slidell. He owned a large lot next to his house. Moe did not have a riding lawnmower. Back then, most folks didn't. So Big Moe tied a rope to a regular push lawnmower to the back of his four-wheeler so he could drive the four-wheeler around the lot, towing the running lawnmower. He was minding his own business, cutting his lot that way, when a photographer from the *Times Picayune*—the daily paper of New Orleans—happened by and photographed him. He had a huge photo on the front page of the metro section of the paper that weekend. It was priceless. The photo truly captured John Frost as his alter ego, Big Moe.

There is another Moe story that I will never forget. Do you know that sometimes burglars will actually take a shit in the victim's home or business? I have seen this on several occasions. I don't know if it's fear or an adrenaline rush or some sort of perverted dominance thing, but if you ask policemen who have been on the job for a while, they will attest to this fact. And the criminals rarely use the toilet. They'll just squat and drop their burden whenever the feeling hits.

One day, the tactical unit was patrolling the first district when dispatch put out a possible burglary in progress call on Saint Charles Avenue. This was about three blocks off Canal Street. The area had office buildings and shops, all of which were multilevel. We knew that most of the first district officers were tied up on other calls, so since we were in the area, we told dispatch we would respond. Three cars from the tactical unit showed up on the scene. Big Moe and Dennis along with Debbie and Conrad arrived about the same time as B. J. and me.

The front door of the building had been forced open, and as we walked in, directly in front of us was a huge wooden stairway leading to the upper floors. Right at the bottom of the stairs, a burglar had left a huge pile of "how do you do?" poo. We searched the bottom floor, and as we climbed the stairs to search the upper building, we cautioned each other about the pile as if it was a live rattlesnake.

Searching a building for a burglar is challenging. I had done it hundreds of times. He could be hiding anywhere or nowhere because he got away before you arrived. The trick was not to become complacent. You should expect that this asshole could be behind any door or hiding in any room or closet. You must tell yourself that he is going to be wherever you are searching at that time. When you open a closet and there's a big burly asshole standing there, you aren't surprised. That's why it's a good thing to have your finger indexed on your weapon and not on your trigger. If you are startled or surprised, you may flinch. A simple uncontrollable physical reaction for you could equal a gaping hole through the chest of a knucklehead. Then the higher-ups are going to want you to explain why you blew a hole in an unarmed dumbass burglar.

The building we were searching was five stories tall. A team would take a floor, while the other teams went to the next two floors up. I was using the above modus operandi, as were the other officers in their search. My teammates were going here and there. I somehow ended up on the top floor with Big Moe.

"I already searched this floor," he told me when I arrived.

"Then you won't mind if I search it again," I told him.

"Whatever you want," he said as he went past me and down the stairs.

I searched the top floor with negative results. We had arrived too late, and the perpetrator or perpetrators had already gone. I started my descent from the fifth floor. Upon reaching the bottom of the staircase, I observed that the huge pile of criminal crap had morphed into one giant Frankenstein footprint.

"Moe!" I screamed

"It wasn't me, it wasn't me," came the loud return from the street.

I carefully made my way out to the street, avoiding the large poo prints that had been left on the floor by the offending boot. I found all the others laughing hysterically as Moe scraped his boot against the curb in an attempt to free himself of the burglar's excrement. He was fuming mad. I thought it best not to antagonize him now. I went to my unit and got a roll of paper towels and a plastic gallon jug of the water that B. J. and I always kept in our vehicle. He took the water and towels and thanked me. In retrospect, I think he was thanking me for not continuing his embarrassment and not necessarily for the cleanup gear.

One sunny morning, about a month later, B. J. and I got the call to meet a homicide unit at the Sugarhouse Hotel on Julia Street. When we arrived, several district officers told us that they were on the ninth floor. Still wondering why homicide would need us, we took the elevator to the ninth floor. Upon our arrival, we could see that a room with a view facing Julia Street was open and a lot of homicide suits were standing around. We walked in to find Sergeant Stone Face, the sergeant detective in charge of this homicide shift, talking to two men in suits seated on the bed. I learned later that the two suits on the bed were DEA agents. By this time, their boss had arrived, along with his entourage.

Stone Face was his usual self. He told them through his permanent scowl that he did not give a shit what they thought. This was now a homicide investigation, and it fell squarely into his purview. He said there wasn't going to be any argument about that. He advised the DEA agents that they could answer his questions now or he would just throw them in a unit and take them to police headquarters until they decided it was in their best interest to talk.

You could see that their resident agent in charge was a typical federal bureaucrat who was not used to being spoken to in that manner. But he immediately cowered to Stone Face. I only saw Stone Face smile a handful of times. He was a gruff, rough son of a bitch. I heard a story that the day he was born, he slapped his mother for waking him up. I know what you're probably asking yourself: How would a SWAT officer know so much about a homicide sergeant? Well, that's because about a year later I would be working directly for him, after B. J. and I were transferred to the detective bureau and assigned to the homicide division.

After witnessing Stone Face speaking to the DEA agents, I began to look around the room. I had heard him say this was a homicide investigation, only there was nobody dead in the room. I walked up to a uniformed guy and asked him where the dead person was. He walked us out to the small balcony of the room. The french doors were wide open. He went to the railing and pointed.

"That's him down there," the uniformed officer said.

I looked down and saw a man's body crumpled up and broken from a fall. The corpse was still holding a 9 mm Mac-10. He had not fallen to the ground but had landed on a metal ceiling of a subroof three stories above street level. Then the officer pointed out another interesting detail.

"Looks like he tried to jump from this balcony to the balcony of the room next door. See the scrapes?"

The balconies were not wrought iron. They were made of brick on all three sides. There were bloody scrapes and a few fingernails still sticking to the brick on the balcony in question.

I thought what a dumb way to go. If he had made the jump, all the DEA would have had to do was go down the hall one door and bang on that one. He would have never gotten away jumping from balcony to balcony. It wasn't really that far to jump. If he had left the Mac 10 behind, he might have made it. Panic made for very bad decision making. But I doubted the coroner's office would conclude panic as a cause of death. But it sure came before the bone-crushing fall he had taken.

As B. J. and I were looking at the dead perpetrator, Stone Face came up behind us.

"I'm sure he's dead. If he's playing possum, that hot roof would have moved him around by now," he said gruffly. "You see what he's holding?"

"Yes, sir. A Mac-10," B. J. replied.

"You guys know anything about that weapon?" he asked

"Yes, sir. They're simple. Not much to them," I said confidently.

"I want one of you to go down on a rope, clear that weapon, and tie it to the rope so we can pull it up. Then we're gonna lower down a body bag. Put him in the bag, tie it off, and we'll pull it up. Then we'll pull you back up," he ordered. "Either of you got any experience at that shit?"

I looked at B. J. He was looking at me and saying with his eyes, *Please God, tell him you know something about rappelling.*

"No problem, Sarge. I was in the marines. I've done some tactical rappelling," I told him.

"Good. I don't want no firemen having to go get that guy. Besides, I need a cop to clear that weapon. Can't take a chance if a fireman got hurt or discharged it in the attempt. That's why you gotta do it. I sent one of my guys to the sporting goods store on Carrollton. He's going to get a rappelling rope and whatever other equipment they think we're gonna need," he told us.

"If he doesn't stop off to get Chinese, he ought to be here any minute. If he did stop off, I'm going to throw him off this balcony. Then I'll lower you down two body bags," Stone Face said. Since he said it through his scowl, I could not tell if he was joking.

The detective arrived with the rope and other necessary equipment, including a readymade rappelling seat. It was of high-quality nylon and adjustable. The seat was the apparatus that went around my waist and around my legs. It came together in the front. This was the seat I would sit in and my main support.

He had also bought several carabiners. A carabiner is a metal loop with a locking metal gate. You run the rope through it, and on a true rappel, you can control the speed of the descent by holding the working end of the rope in the small of your back. I wasn't going to have to worry about that, since this was not really a rappel. They would tie the rope off to the railing on the far side of the balcony, and four or five detectives and uniform cops would slowly lower me down.

Wong was giddy with excitement. Any time I had to take a big bite out of a shit sandwich, he was like a teenage girl at a Beatles concert.

I checked the knots they had used to tie the rope off to the balcony rail. They had wrapped the rail many times before even starting the knots. They had finished it off with about ten thousand half hitches. After inspecting it, I figured it would hold. Besides, there were still four policemen holding the rope, along with Wong. I knew that no matter what happened, Wong would never let go of the rope. I had confidence in the seat, and I had tied a bowline knot through the carabiner that was hooked to my seat. As I got ready to climb over the balcony, I noticed many people on the balconies of the building across the street. They were just out to see the show. I figured if something gave way, I had a good chance of survival because I would be landing on the dead guy, who would break some of the fall.

My only apprehension was when I first climbed out over the balcony and let the seat and rope take my weight. After everything held, it was fine. The guys had set a blanket they got from the room over the railing so as not to chafe the rope as they payed it out. Before I knew it, I was standing over the perpetrator. I checked him for vital signs and found none. I removed the weapon from his hand and cleared it. I put the magazine in my pocket. I looked inside the chamber to be sure it was clear before tying it to the rope. After it was secured on the end of the rope, they pulled it up.

After hoisting the weapon up, they tied a body bag onto the rope and lowered it down. I unzipped the body bag and laid it out. Then I had to move the perpetrator onto the bag. If there was any doubt that he was dead before this, I assure you he was dead then. As I moved him, I heard all the broken bones crunching against each other. He was smashed up bad inside, but there was no blood or gore outside. After I zipped the bag up, I had to figure out how best to secure the bag to the rope. This was not a blue plastic Hurricane Katrina body bag. Real body bags are ten times stronger. They're black and heavy-duty. All four corners have a reinforced nylon loop sewed into them. I wanted to be sure that however I tied the bag, it would not give way. I ran the rope through two handles on one side of the bag. Then I tied a bowline knot to secure them together. As they pulled him up, I watched their progress. I confess that I relocated away from the drop zone just in case my knot did not hold.

My knot held, and they dragged him up and over the balcony. They lowered the rope to me, and I again tied it through the carabiner hooked to the seat with a bowline knot. Together, the officers and Wong pulled me up to the balcony. I got over the rail and started taking off the seat and untying my belt from the rope. That's when everybody came over to me and patted me on the back.

"Shit, man. I would have never done that," several officers told me.

"Good job," Stone Face said.

I wish I could say that I basked in the adulation. But I couldn't help but wonder why these cops would never have done that. So I asked Wong.

"Shit, dude. They were bitching and complaining about how heavy the guy was," he told me, laughing. "I thought they were gonna let go at any minute. When they had you on the line, they were all grunting and shit." He giggled.

Oh, that's just great, I thought. *I checked the knots, I checked the seat, but I never thought to check the physical conditioning of the cops who would be working the line.*

In September 1987, Wong told me he wanted to leave SWAT and go to the detective bureau. It was in the afternoon, and we had been riding around all day. I don't know what took him so long to talk to me about it.

I said, "You kidding me? Why do you want to become a suit? We have good friends here, and everything is working well."

He gave me all the usual bullshit about going to the detective bureau and the opportunity to further his law enforcement career, get additional experience, and get to see and do something different and new.

Our conversation got a bit heated. I told him I thought he was just going to join that elitist club of large ego chumps. I was a little bent. I didn't know why he wanted to break up our partnership after all these years. He told me he had put in to go to the intelligence section and had already interviewed for the job.

I said, "That's news to me. I guess that is why you're broaching the subject today, because you must be on the short list so you waited this long to tell me."

I did not consider then how hard it must've been for him to talk to me about it. He knew that as a partner, I only trusted him. He also knew that I had no prospective partners to ride with after he left. He knew I was not going to take the news well. At least he found the nuts to tell me before he got transferred.

So B. J. had interviewed for a detective position in the intelligence section. I wasn't even sure what the intelligence section did. I knew they collected all the crime stats and any information that we street guys sent to them. Then they computed, distilled, discombobulated, excreted, ingested, and compiled all that information. Then, when they had that shiny nugget of criminal intelligence, they shelved it. Information is power, is it not? In my entire career, I had never seen any bulletin of information or warning disseminated from the intelligence section. Perhaps it only went to the highest of positions, delivered directly into those persons' hands by a blind kid they hired to be sure he could not clandestinely read it. Then after they had read it, they rubbed it over their nether regions and burned it as per the enclosed instructions. They then promptly forgot about it.

Not only did I have to wear this albatross of Wong's transfer around my neck, but I was also sworn to absolute secrecy on the information. I could not talk it over with anyone else. No venting and no validations of my feelings from my compatriots. I just had to suck it up and wait.

The NFL was on strike around that time. As I am not a sports fan and wasn't then, I really don't remember what the strike was about.

Perhaps they were trying to ration Gatorade or cut down on excessive post-touchdown celebratory dances. I don't know. I do know that tactical platoon two was sent to the Superdome to act as security for the New Orleans Saints scab team's practice. Wong and I were sitting in the front row seats at the fifty-yard line, observing the practice.

That's when we saw Lieutenant Keith Mason, the head of the NOPD Intelligence Section, walking past us between the field and our seats.

"Keith, Keith, hey Keith, Keith, hey Keith," Wong called to him. He waved his arms like a castaway on a deserted island would at the first boat he had seen in years. The lieutenant finally looked up and spotted B. J.

"Hi, Mike," he acknowledged and gave a half-hearted wave.

I watched the large joyful balloon that was B. J. Wong deflate before my eyes.

"I guess you ain't going to intelligence," I said matter-of-factly.

Wong said nothing in response. He was crushed. It was a good thing the lieutenant did not come over to talk to us. It would have only caused further embarrassment to Wong.

"I'm still going to try to get to the detective bureau," he told me that evening as we rode back to the office.

"Yeah, go ahead, but you're still gonna be riding with me for the next couple months. You could've done worse," I said.

Living in New Orleans was not all one big party. Lots of people who visit fall in love with the city. Some of those people move to New Orleans permanently. If you are one of those people, I suggest you date New Orleans for about six months before you marry her. Like a first date, she's not going to show you all the bad things about herself. She's going to be charming and fun loving, up for anything and willing to do whatever it takes to make you happy. She probably won't tell you about that narcotics arrest; since she got them to drop the prostitution charge in a plea bargain deal, she was able to get the whole thing expunged. She's quite engaging. She may say something like this, "But enough about me. Let's talk about you, sweetie. How much money do you have in your bank accounts?"

I was driving my personal truck when I parked in a spot where I knew I should not. I thought I was only going to be gone for about five minutes. I figured I would get back in time. After returning ten minutes later, I found a parking ticket on my truck. Okay, they got me. I knew what I did was wrong. I had rolled the dice and played the odds; now I was going to have to pay up. I wasn't mad. Hell, I deserved it. I took the little blue parking ticket and envelope off my windshield, stuffed them in my shirt pocket, and read it over when I got home. I don't remember exactly how much it was, fifty or seventy-five dollars. It was an expensive lesson for me: Don't do stuff that you're not willing to pay for. I sat down and wrote out a check to the City of New Orleans. It was December 21, 1987. I mailed it the next day.

I figured that this event was over, and I had paid my dues in full. Until the first week of February 1988 when I got a letter in the mail from the City of New Orleans. It gleefully told me that I owed more money. It officially notified me that I had not paid the fine on the ticket within two weeks of getting it, so I owed a late fee. Since I had not called them within the two-week period to schedule a time to contest the ticket with a judge, that right had been forfeited. Gentle reader, you cannot imagine how pissed off I was. Since I received the letter on a Friday afternoon, I had to wait until Monday to go down there.

Traffic ticket court was in a large building on Canal Street, about half a block off Broad Avenue. It had huge marble steps in front of it that were greenish gray in color. I don't know if the court is still there today. It could now be a multistory paintball experience or a chicken joint. Who knows? I got there and waited in line until it was my turn to approach the high potentate of Ticketium. I explained my situation to a very unsympathetic public servant. I told her I mailed the ticket via the US Postal Service on December 22, 1987. I mailed the letter in New Orleans. I told her there was no way they had not gotten it before January 4. I requested that she check the envelope's postmark. That should have alleviated any question as to when they received my payment.

She looked at me for a second through her glasses. Then she raised her nose and chin about three inches and scowled at me through the bottom of her spectacles.

"We do not use postmarks to certify when we open something," she said, practically growling.

"Then what do you use to certify when you receive something?" I asked in a forced pleasant tone.

"When we open our mail, we stamp it with a time-date machine," she said.

"Wait ..." I said. "You guys certify when you receive something, and you guys are the determining certifiers as to whether something is late? You don't use the postmark set by the United States Postal Service, an official agency of the United States government, who does not stand to profit by whether or not something is dated that could lead it to be considered late? You, the profiting entity, disregard the postmark and stamp it when you get around to opening it, possibly causing a citizen to have to pay more money in a late fee that you in turn collect to the profit of your department? You don't see the conflict of interest there?"

"That's the way we do it, sir," she said in a patronizing tone.

"Let me tell you what I think happened here," I said through clenched teeth. "I mailed that ticket back in the provided envelope on the twenty-second of December. It arrived here on the twenty-fourth of December. Then it sat on somebody's desk through the entire holiday season. It was sitting there when you guys were clinking glasses and doing the conga with Santa Claus. It was sitting there when Opie was lighting firecrackers along with Jasper's farts on New Year's Eve. Then, when you and the office toadies got back to work and started on the pile of mail that had grown during your holiday malingering and finally opened my letter on January 5, 1988, a professional lackey stamped my damn envelope with your corrupt shitty little time-date machine."

She did not have to respond. Just as I finished my rant, a security guard from the courtroom tapped me on the shoulder. He advised me that the judge wanted me to leave because I was too loud. I leaned toward the little mouth hole in the glass. I told her in a low voice that there would be no way in hell that they would ever get a late fee out of me. I then exited the building. I never heard another thing about that ticket again or the late fee. I don't think it was my powers of persuasion that changed her mind. I think she reconsidered that perhaps I could use my position to start a shit storm for them. It just wasn't worth the late fee because there was no way they could explain what had happened.

My scenario of events was probably closer to the truth.

CHAPTER FIFTEEN

As the year 1988 started things seemed to be going well for everyone at the Dreux. The Satisfier's business was doing well, and everyone else had a good full-time job. I was still seeing my friends every weekend if my schedule permitted. Tony Amato was on the Louisiana State Police, promoting up and doing well. He and his wife were living in Baton Rouge. Tony did not make as many trips to New Orleans as he used to because he and his wife were occupied with their lives in the capital city.

Jerry came by the club every blue moon. They were always strange visits. Strange in the fact that neither he nor anyone else could discern any previous absence. He would laugh, joke, and cut up like he had been there just last week. Everyone else acted the same way. I guess when you walked out of the reflective front door, time stopped inside the Dreux Club. Everyone and everything stayed in suspended animation, waiting for your return. Maybe Barry was hiding some sort of nuclear powered miniaturized time machine in one the chest coolers. If he was in possession of some sort of alien technology, I thanked God he had it. That place was the only thing that kept me sane.

I knew B. J. was still trying to get to the detective bureau. Wong was a good cop, and anyone who knew anything about him would be a fool not to want him on his or her team. I knew our time together in SWAT was short. Sergeant Gerry Kelly had turned in his papers for retirement. Headquarters management decided they would squeeze as much of his leadership experience out of him as they could before he left. They transferred him out of SWAT and into a platoon sergeant position in the third district. I was aggravated by their decision, but I could see why they did it. They wanted the new recruits and younger officers to learn from a very experienced policeman. Kelly didn't care. He had his sights on retirement, and his transfer did not stop us from getting together socially.

Gertie was still living with Kyle. They had a nice house off Harrison Avenue in Lakeview. Kyle had a job downtown at a major oil company's headquarters building. I didn't know what his job was. He could've been busting up exploratory core samples with a little rock hammer or bringing coffee to executives who were too important to get it themselves. Either way, I really didn't care. Kyle never came to the club or exhibited any kind of behavior that would suggest he was the least bit interested in Gertie's lifelong friends. I still don't know what she saw in that oaf. I guess I was just pissed off that it wasn't me. I wasn't dating anyone and hadn't for a long time. In my job, I did not interact with a lot of people who were in the dating pool. When women had been raped, beaten, robbed, or shot, they tended not to be interested in the guy helping them as a potential date. I guess they had other things on their mind.

I didn't like going to those plastic disco or cowboy bars that were in style back then. Before the movie *Urban Cowboy* came out, you never saw cowboys in New Orleans. Cowboys were over in Texas. After that movie, every swinging dick wanted to be a cowboy—cowboy boots, cowboy hats, cowboy shirts, and all looking for cowgirls. Have you ever heard a real, no shit New Orleans accent? Could you just imagine that accent coming out of a cowboy? A real New Orleans accent can easily be mistaken as a Boston or a Brooklyn accent. Only the New Orleanians change the *er*'s on words to *a*'s. Better is betta. Over is ova. You get the idea. It is not a cowboy's accent to hear, "Ah bet ya neva seen no cowboy bigga and betta than me? Have ya, mothafucka?" Poor dumbasses. It's a shame when you have to reinvent your life every time Hollywood comes out with a successful movie. I guess when you get tired of being a cowboy, you could always become a racecar driver or secret agent.

I don't like change. I get comfortable doing things one way. I get good at it. I find the routine satisfying. Don't get me wrong. I can change. I make the necessary adaptations and push until I find that rut of knowledge and expertise where I can become comfortable again. Back then, I knew the upheaval of change was lurking right around the corner for me like the demon who haunted public bathrooms, the fiend who would eat all the toilet paper and then weave a fog so you would not notice it was all gone before you went.

When B. J. left to go to the detective bureau, everything was going to change. I had been riding with B. J. for about nine years at this point. Now I would have to try to find someone who could deal with my eclectic personality for eight to ten hours a day. That was not going to be easy. Everyone in the SWAT unit already had partners. I felt very uneasy about the future. The fact that I did not have someone at home to talk to and receive support from made me feel even more isolated and alone.

One weekend, the weather was nice, so I walked from my house to the Dreux Club. I wasn't going to attempt to talk to any of them about my issues at work. It wasn't that they wouldn't understand, but I did not want to burden them with any of my troubles. When I arrived, the Satisfier was sitting alone at the bar. I pulled up a stool and sat next to him. Without me saying a word, Barry came over and set a longneck bottle of Dixie in front of me. *Ah, routine.*

"So what's going on with you, Steve?" I asked.

"Plenty," he said.

"The garage is going well I hear."

"Too well. It's getting bigger than me. I can't keep up with all the business. It's taking me longer and longer to complete repairs, and customers don't like that. I'm going to have to hire an employee."

"What's the problem there?"

"My fixing cars has always been a one-man job. I'm used to working by myself, for myself. I've never had any other job. Now I'm gonna have to be the boss of somebody and do my job along with the books, ordering supplies, keeping up with the paperwork, paying the bills. This is incredibly stressful for me. How am I gonna hire somebody? I don't know anybody with the skills who needs work. I don't know how to interview someone for a job. How do I know I'm not getting an idiot or, worse, a thief?"

"That's a tough spot, a real dilemma," I said. "Let's just break this down into logical steps. First, the person you want needs to know you're looking for him," I explained. "You know other people in the business. Put out the word that you're looking for somebody. If a friend recommends a guy to you, you could be a little more assured that he is a good guy. When other people hear that you're looking to hire, they may consider leaving where they are now. You certainly don't know the behind-the-scenes goings on of all these repair places. Somebody may want to leave for any number of reasons. If you get no prospects there, take out a help-wanted ad.

"When the person shows up, bring him into your office, look him over from head to toe. Most shitheads dress like shitheads," I informed him. "If he is going to a job interview in a rock 'n' roll t-shirt and cutoffs, he's probably not the guy you want to hire. Are his hands dirty? Is his face washed and hair combed? Does he smell like bad cheese or a baboon's ass? Appearance will tell you two things: First, he's smart enough and cares enough to look good for a job interview. Secondly, if he doesn't give a crap about his appearance, he's not gonna give a crap about the work he'll be doing for you. Ask for references. See if he gives you the name of a guy who runs a traveling circus."

I continued, "Start asking him all the stuff you want to know. Ask him about repairs that he's done in the past. What was the most difficult repair that he successfully completed? What did he find so difficult about that repair? Those type questions will give you, a seasoned mechanic, insight to his true experience level. Ask him to tell you about himself and then let him talk. If he says he's married with a kid on the way, you can assume certain things. If he tells you he just got out of prison for aggravated battery, but it's okay because he was forced to stop using heroin for a while, you can assume other things. By the end of that conversation, you should have a pretty good idea of who this person is. You should already have an idea of what you would be willing to pay this new employee, depending on his experience. I think the rest you can figure out for yourself," I concluded.

The Satisfier looked at me in disbelief. "Man, I gotta write that stuff down. You pitched all that after only half a beer? How do you know so much about hiring somebody?"

"Because I've been to a lot of interviews and gotten a lot of jobs," I said. "Since I was fifteen years old, I have worked in a fast-food joint, a retail store, Lefty's Moving Service, and as an exterminator, a maintenance man, a gardener, and a shoe salesman."

"I never knew any that," the Satisfier said.

Most of my friends didn't know about all the jobs I'd had. That subject never came up. My hardest preemployment interviews and examinations were to get on the police department and when I changed over to the feds.

"Well, I really feel better now," he confessed. "Now I have a clear path forward. Thanks a bunch, man. I really mean that. The next one's on me," he proclaimed, waving his large hand over our empty beers, indicating to Barry that we wanted a second round.

I was glad I had helped the Satisfier feel better. I was glad that I could help him with the stress and apprehension he was feeling. I wish it could have helped me.

My life was still in disarray. Work was going okay, but I still had no love in my life. Sure, I was dating. But I could not find a woman I could click with. I knew in my heart and in my head that it would never be Gert. All I could do was hope for the best. There was someone for everyone. I always knew that to be true. But I figured that my someone was selling T-shirts in a gift shop in Vancouver or on patrol in Israel's West Bank. I figured I would never meet her. In fact, it would be over a decade before I met Patricia, the women I'm married to today.

As I knew would happen, B. J. was transferred from SWAT to the homicide division. Now I was truly alone. I was a floater. I rode with whoever's partner was unavailable that day. I was the standby guy driving a shit wagon. I had the route of whoever didn't show up. Every route was different, but they always stank.

I languished in that purgatory for three months. Then B. J. reached out to me and told me he could get me into homicide. I was so lonely where I was that I told him sure, do it. A month later, I was a detective. I think B. J. went to homicide for the prestige of the position. I only stayed in homicide for about a year. I hated it. There was only twenty-one of us in the division. That year we had more than 250 homicides. If you were up in the rotation, the next homicide was yours and not only were you responsible for the report and the follow-up investigation, but you were also up for the next suicide. That's because you had to keep the guy behind you in rotation ready to get the next homicide.

The homicide division back then had an unofficial uniform shoulder patch that depicted a vulture standing on a New Orleans Police

Department badge. Under the vulture was a banner that read, "Our Day Starts When Yours Ends." And God, that was the truth.

If it wasn't your case, you would be canvassing the area, finding witnesses and taking notes. If it was your case, you would have all the notes passed to you. Then you would have to attend the victim's autopsy. You could start writing a preliminary report, but you had to wait for the coroner's report to come back before you could complete it.

Everyone from the victim's family to your commanding officers wanted everything yesterday. I used to like to go home and forget about my police work, having done everything I could that day. You couldn't do that in the homicide division. The dead were hanging over you like the sword of Damocles. They wanted justice. They wanted to be avenged. Your bosses wanted these human tragedies documented as thick as phonebooks—a big order for a broke dick who could not type.

The suicides were the easiest. They were truly simple reports. Most, but not all, were easily discerned as self-committed. There are lots of ways an investigator can tell. When they were mine, I used to take their driver's licenses. The licenses assisted in my report writing—name, date of birth, address, etc. I used them to write my reports and then added them to a stack I had in my desk drawer, held together by a rubber band. One day I was reaching for a staple remover and came upon the stack. It had grown to about an inch and a half thick. I started going through it, recognizing every face. Overdosed, .38 to the temple, hung himself, carbon monoxide poisoning, slit wrists—the list went on and on.

Some left notes; some did not. The notes went to the coroner's office with the bodies. I'd go across the street and get a copy for the report. One woman that had scrawled the words "I Hate You" on her mirror at her makeup table before shooting herself in the head in front of it. I had many years on the job. I was as callous as anyone. But I knew this position was draining the humanity out of me. I knew I would have to start looking for another assignment. I did not give a shit about the prestige of being a homicide detective.

A detective in the homicide division made a lot of money, not because the position was so valued that it paid more but rather because the fact that they worked all those hours. We had nearly unlimited overtime. I couldn't have cared less about the money, but it became a factor in my leaving homicide. The detective whose place I took in the unit was looking to get back. He had gone to the district attorney's office. The DA's office had about eight detectives assigned to it from the police department. He approached me and asked me if I was interested in a swap. The switch was totally up to police management. The DA's office had no say in the personnel that were sent to assist them. He had already spoken to my lieutenant, the commander of the homicide division.

I was interested in making the move, so I went to talk to my lieutenant about it. He told me he had no issues about the trade and that he could make it happen by the end of that week. Then he told me to close the door to his office. He proceeded to remind me that I was a detective of the New Orleans Police Department.

"You'll be working with all civilians," he stated, "They are not the police. Your first and foremost loyalty is to this department. If you hear or see anything across the street that could in any way hurt the department, you will bring it back to me. Do you understand?"

I assured him that I did. He reached across the desk and shook my hand. Then he told me to get out of his office and leave the door open. As quickly as that, I was in the district attorney's office as a detective.

I settled into my assignment at the district attorney's office quite easily. Each police detective was assigned a section of court. These detectives would complete additional investigations and tie up loose ends of cases going to prosecution. The assistant district attorneys were basically inexperienced lawyers straight out of law school. They might have spent a couple of months cutting their teeth in juvenile court, but they were not experienced prosecutors. Each of them was going through on-the-job training. They could have qualified for food stamps with what they were being paid.

As a police detective assigned to the DA's office, I cleaned up police reports, consolidated evidence, and completed any investigations required to prosecute criminals. I found witnesses who had gotten lost or who moved after the time the crime was committed. I found files the assistant district attorneys lost to the system.

I told them from the beginning, "If you don't remove the file from this building, I can find it. Do not take it home. If you go to trial across the street, bring it back. Follow these simple rules, and I will always be able to find your case file."

Some considered me a wizard, but it was actually very simple. If there were multiple defendants, I would check to see if others were assigned to a different section of court. If they had gotten a conviction on one, they might be in the process of closing the file, but the other defendants were still outstanding. There were myriad other situations for which I had remedies. If they strictly adhered to my instructions, I could locate the missing file.

Finding people who had gotten in the wind was a little more challenging. But I had several fixes for that too. On the second floor of the DA's building, the city had given space to the Social Security Administration. They were a totally standalone group of federal employees. You would be surprised what a kind smile, honest conversation, and the occasional box of baked confectioneries received in return. I had several friends on the second floor. I would go down and visit them when I had free time. I wasn't using them; they were my pals.

The assistant district attorneys never gave me any grief. They knew me as an experienced police detective with a bit of an attitude. Many of them became friends with me after their initial put off. Once an assistant district attorney assigned to work for a very foul-tempered judge was caught in a bind. He was in the middle of a trial in which I was to be a witness. He had sent all the required subpoenas to the other witnesses, but he had not sent one to me. He figured he could just advise me a day or two in advance of my need to be in court. Not only did he not advise me a day or two in advance, but he had also completely forgotten that he needed me altogether.

When the point came in the trial when he was supposed to call me, he froze before the judge, just like the cowardly lion in front of the great and powerful Wizard of Oz. He told the judge that he did not know where I was or why I had not responded to the subpoena he had sent me. He said that knowing it wasn't true, but he needed to cover his ass. Even though she had seen me that morning, the judge figured I had just blown off her court. She was pissed. She had to recess and advised him that he had one hour to find me.

Finding me was easy because all he had to do was call across the street. He requested that I show up at that section of court as soon as possible. I did as he requested. I walked into court and was immediately called before the judge. She reamed my ass in open court, in front of everyone, for disregarding my subpoena. She explained to me the importance of being served a subpoena, and said the fact that I had disregarded it was a pothole in the judicial system. This was not a request but an order to appear in court. I was not able to refuse without serious consequences.

I just stared at the ADA. He knew if I ratted him out now, he would be truly fucked. I did not. I told you how I felt about rats. I just stood there and humbly said, "Yes, ma'am." I made a heartfelt apology to the court for my indiscretion, never mentioning I was never subpoenaed or had any idea that I was supposed to be in court that morning or that her dumbass new, inexperienced ADA had never alerted me. She told me that she was considering remanding me as an example for other cops who disregarded her court's subpoenas. It was a good thing I had not been stripped before the court because she would have seen my balls swelling up as big as county fair balloons. Then she ordered me to take the witness stand, and I completed the necessary testimony. I then left the courtroom.

The ADA involved reached out to me via envoys. He knew me and was terrified of talking to me in person. He recruited one of my best ADA friends to approach me and explain his position. I told her to go back to him and tell him that I understood. He had to work with that judge every day. I did not. I told her this was his one and only free pass. I told her to tell him to forget about it. I knew he had not done it maliciously, but a scared dog will bite you. But I cautioned her to tell him that if the dog bit me again, I would put it to sleep.

I made many new friends at the DA's office. The job was not that difficult, and my day ended when I got off work. I still saw Wong all the time because police headquarters was just across the street. One of the best things about that position was that it was Monday through Friday, 8:00 a.m. to 4:00 p.m. I had not had a permanent shift like that my entire time on the police department.

CHAPTER SIXTEEN

Now that I had all my evenings and weekends free—you guessed it—I spent many of them at the Dreux. The decade of the 1980s was drawing to a close. The business and personal lives of my close friends were dragging them in different directions.

Have you ever had a time in your life that you wish you could get back to? A place and time where you were so very happy? Mine would be the early 1980s at the Dreux. We were young, the music was fantastic, and all we cared about was being with each other. Sure, none of us were making much money, but that did not matter then. What mattered were the incredible friendships, the laughter, the sharing of stories, and the love I had for each of them. I don't know what your heaven looks like, but my paradise will be a dark, shitty little bar filled with smoke and hilarity, with my bottomless glass and a huge black cat on my lap.

It was an early afternoon in January 1989 when someone came to my door. Since it was a weekend, I was off. I opened the door to find Tony Amato standing there. He was smiling like the Cheshire cat. But that was Tony; he was always smiling. He was probably smiling when he got shot.

"How's it going?" he asked, pushing past me and proceeding to the kitchen and the refrigerator for a Dixie.

"Make it two, dipshit," I called after him.

When he was living in the back room, we would buy Dixie by the case directly from the brewery. We would stack them next to the refrigerator. It was not uncommon for us to have ten cases stacked there. Once when I was rummaging around, looking for something to eat,

I opened the refrigerator only to find it packed with Dixie, a stick of butter, and ice cubes—the breakfast of heroes.

He made himself at home on the couch in the living room.

"What are you doing in town?" I asked him.

"Came to visit my mom. Dawn took the kids to visit a friend in Florida. I got the whole weekend off," he said. "I figured I'd come by and catch up. You still assigned to the DA's office?"

"I'm still there, having a blast. Every day's a holiday and every meal a feast," I said.

"Oh, still just spinning your wheels?"

"Yeah, Wong is talking about going to the feds. He says he thinks it would be a good move for us. He tells me we could double our pay in the first year. He's getting all this info from Jimmy Sheridan. You know Jimmy left almost two years ago. He's working with United States Customs Service in their Air Operations Group out of Bell Chase. When he is not flying in Citation jets, he's flying as crew in Black Hawk helicopters. Wong says we got all the SWAT experience we could sell them. We just got to pass the Treasury Enforcement Agents Exam first," I explained.

"I heard the TEA test is a bitch," he said.

Tony wasn't kidding. The TEA would be the hardest test I'd ever taken in my entire life. The math section had twenty-five questions. I was never any good at math. Wong and I even got a math teacher friend of his to tutor us. When I took the test, I took half the time allotted just to do two math questions.

I said, "Screw it. I gotta take this shit to the strect."

I knew that psychometricians rarely made the correct answer A. So that left three more. I looked at the last three remaining answers to see which two were very close together and then chose one of them. I guessed the entire remaining twenty-three questions using that theory. The good Lord must've been watching over me because I passed not only that section but the entire test. I had dug a hole and squeezed underneath the largest obstacle standing in my way of becoming a federal agent.

"How is Gertie doing?" Tony asked.

"I guess she's doing well," I said.

"Is she still living with that guy Kyle? I know you don't much care for him."

"I can't understand why women are attracted to guys who are total assholes. Is it some sort of challenge thing? Do they think, sure, he is a self-centered, self-absorbed, narcissistic prick, but I'm so special that my deep love will change him into the man of my dreams? How often have you seen that happen? A leopard doesn't change his spots. That beast will only roll around in his own filth until you can't see the spots. He hasn't changed. He has just successfully fooled you. You won't realize it until you're naked and tied around a barrel after closing time at a traveling carnival with six clowns and a fluffer in line behind you."

"Wow … that's a hell of a vision," Tony said, laughing.

Gertie Chauvin would ultimately find happiness. She would marry a man who took good care of her. But that would be many years down the road. Her life would still be turned upside down many more times by the clowns Kyle, Bobo, Giggles, and Cheese Dick.

"You see Jerry much?" he asked.

"A couple of times since the wedding. His appearances are now getting few and far between. He never brings his wife to the Dreux. I don't know if it's her or just the daily grind that keeps him away," I said.

"That Jerry is something." Tony laughed. "I guess he had to man up and quit all the jokes."

"If he hadn't, somebody would've surely killed him by now," I said.

"How are crazy Greg and the Satisfier making out? I swear Greg hasn't changed one bit in all these years," Tony said, reaching for his beer.

"I don't know if Greg is certifiably crazy, but he can sure see crazy from where he's standing," I said. "He's doing well. He's building toilets and sinks at that big factory over near the lakefront. I hear he's making pretty good money. He's a foreman or some sort of supervisory position now. He is getting serious with some gal he met over there. Greg is still one of the regulars at the club. I see him all the time. They are usually both there together. Her name is Roxanne. She seems like a nice girl. She's cute, has a great sense of humor, and laughs at all the things Greg says. I just wonder when she's going to figure out that about 75 percent of the time she is laughing, he is not trying to be funny. He's just bat shit crazy."

I continued, "I guess Steve is doing the best out of all of us. The garage is kicking ass. He's got five employees and all the business he can handle. I really don't know how much wrench turning he does anymore. I think most of his time is spent on paperwork. I know he's making serious money. Despite being a big shot, he's still the same Satisfier. He takes good care of his mama and is always buying rounds at the Dreux. He has not let success go to his head. If you didn't know about the garage, you would think he was the same knucklehead fixing cars under the trees behind his mama's house. The guy's got a heart of gold," I said, picking up my beer and walking to the kitchen to get two more.

I returned with the beers and a bag of potato chips that I had opened and put them on the coffee table.

"What about Ron? What's he been up to?" Tony asked me while taking the bag of chips into his lap.

"You know Ron," I said. "He is always going to come out on top. He's still at the club all the time. Sometimes he brings his fiancée, sometimes not. I swear, Tony, she looks like a model. She has long brown hair and an incredible figure. She's intelligent and soft-spoken and gets along with everybody. Together they look like they should be on a magazine cover. He's always smiling, just like you. It's enough to make you sick," I bitched.

"You about a jealous asshole," Tony said.

"I'm not jealous of my friends, you moron! I hate everybody who's content and happy!"

After catching him up on all the latest from the Dreux, we decided to go to the club that night. We still had a couple of hours before it opened, so we got some steaks and potatoes and grilled them up out back. It was like old times. We shared stories and talked about our time together in high school. He told me stories from when he was assigned in Okinawa with the marines.

We had a great afternoon of reminiscing. We did not know then that he would be heading off to Iraq for operation Desert Storm in just a few short years. He went with the same Marine Corps unit I was assigned to before I got out. Tony would eventually make the rank of colonel before he finished his Marine Corps Reserves career. In the same next few years, I would become a federal agent. In my first six years there, I would be serving temporary duties in Mexico, Panama, Honduras, and Colombia. We were both in for a shit storm, each of us with his own cross to bear. That day we were lucky enough to have blissful ignorance of the future that awaited us.

Tony and I made it to the Dreux that evening. As luck would have it, almost all our friends were there that night. Jerry was missing, but everyone else was there. For Tony, it was a great reunion. We kept Barry quite busy, but he seemed to be having a great time too. The jukebox was playing and the beer was flowing. It was just like old times. I left the table and went over to the bar. I lit a cigarette and sat down.

"The club is popping tonight," Barry said while wiping the bar in front of me.

"You should be a rich man with all the tips you gonna make tonight," I told him.

"Where you been? I'm already rich," he said. "I am a king, and this is my court," he declared, waving his arm across the entire room.

"Well, Your Majesty, you got all jesters and no subjects," I informed him.

"Just the way I like it," he said with a hearty laugh.

Someone called to him for an order, and he headed to the other side of the bar. Halfway there, he turned to look at me over his shoulder and smile.

I was sitting there, taking in the whole scene, when I noticed Gertie standing next to me. She put her hand on mine and smiled.

"What?" I asked.

"You seem very happy tonight," she observed.

"You know, Gert, I am. I am very happy tonight."

CHAPTER SEVENTEEN

At about eight o'clock on a Sunday morning in February 1989, I got a call from Ron. Ron sounded very upset and told me I had to get to Barry's house right away. I asked him what was the matter, and he told me to come now and then hung up. Since I was already dressed and Barry lived about three blocks away, I was there in a matter of minutes. As I pulled up, I could see Ron pacing in front of Barry's house, smoking a cigarette. I got out of my car and walked up to him. It was then that I could see the tears in his eyes.

"Barry's dead," he whispered.

"What the hell? What do you mean?" I asked. "I just saw him last night. We closed up the club."

"Mrs. Christopher is in there. She and Barry were supposed to go to breakfast this morning. She knocked on the door for quite a while. When she did not get an answer, she used her key and went in. She found him in his bed."

I went inside the house, a house I had been in so many times. The lights were out, and the soft morning light was peeking through the drapes, casting long bright lines throughout the rooms. It had that familiar old Barry's house smell—a pleasant smell of aftershave, hard work, and honesty. I found Mrs. Christopher sitting on his bedside, holding his hand.

"Oh, David," she said as I walked into his room. "He's gone. My baby is gone." She sobbed.

I sat on the bed next to her and put my arm around her. I started to cry too.

"I have lost everything. My dear husband and both my beautiful babies. I so wish it could have been me. Oh baby. Take me with you. Don't leave me here alone," she said, throwing herself over him and sobbing uncontrollably.

All I could do was rub her back as I cried with her. I felt as though my heart had been torn from my chest. I knew that the terrible pain I felt could never compare to her tremendous suffering and loss at this moment. His bedroom was lit by the morning sun, which cast a blue hue through the curtains. It was a very peaceful scene yet so devastatingly final.

Barry was an ashen color. He had been dead for several hours. His eyes were closed, and he had a peaceful smile on his face. As I put my hand over theirs, I could feel that his was cold. I was no doctor, but it looked like it must've been a massive heart attack. He had died in his sleep. He had not suffered. There was no evidence of movement or thrashing around. The blanket and sheet were still in place around him. I leaned over and kissed his forehead. One of my tears fell on his face.

"Did you call the police?" I asked.

"No. I only called Ron. His was the first name in his address book," she said through her tears.

"I will go make the call," I told her. I hugged her again, wiped my eyes, and left the room. I used Barry's house phone to call the police.

The police had to be notified of any unclassified death. Since it was Sunday morning in the third police district, I did not think it would be long before they dispatched a unit. After calling the police department, I walked out to Ron. I told Ron to go inside and call our friends. I advised him to tell them not to come over right now, except Gert. I told him to ask Gert to come over as soon as possible. Mrs. Christopher needed a compassionate woman to help her.

Gert arrived several minutes later and sat with Mrs. Christopher and Barry until the police arrived. They took down all of Barry's personal information. Since I had handled many of these type of calls myself, I got his driver's license out of his wallet to make it easy on both Mrs. Christopher and them. They asked her the usual questions: Had he been under a doctor's care? Was he suffering from any medical problems that she knew of? The answers to all of which were no. They looked around the house for any signs of foul play and found none. I knew the two third district officers, and they asked if I would tell Mrs. Christopher that the coroner's office would have to take Barry for an autopsy to determine the cause of death. I told them that I would take care of it.

About an hour later, the coroner's office arrived. I knew the coroner's investigator from having worked with him on many occasions. I had Mrs. Christopher and Gertie take a seat in the front room as they brought in the gurney. I led them back to Barry's room, and we placed him on the gurney. We then covered him with a sheet and secured his body with straps. As they wheeled him out of the house, Mrs. Christopher broke down, and so did Gertie. They both held each other. I went outside with him until they put him in the van. I told them I would call later that day to advise them which funeral home we were going to use. I stood in the street and watched the van drive away, taking Barry and a large chunk of my soul with it.

Barry's funeral was held the following Saturday. The mass was held at Saint James Major Church. This church was well known to Barry and me, as well as to all our friends from Gentilly. I made my first communion at Saint James Major. Most of my family members had their funerals in this church. It sat just off the corner of Gentilly Boulevard and Lafaye Street. It was constructed of orange-colored brick; the color must've been quite striking when it was built in 1953. It had many rows of hard wooden pews. I figured it did not matter if I had gone to confession recently, since these pews would extort penance from me the longer I sat in them. The church had light marble floors with black veins. The statuary was of a modern design, not the classic old Catholic stereotype.

I sat in the first pew with Mrs. Christopher, along with Gertie, Ron, and Greg. Jerry's wife was not in attendance, and neither was Gertie's boyfriend, Kyle. I did not ask either of them why they had elected not to come. I was hurting, and it would not have made any difference if they had been there.

There were a lot of folks at the ceremony. Many friends of Barry and friends of Mrs. Christopher. It was different from her son Philip's funeral. Then she'd wanted only family. I don't know what changed her mind to have all Barry's friends attend. None of us got up to speak or do readings, as that was not in vogue back then. Barry had a classic Catholic funeral mass. We prayed for his soul and the souls of our dearly departed friends and relatives. We listened to the priest, who promised us that all who die in Christ shall have everlasting life. We had the sacrament of communion, and shortly after, the mass was over.

The guys and I carried Barry's casket out of the church and down the steps to the waiting hearse. We placed his coffin in the hearse, where the funeral director secured it and closed the door. I then met up with Mrs. Christopher and, along with Gertie, Greg, and Ron, got into the following limousine. After a few minutes to allow people to get to their vehicles, the limousine pulled away from the church, followed by the hearse and a procession of vehicles with their headlights on. We then drove to Saint Louis No3, his final resting place.

Saint Louis No3 is the third oldest of the Roman Catholic cemeteries in New Orleans. It is the newest of the Saint Louis Cemeteries, established in 1854. Most of the graves are aboveground vaults. The walls of the cemetery are made up of multilayered tombs. The rows of marble and stone gravesites are truly works of art. Many prominent New Orleanians are buried there, as well as yellow fever victims and early immigrants to the city. The Christophers have a tomb there; my family does as well. Back then it was not a tourist attraction, so it was easy to get into. It was a quiet place of remembrance and reflection. Today, they have closed off one of the two entrances to the cemetery. Now there's only a single way in. It pisses me off when I go to visit Barry or my family's grave that I have to tell the security guard that I'm not with the fucking tour.

The graveside service was short. I was thankful for that because I don't know how much more Mrs. Christopher could take. The priest blessed Barry's tomb and casket once again with holy water, and after several prayers, the service was concluded. We drove back to the church in the limousine. Jerry and the Satisfier drove their vehicles from the cemetery to meet us again at the church, and together we brought Mrs. Christopher home. She had friends come to the house, and her best friend was planning on staying with her for a few days. We stayed for about an hour before each of us kissed her, gave our condolences, and said our goodbyes. I reminded her again that she had my number and told her to call me for whatever she needed and that we would be there no matter what.

After leaving Mrs. Christopher's, we all met at my place for a drink. I don't think I'd ever had the entire group at my place at one time. Each had been there many times but never together. They were all drinking beer, but I needed something a little stronger, so I had rye whiskey on the rocks.

"Man, did you see Mrs. Christopher?" Greg said.

"I could actually feel my heart breaking as I took her hand," Gertie said. "Can you imagine losing a husband and both of your sons within seven years?"

"You know what I was thinking when I saw her?" Greg asked. "You ever seen pictures of soldiers from World War II or Korea? They're black-and-white photos, and their faces look gaunt and their eyes are just staring at nothing."

"They call it the thousand-yard stare," Tony said. "I've seen the photos, and you're right."

"How come they never had a wake?" Greg asked. "They skipped it and went right to the funeral."

"Because I don't think his mom would've survived both a wake and a funeral," Gert said simply.

"Barry's casket sure was beautiful," Ron said. "It must've cost a fortune."

"I doubt it cost that much to construct," the Satisfier said. "Funeral homes make a killing selling caskets. They bring you into a room of sample coffins to look at and compare. It ain't like buying a car that has a sticker price on it. If you gravitate toward a cheaper model, they say, 'Oh, you don't want that one. We sell those to the pet cemetery.'"

"It sure was a beautiful coffin," Gertie said. "If it wasn't wrong to own a coffin like a piece of furniture, I could stack all my mama's china in it."

"Yep, all you gotta do is take off the handles and put a little wood putty in the screw holes, and you got yourself a real family heirloom," Ron said.

"My dad had a nice casket, only his was a double-wide," the Satisfier said.

"Didn't they drive a stake through his heart before they buried him?" Jerry asked.

"Quit talking bad about the dead, Jerry!" Steve reprimanded.

"Sorry, I forgot," Jerry said.

"The Dreux ain't gonna be the same no more," Ron remarked.

"Barry was the Dreux," Greg agreed.

"Barry would come over here often," I said. "He would bring steaks or sausage, and we would grill out back. When I was cooking red beans or jambalaya, I would call him. He was always happy to eat my cooking. Ron, I'm going to need you and Greg to help me cut the grass and keep up Barry's house until Mrs. Christopher decides what she's going to do with it," I told them.

Both acknowledged that they would do whatever she needed.

"I'm going to miss Barry so much," I said.

"We all will," Gert said tearfully.

"I think Barry kept a lot to himself," Jerry remarked.

"Like his wife," Greg said. "Dave, you were best man at their wedding. They divorced after about two years. What happened?"

"She turned out to be someone other than the person he married," I said.

"What was her name again?" Greg asked.

"Her name doesn't matter," I said. "She's gone."

"Sounds like you have issues about it," Tony said.

"I don't like to see any of my friends hurt," I said. "It was a part of his life that was very private to him."

I had no information about where she was, and I had not seen her in years. He and I hadn't talked about her since their divorce. Even now, some thirty years later, I have no idea if she is alive or dead.

"That cat was the only love in his life." Gert sighed.

"I am going to get Fantome and bring her here," I said. "I need you guys to help me find her."

Everyone agreed to assist. They all did attempt to help me find her. We passed the club at all times of the day and night, but no one saw her. Since Barry's death, the club had been closed. It was going on seven days, and I was becoming really worried. I knew no one else would be taking care of her. So where was she eating? Where was she sleeping?

If she'd struck out on her own looking for Barry, who knew where she would end up.

I passed by the club at about noon on Monday. The door was propped open, so I knew someone was inside. I went in and saw a tall skinny man mopping the floors. I introduced myself as a regular and a friend of Barry's. He told me that he was the owner of the Dreux Club. I had known Barry did not own the club, but I had never met the man who did.

I told him I was looking for Fantome.

"Who?" he said.

"The big black cat," I said.

"Oh yeah. That cat was around just after Barry died. I don't want no cat in here, so I put her out. You know anybody who needs a job?" he asked.

I told him that I would ask around.

"If you find someone, just tell them to call the number in the phone book for the club. I got one of those answer machines. Tell them to leave me a message," he said while continuing to mop. "Barry is going to be hard to replace. For the first couple years, I watched the books carefully. After that, I never checked them anymore. I can tell you for sure Barry never stole a penny from me in all those years."

"Look—I'm very interested in finding that cat. Here's my card. I'm going to write my number on the back. Please, if anyone sees her, call me anytime, day or night," I said, handing my card to him. I knew by the careless way he put the card on the bar that I would be foolish to think I would ever get a call from him.

As I drove home late the next night, I figured I would drive by the club to see if I could spot her. As I approached the corner of Franklin and Dreux Avenues, I saw a large black lump in the middle of the road.

"Oh no, no, no! Please, God, no!" I said out loud.

When I got close to the lump, I saw it was only a rolled-up piece of sod that must've fallen off a truck. You cannot imagine my relief. This only made me more determined to find her.

I awoke in the middle of the night that night. It was about two thirty. I immediately thought of Fantome. I got my jacket, shoved my pistol in my waistband, and grabbed my car keys. I then drove to the club. There in the silver moonlight, I saw the old cat. She was sitting and staring at the door of the darkened club, a door that would never be opened for her again. She did not hear me drive up. I got out of the car, and she turned to look at me suspiciously. She started to walk away.

"Fantome, Fantome, come here baby," I called to her.

She stopped and turned to look at me, and I could see recognition in her eyes.

She slowly walked to me, and I picked her up. She was much heavier than I figured she would be. *If this cat starts to claw and bite me, I'm going to be in real trouble*, I thought. But she did not. I carried her to my car, got in, and placed her in the passenger's seat. As I pulled away, she looked past me at the club until I made the corner.

I carried her inside my home and set her down. She did not know it then, but she would never go outside again, and she would never want to. She curiously investigated each of the rooms of my house, smelling all my possessions. She found the litter box I had gotten in preparation for her arrival. She found the food bowl I had bought her with a picture of a fish skeleton on it. She did not seem very impressed with that. As she was completing the inventory of her new home, I put some dry food in her bowl. I set it down, along with a bowl of water. For myself, I opened a longneck bottle of Dixie beer.

I didn't know when she had last eaten. She spent a long while munching her food. I walked to the other room and turned on the television. I watched TV for a few minutes and finished my beer. It was about a quarter after three in the morning now. There was nothing worth watching at that time of night, so I decided to try to catch a few more hours of sleep. I turned off the lights and headed for my bedroom.

I got into bed and lay in the dark for a while. I thanked God for helping me find Fantome. I thought about Barry and his mother. I thought about the club. Ron was right. The Dreux Club was never going to be the same again. I was just starting to fall asleep when it felt like someone had dropped a bowling ball at the bottom of my bed. I could feel Fantome walking up toward my pillow, but I could not see her in the dark. Then I felt her plop down next to my head. She was purring loudly. I could feel her warm fur against my face. This was probably the first time she had been happy since Barry died.

Fantome spent the rest of her life with me. She ultimately became friends with another large black cat named Jazz that found me about a year later. When they weren't sleeping on me, they were curled up together. They were inseparable. Her favorite toy was a realistic life-size rat. She loved it. I'm sure Barry would have gotten a kick out of the fact that she had gotten a rat at my place after all. She was sweet enough to share the rat with Jazz as long as Jazz did not forget to whom it truly belonged.

Printed in the United States
By Bookmasters